Books by Sadie Hartwell

YARNED AND DANGEROUS

A KNIT BEFORE DYING

Published by Kensington Publishing Corporation

A KNIT
BEFORE DYING

SADIE HARTWELL

KENSINGTON BOOKS
www.kensingtonbooks.com

KENSINGTON BOOKS are published by

Kensington Publishing Corp.
119 West 40th Street
New York, NY 10018

All Kensington titles, imprints, and distributed lines are available at special quantity discounts for bulk purchases for sales promotion, premiums, fund-raising, educational, or institutional use.

Special book excerpts or customized printings can also be created to fit specific needs. For details, write or phone the office of the Kensington Sales Manager: Kensington Publishing Corp., 119 West 40th Street, New York, NY 10018. Attn. Sales Department. Phone: 1-800-221-2647.

Kensington and the K logo Reg. U.S. Pat. & TM Off.

eISBN-13: 978-1-61773-721-3
eISBN-10: 1-61773-721-6
First Kensington Electronic Edition: September 2017

ISBN-13: 978-1-61773-720-6
ISBN-10: 1-61773-720-8
First Kensington Trade Paperback Printing: September 2017

10 9 8 7 6 5 4 3 2 1

Printed in the United States of America

To Gail Chianese
For whose friendship I am grateful every day

Knitting is thought to have originated in Egypt more than a thousand years ago. A few hundred years later, driven by the demand for knitted stockings, knitting guilds sprang up in Europe, with men as their only members. Even though most of us aren't getting paid today, and it's mostly women plying the craft, an organized group of knitters can change their world, one stitch at a time.

—From *The History of Needlework* by Cora Lloyd

Chapter 1

"Let's take a break, Evelyn." Josie Blair tossed a skein of pale green South American wool into a basket, put her hands on the scarred wood of her sales counter, and pushed up from her stool into a stretch.

Evelyn stood, a satisfied expression deepening the fine wrinkles around her eyes. "I'm not tired. I could unpack new shipments of yarn all day long. But how about if I make us some tea?"

"That sounds perfect. Would you rather I run down to the general store and get some?" It was March in the picturesque hills of Connecticut, but the sun was shining, and the almost-warm air held the promise of spring.

"Nonsense. We have some of Lorna's vanilla mint right here. I'll put on the electric kettle, and we'll have a cup in no time." She didn't wait for a further response, just turned on her heel and marched toward the back.

Evelyn Graves was practical, efficient, and knew everyone in town. Josie couldn't have asked for a better friend or a better employee at Miss Marple Knits, the shop she'd taken over a few weeks ago. And Lorna Fowler, who worked at Dougie Brewster's general store a block away, could blend tea as well as any professional in New York City. Maybe better.

"I'll just step outside for some fresh air, then," Josie said to the back of Evelyn's permed, strawberry-blond head. Josie wound a soft wool scarf around her neck as she crossed the floor to the front door, then pulled down the sleeves of her hand-knit Aran sweater. The ivory-colored garment, with its complex pattern of cables and twists, was one of many pieces she'd inherited from her great-aunt Cora Lloyd, who'd owned this shop for many years before her untimely death. Every time Josie wore one of Cora's items, the kinship she felt for the woman who'd married her great-uncle Eben grew stronger. She'd never met Cora, because Josie had moved away to New York City years before Cora came into Eben's life. But that didn't mean Josie didn't feel her presence every day, both at home and here at Miss Marple Knits. It was strange and comforting at the same time.

Just as Josie put her hand on the knob, a shadow darkened her view. Fighting off a pang of disappointment—she'd hoped to feel the sun on her face after a morning of stocking shelves—Josie opened the door and stepped out onto Main Street.

But it wasn't a cloud that had blocked out the sun. An enormous moving truck had parked in front of the empty storefront next to Miss Marple Knits.

Hope surged in Josie's chest. Each new business that came into town would bring more and more people to downtown, and that was good for everyone. Thanks to Great-Uncle Eb, with whom she lived in his farmhouse just outside Dorset Falls, Josie was now the proud owner of not only the building that housed the yarn shop, but the adjacent building at number 15 Main Street.

Less than two months ago, Josie had been living in a tiny Brooklyn apartment and trying—unsuccessfully—to make a name for herself as a fashion designer. But here she was now, a business owner and a landlord. Landlady? She'd have to think about what she wanted to be called, but all she knew was that it felt wonderful. And now she even had a tenant.

The back door of the truck slid open with a cringe-inducing scrape of metal. Josie looked into the depths of the cavernous space as it was revealed, a few inches at a time. The truck was packed full. Most of the items inside were covered in dusty blue quilted cloths secured with bungee cords. Desks? Dressers? Tables? Impossible to know until they, and the dozen or so cardboard boxes she could see, were unloaded.

A moment later, a gentleman came from the vicinity of the front of the truck—*gentleman* was the perfect word to describe him, she thought, with his tailored Harris Tweed jacket complete with suede elbow patches, and his precisely cut silver hair neatly combed back to reveal a widow's peak and tortoiseshell glasses. Lyndon Bailey's face lit up with surprise when he spotted Josie.

"Spying on me already, as every good landlady should?" he said with a good-natured chuckle. *Landlady* it was to be, then. "It's good to meet you in person, Miss Blair."

Josie extended her hand to Lyndon as two men about her age, perhaps a bit younger than her thirty years, appeared. Their matching, utilitarian-looking uniforms proclaimed that these were the movers. Good thing. Lyndon did not seem the type who would want to wrangle his own furniture.

"Lyndon, please call me Josie. I didn't expect to see you until next week."

"That's not a problem, is it? I was able to close up my affairs in Hartford more quickly than I expected."

Josie shook her head. The sooner new shops opened in Dorset Falls, the better. And Lyndon had paid a handsome security deposit plus rent for the next six months in advance. She could afford to be flexible on the dates. "Of course not," she said. "I'm thrilled you're here. But where's Harry?"

Lyndon smiled, showing a nice set of teeth. "He's gone to

the Catskills on a buying trip. He'll be along in a day or two."
He gestured toward the movers, who were rather noisily set-
ting up a ramp from the back of the truck to the pavement.
"Can I let them in? The shop is ready?"

"The shop's been ready for a few decades, I'd say. You have
your keys, so move in. I cleaned for you." Well, she couldn't
take all the credit. Evelyn and Lorna had joined her for a vacu-
uming and dusting party, then Josie had treated her friends to
dinner at the Italian restaurant in the next town over.

Lyndon seemed pleased. "One less detail to worry about. I
thank you." His eyes darted toward the truck. The movers
were maneuvering a bulky shape onto the ramp. "You know
these are antiques, right?" he called to them.

The larger of the two men grinned. "Yup. That's why we're
getting paid the big bucks."

"Cheeky," Lyndon said, under his breath, to Josie. He took
a deep breath, then spoke louder. "That sideboard is Second
Empire. Please be extremely cautious."

The man nodded, then went back to muscling the covered
lump down the ramp on a dolly. He and his partner seemed to
be doing a careful job, at least while Lyndon was watching. Presumably they had insurance for any non-careful events. Josie
wasn't sure to what empire Lyndon had been referring—if
there was a second, there must have been a first, she reasoned.
Regardless, the furniture must be old.

"I'm just about to have some tea. Would you like to join me
and my associate Evelyn for some?" Josie asked.

Lyndon hesitated, looking torn. He finally shook his head.
"Very tempting, my dear. But I need to supervise the move.
Perhaps another time."

"Of course. You have work to do. Come over anytime,"
Josie said. She turned back toward her own shop—and felt a little thrill as she thought the words. Her own shop. Would that

ever get old? "And Lyndon," she said over her shoulder, "I'm glad you're here."

"Me too," he said, then turned to the movers. "For goodness' sake, be careful, gentlemen."

Josie left him to it.

When she returned to Miss Marple Knits, she found Evelyn sitting on the flowered loveseat in front of the big window that overlooked Main Street. Two mismatched, oversized mugs sat on the coffee table in front of her. Evelyn had used a knitting magazine as a coaster. Steam rolled off the tops of the cups, and Josie sat down, reaching for one gratefully. She wrapped both hands around the mug, interlacing her fingers to maximize the contact with the china. Within moments, her hands and her insides were warm.

"What are you working on?" Josie asked Evelyn, whose nimble fingers were flying. The woman could knit like the wind. Evelyn paused, pulling up a length of yarn from the center-pull ball from which she was working. Josie still wasn't quite sure why yarn did not come from the manufacturer in balls already wound, but she was proud of herself for having mastered the swift and winder, the simple companion machines Miss Marple Knits had for making usable balls of yarn from just-waiting-to-be-tangled loose skeins.

"Fingerless gloves," Evelyn said. "Simple lace pattern. Perfect for this time of year when it's too warm for full gloves or mittens, but too cool to go without." She held up a configuration of four double-pointed needles attached by sapphire-blue yarn that was forming a ribbed cylindrical cuff.

"Pretty. Too bad they aren't finished. I could have used them out there." Josie took a sip of tea. Heaven.

"What took you so long?" Evelyn's words seemed to come out in time to the gentle *clack-clack-clack* of her bamboo needles, her weapons of choice. Some knitters and crocheters preferred metal, and some preferred wood, Josie had learned, so Miss Marple Knits stocked both.

Josie sipped her tea and reached for a chocolate cookie. She bit into the perfect circle and closed her eyes, savoring the chunks of semisweet chocolate as they melted on her tongue. Evelyn was not just an expert knitter. The woman could bake. After Josie swallowed, she said, "The new owner of the antique store is here, a few days early, and moving in. Hear all that noise?"

"I did hear it, and I've already peeked outside." Evelyn kept her eyes trained on her work. Josie didn't comment, but both women knew Evelyn had a predilection for not exactly legal "peeking" that had proved useful when a murder had been committed not long ago. "I didn't have a good view of the owner. What does he look like?"

"Well, he's in his sixties, preppy. If I didn't know he dealt in antiques, I'd have said he was a tenured professor of history or English at Yale."

This was enough to make Evelyn glance up, though her fingers continued to move as if without conscious effort. "Married?" Her voice was all innocence.

"Couldn't say."

"Doesn't he have a partner in the business? Where's he?"

"Lyndon said he'll be in town soon."

The shop bells tinkled as a customer came in, unzipping her jacket and heading straight for the sock yarns. Evelyn began to put her knitting down, but Josie waved her hand. "I'll tend to the customer. You keep knitting. You're good for business."

Evelyn wound the yarn around her needle again, made the stitch, then gave the yarn a firm tug as she moved on to the next needle in her configuration. Evelyn had explained to Josie that the tug would prevent something she called *laddering*, a line of loose stitches where the needle changes occurred. "Doesn't seem right, you paying me to knit, rather than to do real work in the shop."

"You help more than you know," Josie said, and meant it. "And your knitting away in the front window is the best kind of advertising."

Evelyn's lips pursed. "I might believe that if anyone actually drove down Main Street, Dorset Falls, Connecticut. This place is a ghost town."

Maybe. It had been up to this point. But Josie had a feeling that fortunes might be changing in her newly adopted village. Yarn lovers were beginning to trickle in to Miss Marple Knits, perhaps due to the small amount of advertising Josie had been able to do—her budget was tiny for this—but more likely from word of mouth. It seemed that once a yarn lover heard about a new shop, she would travel quite some distance to check it out.

Josie busied herself behind the counter while her customer filled her basket. Based on the size of the diamond that currently resided on the woman's left hand, which Josie could see sparkling even from across the room, Josie figured this woman had plenty of disposable income. And Miss Marple Knits was an excellent place for her to spend it. Josie did a quick mental calculation. If the woman bought all the yarn in her basket, this sale should be enough to put the shop into the black this month. *Don't jinx it, Josie. The sale's not made yet.*

A half hour later, after the woman had systematically walked the entire perimeter of the shop, stopping to examine the contents of each bin and cubby that lined the walls as well as to thumb through some of the pattern books, she set her overflowing basket on the counter in front of Josie. She smiled, a bit sheepishly. "I can't help myself. The yarn lust overtakes me." She pulled out her credit card as Josie rang up the sale.

"Personally, I'm glad you can't control your desires. Yarn lust keeps me in business." From across the room, Evelyn laughed. Josie and her customer looked at each other, then both burst out laughing too.

Chapter 2

Josie turned up the heater in her ancient Saab, then turned down the radio, which had been emitting its usual static instead of music. It was just after five p.m., and Josie was pleased to see that there was still daylight. While she'd lived in New York and worked in the fashion industry, she'd paid far more attention to the lengthening and shortening of hemlines in response to the seasons than she had to the lengthening and shortening of days. But the longer she stayed in Dorset Falls, the more in tune with the natural world she seemed to become.

If anyone had told her six months ago she'd be living on a farm in rural Connecticut—and actually doing chores on that farm—she'd have said he or she was crazy and signaled the bartender for another round of whatever that person was having. And yet here she was, pulling into the dirt driveway alongside her great-uncle's farmhouse, property that had been in her family for a hundred years. Oh, she hadn't completely ruled out moving back to New York someday. But for now, she found that it was supremely satisfying to be working toward something, toward making a success of Miss Marple Knits, rather than working so someone else—she couldn't help thinking of her horrid former boss, the designer Otto Heinrich—could be successful.

Josie parked to the right of her great-uncle's truck and cut the engine. From somewhere in the vicinity of the house came the sound of barking, then a high-pitched howl. She braced herself as a huge yellow beast bounded off the porch and came to sit just outside her driver's side door, panting.

"Move it, Jethro," Josie said as she opened the door, gently pushing the dog aside and exiting the car. The dog stared at her, his big brown eyes boring into hers. He gave a sharp bark, then raced off in the direction of the bare lilac bush in the middle of the front yard when she threw something.

Josie let out a breath she hadn't known she'd been holding. She and Jethro had made a tentative peace during her residence here, largely thanks to the liberal application of dog treats. But her cat, Coco, still spent a fair amount of time in hiding when Jethro was indoors.

"Oops, can't forget this." Josie leaned back into the car and reached across the seat. The paper bag she pulled out was emitting a delicious smell: hot roast beef grinder with grilled onions. Lorna, who cooked and clerked at the general store, had thoughtfully left off the green peppers, since she knew they didn't agree with Eb.

As Josie shouldered her purse with her free hand and bumped the door closed with her hip, Jethro reappeared, apparently drawn by the scent of the meat. Not that she could blame him. It was all she could do not to rip open the paper here and now and take a bite. Josie held the bag high and made her way up the sagging front porch of the old farmhouse she now called home.

"Eb?" Her uncle didn't answer as she entered the house and kicked off her boots. When she'd arrived here from New York, she'd brought a cute pair of fur-lined clogs. Now she'd traded those in for a pair of water—and mud—proof boots. Here in the country, there were compromises to be made. You could be fashionable and uncomfortable, or less fashionable but warm and dry. These days, surprising herself, Josie was opting for the latter.

The crackling of the wood stove in the kitchen was audible even at this distance. Eb must have loaded it recently, because it was blasting enough heat to smelt iron. With Jethro right at her heels, just waiting for her to make a mistake, Josie didn't dare set down the bag containing the sandwich. So the irritating bead of sweat that was currently rolling down her nose continued to make its descent, and she was unable to wipe it away.

"Eb?" she called again. "I brought dinner." He didn't answer. She reached up and set the bag on top of the refrigerator out of Jethro's reach, then shrugged gratefully out of her sweater and fanned herself with the neck of her T-shirt. The door that led to Eb's workshop, a room that, according to her great-uncle, had formerly been a woodshed, was ajar. Josie peeked in.

Eb looked up at her over the top rims of his black-framed cheaters. His impressive eyebrows were drawn together over his customary scowl. "You brought food?" He went back to work on whatever he'd been fiddling with. "When are you going to learn to cook?"

"You must have finished another lesson in your online charm-school class today," Josie said affectionately. "What's that?" Josie leaned in to get a better look at what Eb was working on, though it was impossible to see over or around the protective wall of junk parts and other detritus that was stacked up in front of him on the table. "Doesn't look like one of your metal sculptures."

Eb snorted. "Sculptures are for *artistes*. Which I ain't. I make thingamajigs. And this one's none of your business." A thin wire popped up behind the wall as though it had just sprung up from a spool, and Eb snatched it back down.

"Speaking of business," Josie said, "when are you going to let me sell some of your thingamajigs at the shop?"

He didn't look up, but reached for a tool of some kind on the small metal table to his right. "Not for sale. When do we eat?"

Eb might not know this, but the sculptures he constructed from bits and pieces of metal from old farming tools and machines—what others might call junk—were quite artistic. When the leaf peepers came to town in the fall, she thought he could make some nice money from his work. Although Eb didn't appear that interested in money, even the sizeable amount he'd inherited from his late wife. As long as he made enough from his hay, pumpkins, and maple syrup to pay his expenses, he seemed content.

"Dinner," he repeated, hammering away at something with a metallic clink. "That meal you eat after lunch but before the fishing shows come on?"

"Coming right up, Your Highness."

Eb gave another snort. "Bring it out here, willya? Trying to finish something." He went back to his hammering.

Good old Eb. He did and said what he wanted, usually not in the politest way, but deep down, Josie had to admit she loved the cantankerous old coot. She certainly owed him. He'd given her a home, the yarn business, the building in which it was housed, and a rental property next door. The least she could do was bring him a meal. The fact that the meal had been prepared by someone else and would undoubtedly be delicious was not lost on her.

Josie returned to the kitchen. Jethro had his front paws up on the refrigerator and appeared to be trying to jump a little higher, but his snout couldn't quite reach the bag from the general store. "Eb," she yelled toward the open door to the workshop. "Call off your hound, or he'll be the only one eating tonight."

A sharp whistle sounded, and Jethro took off. Eb and their neighbor—their very good-looking neighbor, Josie had to admit—were the only two people on the planet who seemed to be able to control Jethro.

Josie pulled two paper plates out of the cupboard, unrolled the grinder from its white paper wrapper, and sliced it into four six-inch sections. The savory aroma of still-warm meat, vegetables, and homemade bread wafted up and filled her nostrils, causing her mouth to water. She placed one piece of sandwich on a plate, then added a few potato chips, poured a glass of apple cider from the fridge, and placed everything on a tray, which she delivered to Eb. There was just room on the small table at his left elbow to set down the tray.

He didn't look up, just gave a small grunt of acknowledgment. Although she could now see around the wall of junk he'd barricaded himself behind, she still had no idea what he was working on. Just a lot of parts she could not identify. Jethro sat at his master's feet, tail wagging, and looking up longingly at Eb's dinner.

Returning to the kitchen, Josie made a plate for herself, then wrapped up the other two pieces of sandwich and put them in the fridge for Eb's lunch tomorrow. She took her plate to the dining room, which was also the foyer since for some reason the front door opened directly into it. Eb had managed to fill up one end of the table with his stuff again—it was a never-ending job keeping flat surfaces clear in this house—but there was room on the other. She sat down and thumbed through the stack of mail.

An electric bill, assorted junk mail, the sale flyer from the grocery store over in Kent. She took a bite of the grinder. *Delicious as always, Lorna,* she thought as her eyes landed on the next item in the pile. The Haus of Heinrich ready-to-wear catalog. Josie wasn't quite sure how she'd gotten on the mailing list, but she wouldn't have put it past Otto Heinrich to add her name manually to the computerized system, just to stick it to her. Not that she cared—much. Her former boss was a lecherous jerk, who'd thought he could not only manipulate her into producing designs and running his online magazine, but also engage her in some office hanky-panky. Still, she flipped the pages one by one as she chewed. The summer designs weren't bad, though why Otto thought leather jackets would sell in July in the northern hemisphere was baffling.

What the—? The lump of roast beef she'd just swallowed stuck in her throat. She dropped the grinder on the plate, made a conscious effort to swallow, and picked up the catalog with both hands.

A svelte model with sculpted cheekbones and dark hair slicked back from her forehead stared up at Josie, her expression almost defiant. She wore a fitted purple sweater, made of fine-gauge cotton and featuring adorably puffed short sleeves, over a long, slim gray skirt.

That jerk! Not the model, of course. Otto. He had stolen her design. Josie thought back to a few weeks ago when she'd submitted this idea to him, along with several others, in a bid to get her job back. Did he have any claim to her drawings? Nope, she'd been officially fired when she submitted them. She turned the pages of the catalog so violently that a small rip appeared. No matter. Two more of the concepts she'd sent him were now being advertised for sale at exorbitant prices.

She pulled out her cell phone and fired off a text. *You are scum, Otto. Rotten, thieving scum.*

A return text came back almost immediately. *Let's do a video chat. You're so beautiful when you're angry.*

Josie threw the phone down in disgust, then set her plate on the floor for Jethro to find. She'd lost her appetite.

As if she sensed that Josie needed her, the black-and-white form of Coco, Josie's cat, brushed up against her leg. Coco jumped up into Josie's lap and began to knead with her front paws, turned around twice, and settled down. Josie ran her hand from head to base of tail, then again, each stroke of the soft fur eliciting a purr from the former stray. "Want to help me plot a murder?" Josie asked, then immediately felt guilty. She'd seen the effects and aftermath of murder up close, and it wasn't pretty. Nor was it something to joke about.

"How about some revenge, then?" Coco purred in response. "Oh, who am I kidding? I could never think of anything good enough. Come on, girl," she said, scooping up the cat. "Let's go for a ride."

By the time Josie pulled up behind Evelyn's big Buick with its vanity plates—KNITTR-1—she'd calmed down. Of course she was still angry—Otto had stolen her ideas and used them for his own gain. But as a practical matter, this happened all the time in the fashion industry. Some designer would start a trend. Other designers would follow suit, until finally the most wearable, economical-to-produce looks were being manufactured overseas and sold in the big-box stores here in the States. It wasn't as if you could patent or even trademark a puff sleeve or a slim skirt. So there was really nothing she could do except tell him off. She sighed and opened the bright blue front door of Miss Marple Knits.

"You made it!" Evelyn said from the vicinity of the couch. "Lorna's bringing the dessert. Brownies, she said."

Josie set down Coco's carrier, then released her. The cat minced out onto the hard wooden floor as if she had all the time in the world, then headed for the squishy pillow covered with a throw that Evelyn had knitted just for her. She settled herself and curled up into a ball.

Evelyn eyed Josie. "You don't look happy. Here—" She patted the seat next to her. "Come sit down, and I'll pour you a cup of coffee. Unless you'd rather have the wine we left in the fridge from the grand reopening? It'll only take a moment to fetch it."

Josie smiled. "That's sweet of you, Evelyn, but you don't need to wait on me. You've been on your feet all day too."

"Hmmph," the older woman said and pulled her knitting out of her bag.

"Josie's right, Evelyn," Helen Crawford said. "You need to save your strength for our next trip to the casino. I feel lucky." Helen took a sip from a mug that read *She Who Dies With the Most Yarn, Wins.*

"Where are Margo and Gwen?" Josie asked. Since Helen and Evelyn had been boycotting the Dorset Falls Charity Knitters Association meetings, a new, informal knitting circle had sprung up with Miss Marple Knits as the epicenter. It didn't matter—much—that Josie didn't knit. She already treasured the friendships that were growing, stitch by stitch, in her yarn shop.

Helen opened her mouth to answer, when a loud scuffing noise, as if something heavy were being dragged across the floor, sounded from the shop next door, followed by a thud that produced vibrations Josie could feel under her feet, even from this far away. Three heads turned toward the wall.

Josie paused, listening, then headed for the door without bothering to put her coat back on. She turned back to her friends. "I'll go check to see if Lyndon's okay. That sounded like something heavy falling over."

Evelyn and Helen simultaneously pulled the stitches on their needles back so they wouldn't slide off, set their work down, and stood, as perfectly synchronized as a pair of knitting Rockettes. "We'll come too," Helen said.

"Yes, *both* of us," Evelyn responded, giving Helen the eye. Josie was sure they were genuinely concerned. She was also sure the pair of rather competitive single seniors wanted a better look at their potential quarry, Lyndon Bailey.

"Follow me, then," Josie said, and hustled out the door.

Josie reached the antique shop first. The lights were on, which she hadn't noticed when she'd pulled up out front earlier, having been preoccupied with Otto and the catalog. She opened the heavy wooden door. "Lyndon? It's Josie. Are you all right?"

Lyndon stood over what appeared to be a log wrapped in a quilted moving blanket, which lay prone on the floor. He seemed to be intact. "Ms. Blair," he said. "How nice of you to drop by. And who are your stunning companions?"

Helen reached him first and stuck out her hand, lightning fast. "Helen. Helen Crawford," she said, gazing significantly into his eyes. "We heard a terrible noise. Are you sure you're not injured?"

From the corner of her eye, Josie could see Evelyn frowning.

Lyndon took Helen's hand. "I am perfectly fine, dear lady, and I thank you for your concern. And you as well," he said, turning toward Evelyn, dropping Helen's hand and offering Evelyn his freed digits, which she took with alacrity and held, while gazing up at him coyly from beneath her lashes. She even managed a faint blush. Score one for Evelyn.

Lyndon looked at Josie, his expression benign. "Perhaps you could unwrap that end of the object on the floor?" He gently disentangled his hand from Evelyn's and bent down, peeling back the mover's quilt that covered the log. Josie pulled back her end of the padded fabric to reveal a section of a fluted column, covered in weathered white paint, which had probably once graced a classical-style home. Lyndon's end featured carved scrollwork, which he was examining carefully. Finally, he stood, placing his hands into the pockets of his jacket.

"I was lucky," he said. "I was moving this architectural column, and it fell over. I jumped out of the way just in time. Fortunately, there was no damage to it. Or to me." He gave a little chuckle.

Helen jumped in. "Well, you need to be more careful," she tutted. "We wouldn't want anything to happen to you."

While Evelyn and Helen fussed over Lyndon, Josie looked

around the shop. Lyndon had made good progress setting things up just since this morning. If he kept up this pace, he could open for business anytime.

There was certainly a nice assortment of merchandise. An antique bicycle, the kind with one giant front wheel and one tiny one in the back, leaned up against the exposed brick wall. She couldn't imagine who'd want to buy such a thing, let alone ride it, but it was fun to look at. A brown wicker rocker sat next to a marble-topped side table containing a china tea set with a delicate pattern of pink roses. Empty bookshelves lined another wall. She guessed that the boxes stacked in front of them contained books waiting to be arranged. Josie made a mental note to come back over in a few days to see if there were any old books about needlework. They would be nice to display for her customers. Evelyn or Helen might even get a kick out of knitting up some of the old patterns.

Her eyes fell on a cardboard box near her feet. One flap of the top was open. She bent down and opened the other. Inside the box was a jumble of fabric and needlework items, mostly white or ecru, but some with a bit of color. She pulled out a piece of what appeared to be white linen, edged in a hand-crocheted border. Josie was pleased with herself. She was learning to identify knitting versus crocheting, and usually got it right these days. The piece was about nine inches square and smelled faintly musty, but probably nothing a good washing couldn't eliminate. Another piece was knitted in a lacy pattern of eyelets, strategically placed to form a geometric pattern, which would look lovely against a dark wood table.

Josie straightened. Evelyn and Helen were still fawning over Lyndon, who was receiving the attention politely, but was beginning to look a bit uncomfortable, shifting from one foot to the other and glancing in Josie's direction. "Helen, Evelyn?" Josie said. "We should get back to the shop. The other girls are probably there already, wondering where we are." Actually, it would be a good thing if they'd already arrived. She'd left the door unlocked. Not that there was anything much to tempt a burglar. The bank deposit had been safely made before she went home to take dinner to Eb. And she didn't think there was much of a black market for stolen yarn—though who knew? Good yarn was *expensive.*

Lyndon looked profoundly relieved. "Thank you ladies for stopping by. I should get back to work. I'm hoping to open by the weekend."

Josie glanced down at the box by her feet, as a whim struck her. "Say, Lyndon," she said. "Could I be your first customer? I'd like to buy this box of doilies." What she'd do with them, she couldn't quite say. There were more than she could ever use for their original purpose of protecting wood and upholstered surfaces. Something would come to her, she supposed.

Lyndon's face broke out into a broad smile. "You will save me a lot of work if you take that box off my hands. I just bought these. It'll be a long time before I'm able to sort through them, have them cleaned, and identify which ones are saleable, and even then my profit margin won't be high. How does twenty-five dollars sound?"

"Really? That seems like too little. I wouldn't want to take advantage of you."

"Nonsense. Let's call it a Landlady Special. You can take the box now and get it out of my way, then drop off the money to-morrow."

"Deal." Josie hefted the box and made for the door. She turned. "I'll see you in the morning."

"Bright and early," Lyndon called out. Evelyn and Helen eyed each other. The game was clearly afoot between them, but they followed Josie back to Miss Marple Knits obediently.

"What a charming man," Evelyn said, holding the blue door open for Josie.

"Yes, *extremely* charming," Helen replied.

Poor Lyndon.

Josie set her box down on the counter as a chorus of hellos sounded from the seating area. Her high school friend Lorna Fowler sat in one of the armchairs, and her new friends, Gwen Simmons and Margo Gray, sat on the loveseat. Gwen and Margo were working away, Gwen knitting what appeared to be a bright green and purple child's hat, and Margo crocheting a larger piece, a shawl or perhaps the beginnings of a throw or afghan.

"Where've you been?" Lorna asked. "We found the shop open and no one here." She pulled the foil from a pan of brownies whose crinkled, glossy top shone faintly in the light from the overhead fixtures.

"Just checking things out next door," Josie said. Her stomach growled at the scent, and she remembered she'd only eaten a few bites of her dinner. Brownies would do quite well to take the edge off.

"Thanks for inviting me tonight," Margo said. "It's nice to get away from the bed-and-breakfast—and my husband—for a while." She pulled up some yarn from her ball and made a few stitches, pausing to count them. Crochet was, if it were possible, even more baffling to Josie than knitting, consisting of a complicated one-handed dance of looping and twisting. "Did Lyndon say what time he was finishing tonight?" Margo said. "I'll have Darrell leave the key under the mat for him if it's going to be too late."

"I didn't realize Lyndon was staying with you," Josie said, surprised. "I thought he was moving in upstairs. I rented him the second-floor efficiency apartment as a package deal."

"It's just temporary. He said he wants to get the shop running before he moves in and has to start doing his own cooking and cleaning. His business partner, Harry Oglethorpe, rented a room from me too, though he hasn't checked in yet. I don't think Harry is planning to stay in town full-time. He's on the road a lot."

Josie nodded. "Lyndon said Harry was on a buying trip in

the Catskills. Though where they're going to put anything else over there, I don't know. The shop looks full to me already."

"Well," Lorna said. "There's plenty of space upstairs over every building on Main Street. If they need more storage space, they could certainly find it."

Evelyn and Helen, who had resumed their seats on the couch, were studiously examining their knitting. Helen owned the empty building across the street, but Josie seriously doubted Helen would be renting out space there anytime soon.

Helen piped up, shrewdly changing the subject. "I grew up with Lyndon, you know." She frowned at her knitting, pulled a stitch off her needle, and picked it up again.

Evelyn stared at Helen, then narrowed her eyes just a bit. "Funny you didn't mention that," Evelyn said. "Since we were just talking to him. And we've known for weeks he was opening up next door."

Helen's face was unreadable. "Don't get your purls in a twist, Evelyn. I wasn't sure it was the same fellow. His father was a lawyer, and his mother was a part-time nurse in old Doctor Ryder's office. Lyndon went away to prep school, and his family moved away when we were in fifth grade."

Evelyn didn't look convinced. "Why didn't you say anything to him just now?"

"I wanted to see if he recognized me." Helen set her project down in her lap, then reached for a napkin and one of Lorna's brownies.

"Did he?" Josie said. Helen cut three more brownies and doled them out to Margo, Gwen, and Josie.

"Not yet. But he will. I'm sure of it."

Josie wasn't so sure about that, and from the expressions Margo and Gwen wore, they weren't either. It had to have been more than fifty years since Lyndon and Helen had seen each other. However, this prior relationship might give Helen a slight advantage over Evelyn in the competition. At this early point, though, it seemed like anybody's game.

The brownie was every bit as delicious as the scent had promised. Josie took a sip of her coffee, which intensified the dark chocolate flavor. "How is Darrell?" she asked Margo. "Did his arm heal up from where he cut it?"

Margo paused her work to count a few stitches. "He's fine and back at work. Just a few sutures and a tetanus booster shot. It's a cost of doing business when you're a carpenter."

"I hadn't heard about that. How'd it happen?" Evelyn asked.

"Oh, he got tangled up in a bit of barbed wire out at the old Ryder place. The new owners hired Darrell to build some hops poles, and he was out there taking measurements. No biggie."

"Hop poles?" Josie had no idea what Margo was talking about.

"Hops. As in the plant that beer is made from? I don't know much about it, only that it's a vine and that it's grown on tall poles." Margo smiled, her eyes meeting Josie's. "I hear the new owners are planning to start a craft brewery here in Dorset Falls."

A second new business opening in town? That was almost too good to be true.

Josie opened her mouth to comment, but was interrupted by Evelyn. "Helen? Helen. What's the matter, dear?" Evelyn put her arm around Helen's shoulders. Her friend's head was bowed, and when Helen finally looked up, her eyes glistened with tears. She sniffed, and Evelyn handed her a tissue that she'd procured from somewhere. Probably from the sleeve of her cardigan.

"Oh, I was just thinking about Bea Ryder," Helen said, dabbing at her nose. "She was my friend." A deep breath and a sip of coffee seemed to restore some of Helen's composure. "The reason her house was available is because her younger cousin in Florida lost the tenants a few years ago, couldn't find more, and finally decided to sell."

Josie reached out and took Helen's hand. "I'm sorry you lost your friend," she said. "When did she die?"

The muffled sound of furniture moving came through the wall adjoining the antique shop, but it barely registered this time.

Helen's fingers shook under Josie's. "That's just it. I don't know if she's dead. Not for sure. One day, decades ago now, she disappeared. And never came back. And I miss her every day."

"I remember reading about that," Evelyn said. "It was just after my first husband and I moved here from Massachusetts."

First husband? Josie wondered how many others there had been. Well, there couldn't have been *that* many, could there?

"Of course," Evelyn continued, "the newspapers called her disappearance just that. A disappearance. As though she decided to up and leave Dorset Falls on a whim and might turn up somewhere else someday."

Josie saw Helen's face, which had been soft with memories and tears, harden.

"But most of us thought—and I still think—she was murdered. Though I don't know by whom," Helen said.

A fist tightened around Josie's innards as she recalled the dead, cold body she'd found lying just yards away in the storeroom of Miss Marple Knits, not long ago. Was this little town cursed?

"There must have been some theories," Margo said.

"I don't think I've ever heard this story," Lorna added.

"You're both too young, and it happened a long time ago. But let's not talk about that anymore," Helen said, removing her hand from Josie's and picking up her knitting. She made a few stitches, then seemed to relax, obviously soothed by the repetitive motion, or by the feel of the yarn in her fingers. Knitting was like Valium to these women.

"Then let's talk about going to see a show in New York," Evelyn declared. "There's that new needlecraft musical—the one where the main characters tell the story of their lives while knitting one crazy-long scarf?"

"Singing and dancing while they do it?" Helen said, the usual cheerful lilt returning to her voice.

Josie looked over at Helen, then Evelyn. There were some strange plays produced in New York, but—

"Kidding!" Evelyn said. "But there *should* be a knitting musical. Let's pick out a show, and we'll ask the limo company to send Rodrigo to drive. Josie, you'll come with us. Gwen, Margo, and Lorna too." It wasn't a request. It was an order.

Josie hadn't returned to New York since her move to Dorset Falls. Was she ready to go back? She supposed she'd find out eventually.

Chapter 3

Dougie's General Store, which most locals, now including Josie herself, simply called "the g.s.," was its usual uncrowded self the next morning. Although, even mostly empty, it was still one of the busiest places in Dorset Falls.

At a table near the counter sat just the person Josie never wanted to see, Diantha Humphries, who appeared to be in deep conversation with a man Josie had never met. Josie shifted the box containing the store's standing order of four dozen eggs, which she'd retrieved from her chicken coop only an hour ago, and debated for a moment. There was nowhere to set down the box except where it belonged, which was on the lunch counter. Which was right next to Diantha.

Drat that woman. Why couldn't she have chosen a seat closer to the restrooms? Josie steeled herself. *You've done nothing wrong,* she thought. *It's Diantha's problem if she doesn't like you.*

Josie plastered on a big smile, crossed the wooden floor, and laid her box down on the counter. "Good morning, Diantha.

Lovely spring day, isn't it?" Nothing like a preemptive strike of cheerfulness.

Diantha's face twisted from its usual expression of haughty distaste into one of pure dislike. She set her coffee cup down on the table and glared up at Josie. "Maybe for you," she spat out. "It's been weeks since I've had a good morning or a lovely day, thanks to you. Why don't you go back to the city where you belong, before you cause any more trouble in my town?" The man, who appeared to be in his early sixties, seemed annoyed, whether at being interrupted in his conversation with the old battle-ax, or for some other reason, Josie couldn't say.

Josie resisted the urge to roll her eyes. Diantha was on the town council, at least until elections rolled around in the fall, but unless she'd suddenly been crowned Queen of Dorset Falls, the town most certainly was not all hers. The woman was like a broken record. Every time Josie encountered her, Diantha commanded her to leave. Which gave Josie all the more desire to stay.

Josie opened her mouth to respond when the sound of angry voices punctuated the air. Diantha whipped her head around toward the back of the store. Josie turned too.

"You don't like the way I run things in my own store, you can find another job." The voice was male, and since it was coming from the direction of Douglas Brewster's office, Josie had to assume it was his.

"Dougie," a female voice said. *Lorna,* Josie thought. "Think about what you're doing. You can't cut corners with the food service. Margarine instead of real butter? Powdered eggs? You'll put yourself out of business."

"Fat lot you know about business. You're just the cook and sales clerk here. And don't think I don't know what you're doing. You want to keep buying those fresh eggs from Eben Lloyd and that niece of his. Can you say 'conflict of interest?' "

Josie suppressed a snort. Douglas Brewster, mayor of Dorset

Falls, was rather well versed in the subject of conflict of interest, at least based on what the events during her tenure in town had shown.

"Think about it," Lorna said in a reasonable tone, though there was an underlying hint of agitation. "Other than the occasional pancake breakfast or strawberry supper at the Congregational church, this is the only place in town that serves food. You've got a good thing going. Why would you want to mess with that?"

"I'll remind you that you're my employee, and you'll do what I say. I need to get costs down on this business, and I'll decide how that's going to be done. If continuing to work here is something you'd like to do, then I suggest you shut up and get back to work. And send Rick in."

Lorna stormed out from the back office, her long braid of dark hair bouncing over her left shoulder. Josie watched her draw a deep breath, then another. Lorna picked up a mug made of white china and took a sip, then set it down again. "Cold," she said, to no one in particular. She tossed the contents of the mug down the sink and reached for a jar of tea, presumably to make a fresh cup.

Josie waited a beat. "You okay, Lorna?"

Lorna turned toward her friend. She cut her eyes around the room, where they landed on the man sitting with Diantha, who had apparently heard his summons because he now stood and headed behind the counter toward Dougie's office. "Sorry I didn't notice you. Yeah, everything's just peachy." Josie was sure everything wasn't peachy, but Lorna could hardly unburden herself while Dougie, or Dougie's cohort Diantha, was in earshot.

Josie decided to change the subject. "Who's that guy?" She inclined her head toward the office door.

"Rick Steuben. Some old prep school friend of Dougie's. They're planning a reunion and want me to cook a dinner." Something slapped against the table Diantha was sitting at, probably the newspaper she'd been reading as she drank her coffee.

"Last night was fun, wasn't it? We should do that more often," Josie said. A huff sounded from Diantha's direction.

Lorna gave a rueful smile. "I only felt a little weird, being a nonknitter in a group of experts."

"At least we have each other." Josie returned the smile.

"Disgraceful." Diantha's voice was laced with contempt. "Why don't you sell the shop to somebody who knows what she's doing and be done with it?"

Lorna turned to Diantha. "Great idea! Why don't you make Josie a great big offer? You'll do well in business, with your advanced customer-service skills."

Diantha stood abruptly, throwing her napkin on the table. "*You'd* do well to remember, Miss Fowler, that your employer is a friend of mine. Sounds as if you're on thin ice as it is, so you might want to stay on my good side." She jammed her arms into the sleeves of her coat and grabbed her purse.

"And another thing," she said, jabbing a finger of her free hand in Josie's direction. "If you think you can break up the Dorset Falls Charity Knitters Association by running your own knitting circle at that shop of yours—a shop that has lost my business permanently, I might add—think again." She stormed off.

"That's too bad," Josie called toward Diantha's back. "Because I just got in a shipment of the most unusual blend of opossum, merino, and silk. The colors are glorious." Diantha stopped short, shoulders shaking, then continued toward the front door.

"Opossum yarn? You're kidding." Lorna began to giggle.

"Not kidding. It's a real thing." Josie reminded herself that Dougie was still in the store, even though his office door was shut tight. She lowered her voice. "Seriously—you're not going to get fired, are you?" Josie did a quick mental calculation. There was no way she could take Lorna on at Miss Marple Knits, not yet, anyway.

Lorna shook her head. "I doubt it, unless Dougie can find another cook willing to work both the griddle and the cash register for what he's willing to pay. And the food section of the store makes more profit than anything else. Don't worry about me. I'll be fine."

"I know you will." Josie picked up her empty egg box, which Lorna had unloaded while they'd been sparring with Diantha. "Uh, can I come by later for a couple of stuffed pork chops and some garlic butter green beans for Eb's dinner?" She shrugged. "I've got a busy schedule, you know."

Lorna laughed. "They'll be ready when you get here."

Evelyn wasn't due in to work until later, so it was dark and quiet when Josie entered Miss Marple Knits. She flipped on the light switch, blinked rapidly, and felt rather like Dorothy stepping into Oz for the first time. Yarn in every imaginable color and texture greeted her. Sample knitted and crocheted items hung from hooks on shelves, begging to be touched or, even better, tried on. It didn't matter that she'd seen this same tableau every working day for weeks. The light coming through the big plate-glass windows changed and made the colors more or less vibrant, the details softer or clearer, each time.

Much as she loved Evelyn's company and, Josie freely admitted, needed her expertise, it was nice sometimes to be alone here.

Except she was never alone. Cora, the woman who'd owned this shop for years before Josie, and who'd married Uncle Eb when both were in their late sixties, was everywhere. And the movie still of a snowy-haired actress playing Miss Marple, knitting away, held pride of place on the wall behind the cash register. Someday Josie should look up the woman's name.

"Cora? Miss Jane?" Josie said aloud. "What should we tackle first? Straightening up? Or we could look at the new catalog from that Australian company." Josie almost expected one of them to offer an opinion, but of course they didn't.

Last night's plate of brownies covered in plastic wrap sat on the counter near the cash register. Josie and her friends had made a good dent in the treat, but there were still half a dozen left. Much as she wanted one—it would be *so* delicious with a hot cup of coffee—she resisted. Yankee food was comforting and addictive, and she'd been eating a lot of it, thanks to Lorna and Evelyn. Even though Josie had taken to wearing comfortable sweaters and jeans most days, rather than the torturous heels and tight, slim skirts she'd worn in her New York design career, it wouldn't hurt her to forego these sweets.

Besides, it was likely Evelyn would bring something when she came in this afternoon. Cupcakes, maybe.

That decided it. Josie shrugged back into her coat, then reached for the plate. "I know just what to do with you, my little chocolaty squares of sin." She could kill two birds with one stone, getting rid of the brownies and paying Lyndon for that box of doilies. She headed back out the front door, locking up as the shop bells jingled behind her. A glance up and down Main Street showed the usual landscape of empty storefronts, with nary a car or human in sight, so it was unlikely she'd miss any customers if she didn't open right on time this morning.

Josie walked the few yards to number 15, blowing out a frosty breath. It was nippy this morning, but it would likely warm up later. Balancing the plate in one hand, she knocked on the door of the antique shop with the other.

She peered through the glass, then put an ear up against it. No sound of footsteps coming toward her. She knocked again, then tried the handle. The big oak door, identical to the door of Miss Marple Knits except for the color, swung open in a heavy arc. "Lyndon? It's Josie."

Light blazed from the overhead fixtures, and the door hadn't been locked, so her new tenant had to be here somewhere.

Lyndon seemed to have made more progress last night after Josie and the ladies had left. Some of the furniture had been arranged into vignettes. A comfy-looking vintage chair sat next to a mahogany reading table, which was topped with a china lamp and a stack of old books. A tribe of charmingly tattered brown teddy bears poked their heads out of a wicker baby carriage, their black button eyes still shiny.

A faint rustling sound came from the back of the shop. Josie headed toward it. "Lyndon?" She peered over the pile of boxes on the sales counter. And froze.

A man stood there, his face pale and covered with a light sheen of sweat. He stared at Josie, who took an involuntary step backward, not sure if she should be concerned for the man or afraid of him. At least the counter stood as a buffer between them.

"Are you all right?" she asked, heart racing.

He opened his mouth as if to say something, then looked down. "Call 911," he finally croaked out. Josie rushed around the counter, intending to find a chair and assist the man in sitting down while she called for an ambulance. She stopped short as she rounded the corner.

Her paper plate of brownies dropped to the floor.

Into a puddle of dark liquid that splashed thickly up against the wood counter.

A body lay there, still as stone. Josie's eyes went immediately to a rusty piece of metal—a tool of some kind?—that protruded from the man's chest. She swallowed back bile, so sharp and bitter that it stung her throat and took away her ability to speak for a moment.

"Lyndon," she rasped, reaching for her cell phone.

Chapter 4

Josie kept her eyes trained on the man standing behind the counter, and backed out a few steps into the main floor of the shop. There were plenty of things to hide behind, and plenty of objects available to use as a weapon, if it came to that. Would she remember her self-defense training if she needed it? Like most self-respecting city girls, she'd taken those classes at the neighborhood YMCA, but now she wished she'd kept up on the skills she'd learned. Glancing down at the phone in her hand, she punched in 911.

But based on the gray pallor of Lyndon's skin and the amount of blood on the floor, she knew it was too late.

The man behind the counter drew in a sharp breath, then blew it out again. He seemed to recollect himself. "Is help on the way?"

Josie nodded, mentally calculating the distance to the door. She'd have to turn her back to the man to get out. There were too many things she could trip over on the winding path through the shop's inventory to try to navigate backwards.

The man seemed to have found his voice, though it broke

when words finally came out again. "I just got here, and I found him like that. He didn't respond when I tried to talk to him. Who—who could have done such a thing?"

Josie continued to eye the man warily. He didn't seem to be an immediate threat, and she could hear the sirens wailing in the distance. The police and fire departments were only a couple of blocks away. She realized who this man was.

"You must be Harry," Josie said. "Lyndon's business partner."

He nodded. "Sorry. I should have introduced myself, but . . ." His voice trailed off as he turned his head toward Lyndon. He turned back to Josie, and his prominent Adam's apple bobbed as he gulped. "That can't be an accident," he finally said.

Josie had to agree. She'd seen Lyndon only last night, and he'd seemed tired, but then again he'd been working all day. And a metal . . . thing didn't ordinarily end up in a man's chest. She squeezed her eyes shut. Would she ever get the pictures out of her mind? This was the second body she'd found since she'd returned to Dorset Falls. And it wasn't getting any easier. She broke out into shivers.

Harry came toward her. Josie stepped back involuntarily, the backs of her knees connecting with something, and she landed solidly in the armchair she'd noticed earlier. Was Harry concerned for her? Or was he coming after her? But that didn't make sense. He'd told her to call emergency responders. Harry stopped in his tracks and looked up as a squad car pulled up out front, siren wailing. The door opened.

Help had arrived. Officer Sharla Coogan entered the shop, hand on the butt of her service weapon. The cop's eyes landed on Josie, then moved toward Harry.

"Josie? What's going on?" Sharla stood stock-still.

"It's Lyndon Bailey. The new owner of this shop. He's behind the counter. I think he's dead."

"Show me," Sharla ordered, all business. "What's your name?" she said to Harry. "You lead the way."

"Harry Oglethorpe. I own the shop with Lyndon. Over here," he said, and made for the back of the room.

"You okay?" Sharla whispered. Josie nodded.

Sharla leaned over and examined Lyndon's body when they reached him. Josie stayed where she was. There was nothing she could do, and she couldn't bear to see Lyndon's cold, sightless eyes again.

"You stand over there," Sharla commanded Harry. "I don't want you contaminating the scene any more than you already have. The EMTs should be here any minute, but I don't think they can help." She straightened. "Now suppose," she said to Harry, "you explain this."

Harry's hands shook, and he shoved them into the pockets of his baggy corduroy trousers. "I—I got here about nine o'clock and found Lyndon." He looked Sharla in the eye. "I don't know what happened."

Sharla continued to stare him down. Josie was glad she wasn't on the receiving end of that stare. Sharla was a good cop. Though she was being Bad Cop, or at least Tough Cop, right now.

"I said I don't know." Harry held her gaze.

"Why didn't you call 911 yourself?" Sharla said.

"I just got here!" Harry blurted. "I found him, and then a moment later Josie arrived. I—I guess I was in shock or something."

The door opened, and Detective Bruno Potts, Sharla's superior, came in along with a cold breeze, followed by a couple of volunteer firefighters carrying a bag that presumably held medical equipment. Sharla shook her head at Potts in the direction of Lyndon's body. He quickly assessed the situation and began to bark orders.

Sharla herded Harry toward a Victorian-era couch and commanded him to sit. She returned to Josie.

"You need a drink or anything?" The authoritative tone was gone from her voice.

Josie shook her head. "I'm fine. Or as fine as I can be."

Sharla positioned herself so that she could keep an eye on Harry. "We'll need you to give a statement. Are you up for that?"

If the situation hadn't been so serious, Josie might have laughed. Instead, she said, "Unfortunately, I'm kind of a pro at this by now. But I can't imagine anything I have to say will help."

"Can you give me a quick rundown?" She nodded toward Harry. "I'll have to get him down to the station, then come back and assist Bruno with processing the scene. It would help if I had a little background."

Sharla wasn't exactly angling for Potts's job, but she wasn't averse to learning as much as she could about crime-scene investigation, either. If her mother-in-law, Evelyn, had anything to do with it, Sharla would be state police commissioner someday.

"You know I own this building, thanks to Uncle Eb, right? Well, until yesterday, I'd only spoken to Lyndon once. On the phone. We e-mailed back and forth about the terms of the lease, that sort of thing. Lyndon showed up yesterday with a moving truck. He was alive and well last evening."

"Right. Evelyn said she was coming here last night."

Josie shifted in the armchair, trying to find a comfortable position. Clearly this was a chair that was meant to be looked at, not sat on. "You should join us some night after you put Andrew to bed," Josie said. "Nonknitters of Dorset Falls, unite."

Sharla smiled. "Did you hear or see anything unusual?"

"Not really. At one point we heard a loud noise, and Evelyn, Helen, and I went next door to see what had happened. Lyndon had knocked over an architectural column of some kind, but he was okay. As far as I know, he was alone here," Josie said, anticipating Sharla's next question. "All the girls and I left Miss Marple's about nine thirty, and the lights were still on here when I drove by."

"And what happened this morning?"

"I came here to bring Lyndon some leftover brownies. It must have been just after nine. Harry was standing over the body."

Sharla looked thoughtful. "That time jibes with what he said a few minutes ago. But is he telling the truth about what time *he* got here?"

Josie knew Sharla didn't really expect an answer. But Josie wondered the same thing.

"Do you need me to stay? Should I go to the station now?"

Sharla shook her head. "You can go on back to the shop and come in this afternoon once Evelyn gets there. No need for you to lose business over this, and there'll be cops and CSI techs right next door for at least the rest of the day. You and Evelyn are safe enough."

That made sense. Josie's gut feeling, for what it was worth, was that Lyndon had been specifically targeted, though she couldn't imagine why.

"You wouldn't happen to know Lyndon's next of kin, would you?" Sharla continued. "Of course we can find out, but you'd save us some time."

"Pretty sure he gave me the contact information for a daughter, maybe a niece, on his rental application. I'll check the file and call you."

"Sounds good. See you later at the station."

Harry looked up as Josie passed on her way out the door. "His niece's name is Taylor. Taylor Philbin. Lives near the shore. In Mystic, I think. She works at one of the shops near the Seaport Museum." Josie couldn't quite identify the emotion on his face. Sadness? Disbelief? Guilt?

Sharla noted the name on her pad. "I'll let you know if we need more information," she said to Josie. "You can go now, if you're ready."

Ready to leave another dead body? Josie was more than ready. "I'm sorry, Harry," Josie called.

"Me too," he replied. That could mean a lot of things.

A few minutes later, Josie put her key in the lock of the door of Miss Marple Knits, just as Evelyn walked up behind her. Josie started.

"Sorry, dear," Evelyn said. "What on earth is going on? I heard the sirens. And now here are two police cars and an ambulance out front."

Josie glanced back up Main Street, past the antique shop and toward the general store. Other than Josie's ancient-but-functional Saab and the emergency vehicles, there wasn't a car in sight. Which meant that Evelyn had parked her car at Helen's house a couple of blocks over. Which meant that she'd probably been in Helen's not-quite-empty building across the street again.

Evelyn's eyes followed hers, then landed on Josie's face. "Yes, I was up in the Lair," she admitted. "But I was only looking for my size-eight circular needle and checking my e-mail. We're not doing . . . *that* anymore. No need."

Josie wanted to believe her. She really did. The women entered the shop.

"So what's going on next door?" Evelyn repeated. "Is Lyndon all right?" Evelyn hung up her coat and set her bag down behind the counter.

"Lyndon's dead." At Evelyn's stricken look, Josie wished she'd made the announcement with a bit more tact.

"Dead?" Evelyn's hand went to her throat. "Stroke? Heart attack?"

There wasn't really any tactful way to say it. "It looks like murder." Josie filled Evelyn in on what she knew. "So," she said, "if by chance anyone's surveillance equipment *happened* to be turned on and trained toward the antique shop last night or this morning, that would be information that should be given to Sharla immediately."

Evelyn looked her square in the eye. "I've got nothing. I swear." She held up her pinky and crooked it. "Helen either."

Josie bent her own little finger and linked it with Evelyn's. "Pinky swear accepted. Let's get to work, then."

Routine tasks at the shop soothed Josie's jangled nerves. There were more customers than usual throughout the morning. It was pretty clear people were here to find out what was going on next door. Evelyn seemed more than happy to chat with everyone who came in. Josie busied herself tidying up, reorganizing yarn in the cubbies by color and manufacturer, and straightening up the knitting magazines and free patterns stacked on the coffee table in between ringing up sales. Finally, she paused. The last customer was just leaving the shop, bulging Miss Marple Knits bag in hand. Evelyn was a born salesperson.

"Well," Evelyn said as the door closed, "as awful as this is to say, death seems to be good for business. Though I'd rather make a few less sales and have poor Lyndon still be alive." She retrieved her oversized purse from behind the counter, sat down in one of the chairs facing Main Street where she could see through the window, and pulled out her knitting. It appeared to be a different project from the one she'd been working on last night. Though Josie had been in business only a short time, she'd begun to know the habits of some of her regulars. Some, like Helen, worked on one project from start to finish. Others, like Evelyn, had several pieces going at any one time, and knitted on whatever they felt like or happened to pick up first.

Josie's cell phone rang. The display read *Sharla Coogan*. "We're ready for you, if you can leave the shop," Sharla said when Josie answered.

"Might as well get this over with," Josie said. "I'll be right there."

"Heading for the police station?" Evelyn said, eyes intent on her knitting. "I'll close up. You go give your statement, then go on home afterward. You've had quite a day."

Josie had to agree. It *had* been quite a day. And it wasn't over yet.

Chapter 5

The Dorset Falls police station occupied one half of a two-story brick building a couple of blocks from downtown. The other half housed the volunteer fire department. Josie pushed open the door to the police station and crossed the black-and-white tile floor to the front desk. *Perfect. Not.* Officer Denton was on duty. He made no secret of the fact that he thought she was a kook.

"Well, well. Miss Blair. What brings you by today? Inquiring minds want to know." He smiled, revealing a deep dimple in each cheek. Which seemed incongruous considering his just-short-of-steroidal physique. The guy had a neck approximately the diameter of the column Lyndon had knocked over last night.

Josie bit her tongue to keep from saying what was really on her mind. So what if she'd given the police an unusual theory about the last murder? It hadn't been *that* far-fetched, even though it had turned out to be wrong. "I'm here to give my statement. About Lyndon Bailey's death."

"I heard you found another body. Have a seat. Officer Fleming will be ready for you shortly."

Josie sat in a molded plastic chair with shiny chrome legs. She opened a magazine—*Modern Fisherman*—and put it back down. That would be more Eb's style. Even though she ate fish, she wasn't all that interested in knowing how they were caught.

Her thoughts focused on Lyndon. He'd barely been in town a day. Who would want him dead? He hadn't been here long enough to make any enemies. Helen said he'd lived in Dorset Falls as a child, but it was ridiculous to think that someone from his childhood had borne a grudge against him for the last fifty years or so and had waited all this time to make a move.

Lyndon had arrived almost a week before he was supposed to. Not that there had been any secret about that—the moving truck parked on Main Street had been as conspicuous as a rhinoceros at a tea party, even in Dorset Falls's moribund downtown, and it had been clearly visible from the general store, where most Dorset Falls-ites congregated at some point or another.

Josie hadn't known he was coming early, and if Lyndon hadn't told her, his landlady, that he would be moving into the store before his lease officially started, it stood to reason he hadn't told anyone else, either. But that was just speculation. He might have still been in touch with someone else here, and word could have gotten out.

Still, it seemed far more likely that whoever had killed him had followed him from out of town. But why? Lyndon gave all appearances of being a sweet man, polite and genteel. There'd been no indication that his move to Dorset Falls was precipitated by anything other than perhaps a desire to live in a quiet country village, or nostalgia for his childhood home.

Her thoughts went to Harry. He looked to be a few years younger than Lyndon, probably in his mid-to-late fifties, about the same age as her mother. He didn't have quite the old-fashioned, courtly appeal Lyndon had possessed. Though that might not have been fair, considering the fact that the only time Josie had met him, Harry had been standing over Lyndon's dead body. There was nothing appealing about that scenario.

Could Harry have killed Lyndon? He'd said he'd arrived just before Josie had this morning and found his business partner dead. That could be true. Or not true. His shock had seemed real enough, but maybe he was just a very convincing actor. These two had been partners for some time, according to what little Lyndon had told her when the lease was negotiated. Why wait until now to kill him?

"Miss Blair?" A voice brought her out of her musings. "I'm Officer Fleming. Please come with me."

Josie rose and followed the man into the nonpublic area of the building. He held the door of a sparsely furnished office open for her and motioned for her to sit. Another hard plastic chair.

Officer Fleming appeared to be fresh out of the academy: barely into his twenties, clean shaven, possibly a little nervous based on the way he was drumming his pen on the metal desktop, where it gave off a metallic clink with every tap. Clearly Detective Potts didn't think she had anything of importance to disclose if he was allowing Fleming to practice statement taking on her.

The officer recorded her name, address, and phone number, and she told him what she knew.

"Anything else?" He seemed less nervous, now that the end was in sight. Good thing the kid worked in Dorset Falls rather than New York. He'd be eaten alive there.

"Not that I can think of at the moment."

"Then I'll escort you out. You can call if you remember something." He stood, and Josie followed him back into the vestibule.

Harry Oglethorpe sat in one of the chairs, looking pale and a bit dazed. Officer Fleming frowned. "You've given your statement to one of the other officers, right? He just released you? You can go now," he said to Harry.

Harry looked up. "I don't actually have anywhere to go, except for back to the bed-and-breakfast," he said. "And you've impounded my car, looking for evidence."

Fleming's frown deepened. Harry's tone was even, a bit flat, and not at all accusatory, but the officer was clearly taking note of Harry's words and demeanor. "We can get you a ride," he said.

Harry shook his head. "Thank you. But I suppose I can walk, now that I've had a chance to recover myself. It can't be more than a few blocks."

Josie didn't blame him. She'd rather walk than ride in the back of a police cruiser too. If the police were letting him go, they must not think he was a danger, so she decided to make an offer. "I'll take you to the Gray Lady. Assuming you don't mind a bit of cat hair on the seats."

Harry gave a wan smile. "I'll accept. Cat hair and all."

Ten minutes later, they stood on the porch of Dorset Falls's only hostelry, the Gray Lady Bed and Breakfast. The house was huge, with a three-story turret on one end and an excessive amount of white-painted gingerbread trim. The shutters were forest green, which looked lovely against the dove gray of the rest of the building. The door opened, and Margo hustled them inside.

"Are you both all right?" Margo asked, ever hospitable. "The police have been here and sealed off Lyndon's room. They've already been through yours," she said to Harry, apologetically. "And released it. But if you'd rather move to one of the other two rooms we have, it's no problem."

Harry shook his head. "Where I am is fine. I guess I have

some . . . decisions to make, and this is as nice a place as any to make them. And I can't leave town."

"Come out to the kitchen, then, and let's have a bite to eat. You look done in," she said to Harry. "Not that that's surprising in the least. Josie, why don't you come too?"

They dutifully followed Margo past the ornately carved staircase, down a papered hallway, and through a dark oak door. The kitchen beyond was bright and cheerful. Margo sat them down at the table in the center of the room and went to the fridge.

After several minutes of silence, during which Harry stared out the window and Josie discreetly watched Harry, Margo set sandwiches and glasses of lemonade in front of her guests. "Eat something, Harry," Margo urged.

Josie took a bite of her sandwich. Turkey on wheat bread with lettuce and a thick slice of avocado. Delicious.

Harry picked up his sandwich and took an unenthusiastic bite. He chewed, swallowed, and set it down again. "I'm afraid I'm not very hungry," he said.

"Understandable," Josie said. "But unless the police gave you something from a vending machine down at the station, odds are you haven't eaten all day. And it would be a shame to waste this."

"You're both very kind," he said. "As soon as I get my car back, I guess I'll be heading home to my condo in Wethersfield. But I expect that won't be for a few days at least." He nibbled at the sandwich again, then sipped at the drink.

Josie wasn't quite sure how to bring up the subject, and now probably wasn't the time, but she decided to go for it. "What, uh, do you plan to do—"

"About the shop?" he cut in. "I can see you feel bad about asking, but don't. We're all businesspeople here." He set down his glass. "I don't know. Lyndon was always the face of the business, better at sales, and I did most of the buying. Behind the scenes."

"Well," Josie said, "the rent is paid for six months in advance." She mentally crossed her fingers and rubbed an imaginary rabbit's foot. Even though she wasn't legally obligated to return any money, she'd feel morally obligated to at least offer.

Harry waved his hand. "I'm not going to try to get out of the lease. I have a feeling tenants aren't exactly knocking at your door looking for rental space. Nothing personal," he said apologetically.

"Dorset Falls isn't a hotbed of commerce, that's for sure," Margo said.

Yet, Josie amended. She had a gut feeling about this town, but wasn't about to say anything aloud.

Harry rose, placing his napkin on the table. "Margo, I believe I'll go upstairs now. I have a lot to think about."

Margo rose. "Of course. I'll put the rest of your sandwich in a bag in the fridge, then if you get hungry later you can come back for it."

When he was gone, Margo inclined her head toward the door. Josie could hear the footsteps ascending the staircase to the rooms above. Still, Josie lowered her voice. "What do you think about him?"

Margo's expression was thoughtful. "Not much to think. He showed up here last night after I got home and went straight to his room. That was the first time I met him."

"Harry seems . . . reserved," Josie said. "Standoffish? Although he did find his business partner dead this morning, so I suppose his demeanor today might not be an accurate reflection of his usual personality."

"You also found a body this morning," Margo pointed out. "What about you?"

"It was a shock, of course. I wish I could unsee poor Lyndon lying on that floor." Josie gave her lemonade a stir and took a sip. "Just out of curiosity, what time *did* Harry arrive last night?"

"Just after the eleven o'clock news started. Darrell had dozed off in his recliner, so I had to let Harry in and take him upstairs."

"Lyndon was still at the antique store when we left last night—or at least the lights were on over there. Did he come back?"

Margo eyed her. "I see where you're going with this. I don't know. I didn't see him, and Darrell didn't mention it. But all guests have a key to the outer door, as well as keys to their rooms. So Lyndon could have come in quietly after we went to bed."

"Was his bed slept in?"

"Hard to tell. When I looked in after the police left, the covers were off. Whether the police did that looking for evidence, or Lyndon did, I can't say."

So Harry had come into town after Josie had last seen Lyndon alive. Or at least he'd shown up here at the Gray Lady then, which wasn't quite the same thing. And he could have left anytime during the night. Or, assuming Lyndon did come back to the Gray Lady last night, Harry could have followed Lyndon to the antique shop early this morning. However it happened, and whether Lyndon was killed last night, or this morning, Harry could have managed it.

Don't speculate, she reminded herself. *The police are handling it.* Still, she couldn't help but ask, "Did the police find anything?"

Margo shook her head. "Not that they told me. As far as I know, Lyndon only had a few clothes here, which they took along with them. The detective wasn't here long collecting evidence in either Lyndon's or Harry's room, so I'm assuming there wasn't much of anything to find."

"What about Lyndon's car? Did the police take that too?"

The timer buzzed on the oven. Margo rose. "Rusty Simmons brought the tow truck over himself a little while ago and took it away." She pulled a hot casserole from the oven. The heavenly fragrance of homemade lasagna wafted across the room and filled Josie's nostrils. As nicely as she'd settled into the rural life of Dorset Falls, there were some things she missed, like her favorite little Italian restaurant around the corner from her Brooklyn apartment.

"Which reminds me," Margo continued, placing the hot dish on a trivet on her granite countertop and setting the potholders beside it. "Maybe Rusty can rent Harry his loaner car. Then Harry can at least get out of the house and drive around town. Not that there are all that many places to go. You want some of this to take home?" She pointed to the dish on the counter.

Tempting. Oh, so tempting. "Well, I was going to get dinner from the g.s. tonight. Truth is Eb's been needling me about not cooking. Much as I hate to admit he's right . . ."

Margo gave a little chuckle. "I understand. Your countrification process has begun. Take this." She opened a cupboard and pulled out a Mason jar filled with a dark red substance. "Homemade sauce. Can you use a knife? A frying pan? Can you boil water?"

Josie nodded. "I even know how to turn the knob and light the burner."

"Then you can handle this." Margo rummaged in a drawer until she found a piece of paper and a pen. She wrote down some instructions and handed them to Josie, who read through them.

"Thanks, Margo. I'll cancel my order from Lorna. I can't wait to see the look on Eb's face when I set a mostly home-cooked meal in front of him." Oh, he'd find something else to bug Josie about. That was just his nature. But it would be satisfying just the same.

Chapter 6

Josie scrubbed out the last pot, gave it a rinse, and put it in the dish drainer to her right. She'd probably used more utensils and dishes than were strictly necessary, but the spaghetti and meat sauce had been quite tasty, if she did say so herself. Eb had merely grunted as he walked past her from his workshop and through the kitchen while she'd been sautéing onions and ground beef. When they'd sat down to eat at one end of the dining room table, which she'd had to clear of mail and newspapers yet again, he'd looked at the meal skeptically. "Needs garlic," he'd said, mopping up sauce from his second helping.

Buoyed by her relative success in the kitchen, she turned on the small light over the stove and left the room. It was time to tackle something she'd been avoiding.

Eb was sitting in his ugly but comfortable velour armchair by the window as she passed the dining room—at least, she supposed it was comfortable. She'd never sat in the thing. It felt like an invasion of his privacy, somehow. "Did you beat your time on the crossword yet?"

Her great-uncle grunted. "No. What the hell's a 'stet' anyway?" He penciled in a couple of letters. "Gotcha, you little devil."

"I'll be in the morning-borning room." Eb gave another grunt. He was extra talkative this evening.

Josie walked through the adjacent living room, which was furnished with another rust-colored velour armchair and a couch covered in a floral slipcover. That must have been Cora's doing, as Josie couldn't see Eb choosing that particular pattern. She paused long enough to fold up a knitted afghan and rearrange the throw pillows—also Cora's handiwork. Was there anything else to be tidied up? She gave herself a mental flick on the head. *Stop avoiding and just do it, Josephine.*

The door to Cora's room was tucked into a corner of the living room, and Josie made her way toward it. In actuality, Cora hadn't occupied the space for that long. She'd only lived in this house for six months or so before she died. But like Miss Marple Knits, the house retained traces of her. In the old days, this was what was called the borning room, where generations of Lloyds had entered the world and where they'd been brought in their final illnesses. Cora had used it as an office and a sort of private knitting salon—no doubt to get away from Eb's predilection for outdoorsy reality shows. Not long after she'd moved in, Josie had dubbed it the morning-borning room, and the name had stuck.

And now it was hers.

She crossed the room to the desk and sat down, then opened the lid of her laptop.

And took a deep breath.

While she waited for the video to load, she reached into the deep bottom drawer of the desk and pulled out a pair of size 10.5 knitting needles and a ball of chunky, cream-colored yarn she'd wound herself at the shop. Coco leaped up onto the desk and settled onto a stack of paper.

A well-manicured and bejeweled pair of hands appeared on

the screen as the words *Learn to Knit* scrolled across. A friendly, disembodied voice spoke.

"You say you want to learn to knit? Well, you've come to the right place. Or the right video, at least."

"Okay, lady, let's do this." Josie watched the screen. She'd mastered the initial slipknot and placed one on the needle. But that was as far as she'd gotten in quite a few tries. Casting on still eluded her. From what she'd been able to determine, there were several different methods of getting those initial stitches on the needle. And none of them had worked. Yet.

Josie wasn't sure why she was so determined to do this on her own. It would have been a simple matter to have Evelyn teach her. In fact, they'd talked about offering classes, but that was for sometime in the future. Dorset Falls didn't seem to have a nonknitting population large enough to make it worthwhile. But as their out-of-town business grew, they could revisit the idea.

Maybe it was just a matter of pride. She'd been to fashion school—and had the student loans from her MFA to prove it. Sewing was no problem, though she didn't do much of it anymore. So she wasn't totally without skills. And she had a sneaking suspicion that knitting wasn't as difficult as it looked, though knitting *well* clearly took some practice.

Maybe . . . maybe she just wanted it to be hers. The Miss Marple Knits business, the building at number 13 Main Street, her comfy room upstairs here at the farmhouse, all these things had been given to her. And she was beyond grateful for the new direction her life had taken. So maybe that's all it was. She needed to own the knitting itself. And she was determined to figure it out.

Josie realized that while she'd been ruminating, the hands on the screen had not only produced a line of cast-on stitches, but had knit a couple of rows. She ran the video back to the beginning. This time, she'd pay attention.

A half hour later, Josie blew out a frustrated breath. This was ridiculous. How hard could it be? And yet she still hadn't managed a single stitch. She tossed the needles and the yarn back into the drawer and tapped it closed with her knee.

"Who says a yarn shop owner needs to know this stuff anyway?" Coco didn't answer, just looked at her with one eye. Josie gave her a long stroke, from ears to tail, and Coco gave a contented purr.

Josie leaned back in the office chair. It was too early to go to bed. The television in the living room blared. Eb—who was the slightest bit hard of hearing, though he'd never admit it—must have quit crosswording and turned it on. It was a pretty good bet he wasn't watching *Project Runway* or *America's Next Top Model* or even a costume drama on PBS.

Josie might not be able to knit, but there was one thing she could do. She closed out of the video and typed in *www.miss marpleknits.com*. She'd bought the domain name just after she took over the shop, and had begun building a website, using a template provided by her host. It had been surprisingly easy. The blog portion of it was up and running, even if she didn't have any yarn or tools and supplies up for sale yet. That would come.

It didn't appear that anyone other than a couple of people in Malaysia had read her previous posts. But she wrote another one anyway, describing the new opossum-blend yarn that had just come in. Josie hadn't been the world's greatest fashion designer—at least, that's what Otto Heinrich had repeatedly told her—but she'd been good at writing about it. She scheduled the post and closed out.

Coco padded along behind her as she made her way through the living room. Odd. The television was on, but Eb wasn't there. That was unlike him. He didn't like to waste electricity. Or words, or anything else. She carried her mug through the dining room to the kitchen and deposited the cup in the sink, running some water into it. Eb's workshop door was ajar, and a thin line of light shone around the edges.

"Eb? You want me to leave the TV on for you? I'm going upstairs to read, then go to bed."

Eb's gray head poked out from around the stack of junk barricading him into his worktable. "Turn it off." He disappeared again. A faint whirring noise was just barely audible.

"What are you doing in here so late?" Eb was a taciturn creature of habit. In the time she'd lived here, she'd never seen him do anything in the evenings other than solving a crossword, reading the newspaper, or watching shows about how to catch sometimes nasty giant animals that lived in bodies of water.

There was a silence, then he poked his head around again. "Idea for a thingamajig hit. Had to start." He stared out at her from under his iron-gray brows. "G'nite."

Well, fine. The old coot. See if she ever showed an interest in his work again. "Good night, Eb."

A grunt came from behind the junk wall, followed by an answering howl from Jethro, who must have been at his master's feet.

Ten minutes later, Josie had washed and moisturized her face, brushed her teeth, changed into fleece pajamas, and settled under the quilt with a mystery novel. The lamp gave off a soft glow as she read herself to sleep.

On her way into town the next morning, Josie decided to take the long way around and drive past the Woodruff farm. The feathered ladies in her chicken coop had laid a few more eggs than usual, so it was only neighborly to drop the excess off next door. Oh, who was she kidding? She hadn't seen Mitch Woodruff in a few days and, well, she wanted to. Not caring to analyze her wants any further, she pulled into the driveway by the barns, in front of a large, fenced enclosure.

More than a dozen curious, adorably goofy faces appeared on the other side of the fence. Some were dark chocolate brown, others were creamy white, or pale gray. But she was looking for one in particular. She exited the car and approached the fence.

"Stella! There you are, sweetie. You've grown." Josie reached her hand through the mesh of the fence and patted the cria—the one who'd been born the day Josie had officially opened Miss Marple Knits as her own, and whom she'd named—on the soft fluff of fawn-colored fiber that crowned her little head. The other alpacas, females only as the males had a separate enclosure, crowded round Josie, staring. Stella held her own against the herd.

Josie pulled back her hand, wishing she'd brought Stella a special treat. But she had no idea if alpacas could even have treats, or what a treat would consist of. Footsteps sounded behind her, coming from the direction of the barn. She turned.

Mitch Woodruff strode toward her, wearing a hooded Cornell sweatshirt under a canvas Carhartt jacket. Her heart, the treacherous thing, fluttered as he flashed a big grin at her. "Hey, Josie," he said. "Come to visit Stella?"

This was ridiculous. Good-looking men were a dime a dozen in New York City. In fact, she'd turned down advances from more classically beautiful guys. Though perhaps they shouldn't count. Most of them had been more interested in her connections at the Haus of Heinrich than in her.

But good-looking, kind, funny, and loyal guys, well, those didn't just grow on trees. Or next door.

"Uh, yeah. And to bring you and Roy some eggs. They're on the front seat. The hens have been working overtime."

"Thanks." He smiled again, showing either great genetics or great orthodontic work. "She's getting big, isn't she? Pretty soon, we'll have to put her on a halter and start training. The spring alpaca shows are coming up." He put his hands in the pockets of his Levi's. Josie didn't have to look at his back pocket, tempting as that was, to know his brand of jeans. Mitch always wore Levi's.

"I was thinking maybe I'd go to one of the shows with you, sometime. To check out the yarns and see if I want to carry them in the shop." Great. She'd just invited herself to horn in on his business.

Mitch didn't seem to mind. "That's a great idea. I've been selling the fiber to a collective, one that sells to a larger company that spins and distributes the yarn. But once I expand the herd, I might look into producing some small runs of artisan yarns. Maybe you could help me with that?"

The possibility was interesting. "Sure," Josie said. "We could give it a test run through Miss Marple Knits. I want to start an online shop."

Mitch nodded. "Good thinking. You're a smart business owner."

Josie didn't know about that. There was so much to learn. But she was getting the hang of it. She looked out into the field beyond. "Is that a hops pole?"

Mitch looked in the direction she indicated. "Dorset Falls is becoming hops happy, isn't it? But no. That's Roy's antenna. He bought a ham radio setup from Art Cote down the road. Art fleeced him, but it's been keeping Gramps occupied."

"Well, a hobby's good."

Mitch gave a slight frown, then looked off toward the animals. "Honestly, between you and me? He's acting . . . odd." He turned back to her. "Odder than usual," he said.

Which was what Josie had been thinking the last time she'd seen him a few days ago at the general store. "You think he's sick? I worry about Eb all the time, even though he'd kick me out if he heard me say it."

"No, not physically sick. But have you noticed he and Eb have been in an unusually long truce?"

The legendary feud between Eben Lloyd and Roy Woodruff

reached back decades. Even further in an ancestral sense, because it seemed their fathers had been enemies as well. No one knew what had started it—and if Eben or Roy knew, they weren't talking. From what Josie had witnessed, and Mitch had confirmed, the two bachelor farmers were masters of pranking and sabotaging each other, but they always stopped short of physical harm.

"The last thing I knew, Roy had cut Eb's maple sap lines, which you fixed, thanks, and Eb somehow managed to sign Roy up on an online dating site under the name 'Farmer Fabio.'"

Mitch chuckled. "That was a good one. Eb was nice enough to include a phone number in the profile, and Roy's still getting phone calls. We've stopped answering and just let the machine pick up now."

"So it's Roy's turn, right? Maybe he's . . . fresh out of ideas?"

"I'd like to think so," Mitch said. "Though they don't always stick strictly to the rotation." Mitch's border collie, Pepper, raced from around Josie's car and stopped at Mitch's feet. The dog looked up adoringly. Josie couldn't blame her. Mitch reached down and scratched Pepper behind the ears. "But Roy seems . . . preoccupied. A little on edge." He shook his head. "I'm just keeping my eyes and ears open. Whatever it is, it'll either blow up or blow over."

"If I hear anything, I'll let you know." Josie opened the car door and pulled out the disposable container of eggs, handing them to Mitch. "I should get to the shop."

"And I should get back to work. I'm glad you stopped by."

Josie was too.

Chapter 7

Evelyn was already at Miss Marple Knits when Josie arrived. As Josie hung up her jacket and scarf—the day promised to be warm, so she'd be overdressed by the afternoon—Evelyn poured a cup of tea and set the mug on the counter.

"You have to try this," Evelyn demanded. "Lorna is a tea genius. See if you can tell what it is."

Josie laughed. "Tea genius. We'll have to tell her that." She picked up the mug by the handle rather than wrapping her fingers around the middle. Fragrant steam rolled off the top, and Josie inhaled. "Raspberry?" She took a sip. "Definitely raspberry, but with something richer, almost buttery mixed in—"

"Hazelnut," Evelyn interrupted. "It's Linzer torte. Taste the cinnamon too, with just a hint of clove? This is magnificent." Her expression dared anyone to disagree.

Which Josie did not. "Delicious."

"She should be selling this and making money for herself, not letting Douglas Brewster take all the credit. And all the profits."

Lorna must have thought about taking her tea business out

on her own. Maybe she just needed some encouragement. Next time Josie saw her, not at the g.s., she'd butt in and mention it. In fact, that was a good excuse, not that she needed one, to schedule another after-hours knit-in here at Miss Marple Knits.

Josie booted up the shop's electronics. "I saw the crime-scene tape still up next door. The police aren't done?" Her eyes fell on a cardboard box at the far end of the counter. Oh, right. The box of doilies she'd bought from Lyndon the night before he died. She walked to the end of the counter and opened the box. At some point, she supposed, she'd have to pay Harry for them.

"You'd think I'd have some details, wouldn't you, since my daughter-in-law is on the police force—underutilized, I might add." Evelyn was just the slightest bit huffy. "But no, Sharla won't tell me anything."

"I wonder if there's even a suspect." Josie was still inclined to think it was someone who'd followed Lyndon here, maybe from Hartford. And hopefully whoever it was, was gone. And would be caught soon.

"If there is, I haven't heard. From anyone."

"Maybe it was a robbery gone bad. I wonder if there was anything missing from the shop," Josie mused, opening the second set of flaps on the box. "Though I don't see how anyone could tell, unless there was an inventory of some kind. The place was—still is—full of stuff. Harry might know."

Evelyn considered. "But why would a thief try to rob a shop with all the lights blazing and the owner right there in plain sight, obviously just moving in? And with us right next door, unless it happened after we went home? Why not go down to the general store, which was closed and would probably have a bigger cash drawer? No, poor Lyndon was specifically targeted."

"Yeah, I think so too," Josie said. "But why? He seemed so nice. Of course, the other question is whether he was murdered last night, or early this morning. Not that I suppose it matters. The poor man is dead." She dumped the contents of the box on the counter.

Evelyn leaned in. "Doilies," she announced. "Don't have much use for those anymore. Never cared for them myself, either to make them or have them in the house. Reminded me of my mother. Old-fashioned."

Josie picked one up and held it to the light. "I think it's pretty," Josie said. "Such tiny stitches, and look at that intricate pattern someone had to keep track of. This must have taken hours and hours to create." She laid it on the counter and gently smoothed it out. The heat from her hand released a faintly musty odor from the item.

"Yes, you have to pay attention when you're crocheting them. It's easy to lose your place in the charts. I always liked knitting better."

Josie pawed through the pile. "Look, here's a matching one."

"They were often made in sets." Evelyn took her big purse over to the couch and pulled out her knitting. Perhaps she needed an antidote to all the crocheted items she'd just seen. Josie had observed that while some knitters were also crocheters, most people preferred one discipline to the other. "I imagine you'll find more," Evelyn said, stabbing and looping away at the knitted fabric. Josie watched her for a few moments. It always fascinated Josie to see a knitter get into her flow state. Josie herself was a long way from experiencing that, based on last night's unsuccessful attempt.

She continued to sort through the doilies. "What's this? I'm pretty sure it's not crocheted. Or knitted." What else could there be?

Evelyn didn't look up, but pulled another length of yarn out of the ball she was working from. "Is it made of loops and coils, rather than stitches?"

"Yes, that's exactly it. Loops and coils."

"Tatting. It's done with a shuttle instead of a needle or a hook, and it's rather tricky to learn. Tension is super important. Almost nobody does it anymore."

Tatting? Josie had never heard of it. She pulled another piece out. This one was definitely knitted. About six inches square, made of an ecru-colored thread, it didn't seem to have an identifiable pattern like the others. In fact, the placement of the eyelets was quite random. Holding the doily up to the light, Josie refocused her eyes in case she'd missed something. Nope. The piece had a certain charm to it, despite the fact that it wasn't nearly as attractive as the other doilies in the box. Perhaps it had been made by an inexperienced knitter, even a child. Josie shook her head. It was still miles better than anything she herself could produce. She tossed it back into the box.

"Say, Evelyn. What's the best way to clean these? They have a funky smell. I don't see any mildew or big stains, though."

Evelyn deigned to look up from the project in her lap. "What are you going to do with those? You could have bought nice new yarn for twenty-five dollars." Her tone was faintly accusatory, but Josie understood. "It'll be a fair amount of work to launder, shape, and starch them. And it's all got to be done by hand, no washing machine."

Josie caught her lower lip between her teeth. "I don't really know. But they're pretty. Decorative." And somebody had put a lot of time into each one. That needed to be respected.

"Decorative dust catchers. But you're creative. You'll think of something. To clean them, run a sink full of lukewarm water and squirt in some plain, white dishwashing liquid." Evelyn said the name of the brand, which Josie remembered from her childhood but wasn't sure they even made anymore. "I have to go shopping at the big supermarket in Kent, so I'll pick some up for you. Then you'll soak them for a while, gently swish them around, and then we'll need to lay them out flat and pin them to shape on a template to dry. You can starch or not."

"Will that take care of the odor?"

"Maybe, maybe not. Your best bet is to put them out in the sun and air, which you can do before you wash them. Does dear Eben have a clothesline back at the farm?"

Good old Evelyn. She hadn't given up on Eben Lloyd. Josie pictured the backyard. There was some pulley-type hardware outside the back door, but no line attached. Eb had probably taken it down for the winter. Well, she could ask him to put up a line for her. If he was in a good mood, he might even do it. As long as she fed him first.

"Yeah. I'll take these home tonight." Josie put the doilies back into the box and stowed it under the counter, next to her purse so she wouldn't forget it.

The shop bell tinkled, and Evelyn and Josie both turned their attention to the door. A man walked in. He wore a nice pair of Oakley sunglasses, dark-wash jeans, and a sport coat over a black T-shirt. His hair was pulled back into a ponytail. His skin was tanned. He clearly was not a yarn connoisseur, because his eyes went straight to Josie; he seemed not at all interested in the contents of the shop.

Josie opened her mouth to greet him, but he preempted her. "The shop next door. Where's the owner? Why is there crime-scene tape across the door?" He was asking questions, but this was clearly a man used to giving orders.

She was familiar with the type, having lived and worked in New York for years, though she supposed the Big Apple hadn't cornered the market on bossiness. Just look at Diantha Humphries. But unless Josie missed her guess, this guy wasn't a New Yorker. His clothes, appearance, and attitude suggested West Coast. California, probably.

"And you are?" There wasn't really any reason not to give him the information, but Josie wasn't above making him work for it. From the corner of her eye, she could see Evelyn, whose lips were turned up imperceptibly as she watched the exchange.

The man seemed slightly taken aback, but recovered himself. "Forgive me," he said solicitously. "Kai Norton. I'm looking for Lyndon Bailey. Isn't that his shop next door? Was there a break-in?"

What was up with this guy? There was a touch of glee in his voice. He'd either not heard about the murder, or he didn't care, or—

Her stomach gave a little clench. This guy was clearly from out of town, and now he was looking for Lyndon. Didn't they say a criminal always returned to the scene of the crime? Evelyn must have had the same thought, because she was now sitting at attention and had put her hand into her big purse. Josie hoped she was holding her cell phone, ready to call for help if necessary.

"Are you a friend? Relative?"

"Business associate. Why all the questions? I just want to find Lyndon. Now more than ever, if there's been some issue at the antique store." His face held no concern, just more of that . . . glee. There was no other word for it.

"Well, Mr. Norton, I'm sorry to have to tell you this, but Lyndon was found dead in his shop."

Norton's face froze. "Dead?" he said after a beat. Impossible to say what the man's emotions or thoughts were, but Josie could almost see the wheels turning. "Does Taylor know?"

Taylor? Right. Taylor Philbin. It wasn't outside the realm of possibility that this guy knew Lyndon's niece, but still . . .

"I imagine the police have notified her by now," Josie said.

"Police? Then they suspect foul play?"

"I can't tell you what they suspect. If you were doing business with Lyndon, I'm sure they'll want to talk to you." Time to get this guy out of here.

He handed her a card. "Here's my contact information. Is there anywhere to stay in this town? I'd planned to get a room farther south, but now I'd like to be here when Taylor arrives."

Josie gave him the address of the Gray Lady Bed-and-Breakfast. And hoped she wasn't making a mistake.

When he'd gone, she looked at the card in her hand. "Kai Norton. Norton Television Productions." Evelyn put her knitting into her bag and came to take a look.

"Television?" she said. "What would a television producer want with Lyndon? Or Lyndon's niece?"

Josie wondered the same thing. She pulled out her cell phone to give Margo a heads-up. Margo and Darrell could make their own decision about whether to give the guy a room. He'd not seemed to be the world's most compassionate guy, but he didn't have *Psycho Killer* tattooed on his forehead either. While Josie waited for the call to connect, she said to Evelyn, "The bigger question, I think, is why didn't Kai Norton ask about Lyndon's business partner?"

"Harry," they said at the same time.

Chapter 8

Josie left Evelyn in charge of Miss Marple Knits and dialing her daughter-in-law, Sharla, presumably to give *her* a heads-up. Through the crisscrossed yellow tape, Josie could see in the windows of the antique shop. The place appeared empty. She wondered what had happened to Lyndon's body. The closest hospital was a thirty-minute drive away, and she didn't know where the closest funeral home was, but she was pretty sure Dorset Falls didn't have one.

As she walked toward the general store, her mind whirred. What was going on here? Lyndon was dead before he'd even opened for business. Harry had been standing over Lyndon, looking dazed, when Josie arrived. Was he dazed because his business partner was dead? Or because he'd caused the death? And what was that murder weapon, anyway? From the limited view she'd had, it appeared to be two flat pieces of rusty metal, connected in a U-shape. It had looked old, and it was a reasonable assumption it was some antique thingie from the shop. Had Lyndon had an argument with someone that had turned violent, and the thing had been handy? If the death had been premeditated, wouldn't the killer have brought a more traditional weapon, like a knife or a gun?

The general store was busier than usual when she entered. Every visible head turned, so she raised her hand in a group greeting. Josie made her way to the lunch counter in the back. The specials board listed Hungarian goulash and chicken tortilla soups, in addition to the usual tomato bisque and chicken noodle. It wasn't quite lunchtime, but she figured she'd get it to go, then she and Evelyn could eat later.

Lorna appeared behind the counter, wiping her hands on her apron. Her face broke into a grin when she saw Josie. "Tea? I've got a new flavor I'm testing."

"If it's Linzer torte, it's a winner. Evelyn made me some earlier. We should, uh, talk more about that sometime," Josie said, with a glance toward Dougie's office. She could hardly suggest to Lorna here that she go into business for herself.

"We should." Lorna turned her head. "Taking my break, Dougie," she called.

"Make it quick," came the response.

Lorna made two cups of tea, and they carried their mugs to a table in the farthest corner.

"He's grouchy. Grouchier than usual." Lorna kept her voice low.

"Tell me about it. I live with the King of the Grumps every day. You look tired." Her friend's eyes were ringed with dark circles.

"I am. Dougie's got his friend in town, so I'm doing pretty much everything here so they have time to reminisce about their prep-school football days—oh, heck."

Josie turned to see what had Lorna pseudo-cussing. An elderly man in a motorized wheelchair was whirring across the floor. He pulled to a stop in front of Lorna and Josie, then adjusted his glasses. "Who's this?" he demanded.

Lorna answered. "This is Josie Blair. She owns the yarn shop now. Josie, this is Alden Brewster."

"Nice to meet you, Mr. Brewster. Are you Dougie's—"

"Father. You Eben Lloyd's niece?" He looked Josie up and down and apparently liked what he saw, because he waggled an eyebrow at her.

You should have seen me in New York, Pops. "Yes. He and my grandfather were brothers."

"He's a mean old bastard. But I can respect that." He pointed a finger at Lorna. "You. Girl. Open up that door for me so I can go talk to my son."

Lorna rose and did as she was asked. He followed her through the opening in the counter and wheeled himself up to Dougie's door. "Let me in, moron," he yelled. The door opened, and Alden rolled through.

When Lorna returned, Josie said in a low voice, "We really have to get you out of here. Nobody should have to put up with that."

Lorna smiled. "It's okay. Well, it's not really okay, of course. But for right now, this job is a means to an end." She clearly didn't want to talk about what that end was, which Josie knew was her right.

"I didn't know Dougie had a father. I mean a living father," Josie amended. "I haven't seen him around town."

"He goes to Florida every winter and just got back. He's not in town much anyway. Lives in a big house out by the lake and only comes into town to torment Dougie."

The door to Dougie's office opened. "I have to get back to work," Lorna said quickly.

"Understood. I'll talk to you soon." But Lorna was already back behind the counter by the time Alden, Dougie, and another man paraded out. Josie remembered she'd seen him the other day. What was his name? Rick . . . Steuben, that was it. Dougie's prep-school friend. He must have been pretty proud of his alma mater, because he wore an athletic-style jacket with *Collingswood Academy* emblazoned on the left side of his chest.

He appeared to be the same age as Dougie, which only made sense if they'd gone to school together, but appeared to be in better shape. Better looking too. He was wearing his age well. Josie thought of her mom, who, to her knowledge, hadn't been on a date in years. But no. Any friend of Dougie's was bound to be a jerk. And maybe her mother already had a secret dating life she hadn't mentioned. The three men filed out the front door without a backward glance.

Josie waited till she was sure the coast was clear, then approached Lorna at the counter again. "I should get back to the shop. Two goulashes, please."

Lorna ladled out two cups of soup, topped them with lids, and put them into a bag. "There's extra bread in there." She smiled.

"Not that I need the extra bread, but I appreciate it. I'll talk to you soon." Josie headed back to Miss Marple Knits.

When she got there, Officer Sharla Coogan was leaned up against the back counter. She and Evelyn were staring at a cell phone, broad grins on each of their faces. They looked up when Josie approached. Sharla looked a bit apologetic, but Evelyn just looked proud. "We're watching a video of Andrew. He's learning to ride a bike."

"Sorry, Josie. We can do this later, not gush over my kid on company time," Sharla said.

"Don't worry about it. Andrew's adorable."

"I know," she said. "Most of the time." Sharla went into cop mode. "Mom says someone was here looking for Lyndon?"

Josie reached into the pocket of her jeans and pulled out the card, which she handed to Sharla. "He said he was Lyndon's business associate. I wonder what a California television producer would want with a Connecticut antique dealer?"

"I don't know either," Sharla said, "but I think I'll give him a call."

Josie pulled out her cell phone and typed *Norton Television*

Productions into her search bar. "It says here that they produce reality-type shows. Could Norton have been looking for Lyndon to supply him with antique set props or something?"

"But Harry was the buyer in the partnership. Why wouldn't Norton be dealing with him?" Evelyn asked. "Remember, Norton never said a word about Harry."

"But he did mention Lyndon's niece, Taylor, right?" Sharla flipped open her notebook. "Taylor Philbin. Age twenty-seven. Runs a gift shop at the shore. I imagine she'll be here to claim the body anytime."

Josie secretly willed Sharla to go on, but she had apparently said all she could. They already knew all this, except Taylor's age, so it wasn't as if Sharla was spilling anything she shouldn't.

"Sharla," Josie said. "I've been wondering about something. What was the murder weapon? I've never seen anything like that. If you can say, of course."

"You saw the scene, so there's no reason I can't confirm it for you. Cause of death was exsanguination—bleeding out— due to a stab wound. The implement was a pair of antique sheep shears."

Sheep shears. Josie saw Lyndon's body again, this time in her mind's eye. She blinked, trying to clear the image.

"And before either of you asks," Sharla continued, "we're still following leads. Not ready to make an arrest yet. Can I keep this card?"

Josie nodded. She had no reason to call the television producer for anything. "He might be staying over at the Gray Lady," she said.

"Not sure that's such a good idea," Sharla said, and left.

"What did that mean?" Evelyn said when she'd gone.

"I'd say it means Harry hasn't been cleared."

Chapter 9

By the time Josie and Evelyn closed up Miss Marple Knits for the day, the crime-scene tape had come down next door. Josie decided to drive by the Gray Lady Bed-and-Breakfast to check on Harry and give him the news. And if she found out whether Kai Norton had taken a room there, so much the better. Curiosity was eating away at her over what his business had been with Lyndon.

Dorset Falls was a pretty little place, if you didn't count the mostly empty downtown. And the murders. Lawns in front of the saltboxes and Victorians and smaller ranch-style homes were still brown from winter, but here and there cheerful spots of purple, white, and gold appeared in the form of crocuses. It was still too early for tulips and daffodils, she supposed, though she didn't have the gardening gene. She pulled in at the Gray Lady and put her car into park.

Margo greeted her at the door. "I heard your car. It has a, uh, distinctive sound."

"If by 'distinctive' you mean 'needs a tune-up,' you're correct." Josie laughed. "I've got an appointment with Rusty next week."

"Thanks for sending that California guy. He decided to stay."

Josie felt a little nugget of worry form. "Just be careful, okay?"

Margo held up a hand. "Noted. Two strangers in Dorset Falls at the same time a man dies suspiciously always ups the alert level around here. Come on in," she said. "Let's sit in the front room. I just mopped the kitchen floor."

Margo showed Josie into a room with ceilings at least ten feet high. Elaborate oak molding framed every window and door and lined the baseboards and the ceiling. The walls were papered in a design of exotic birds and elegant scrollwork. The over-the-top décor would have looked ridiculous at the farmhouse, but it was just right here. Even doilies would have worked.

"I can't stay too long, and I'm sure you'll want to be getting dinner on the table. I actually wanted to speak to Harry, if he's around. Not that I don't want to talk to you," Josie added.

"No offense taken. And yes, Harry's here. He's been in his room most of the day. Not sure what he's doing up there, but he asked for the Wi-Fi password, so he must have a computer with him. Work, maybe."

From off in the distance, a phone rang. Margo jumped up. "That's the business line. You can go on up and see Harry. His door will be second on the right at the top of the stairs." She hustled off as the rings continued.

Josie ascended the grand staircase. There was a landing at the top. She paused. At the far end of the hallway, she could see Harry with his hand on the handle of a door. He jiggled the knob, but the door was apparently locked. He moved in her direction and tried the next door, which also appeared to be locked. What was he doing? Unless Margo had misspoken about which room was his, he was trying to get into rooms that weren't his own.

He was bound to notice her eventually, so Josie decided on a preemptive strike. "Harry?"

He started. "Josie. You gave me a fright. It's nice to see you again."

Was it? He seemed agitated.

"I didn't have your cell number, so I thought I'd come by and let you know you can get back into the antique shop. At least I think you can. The crime-scene tape is down."

"They've released Lyndon's room here, too." Harry's face was expressionless, but he still seemed on edge.

"I hate to ask," Josie said as they walked downstairs and back into the front room. "But have you given any more thought as to whether you're going to open the antique store? Of course you have the place for six months, but—"

"You need to know whether you should start lining up a new tenant. I wish I knew. Lyndon and I had a legally binding partnership agreement. We each owned half of the business, each to inherit the other's half upon one partner's death. But we've got stuff stored in several places around the state, and not all of it belongs to the business. Some of it I bought personally, and some Lyndon bought for himself. It's going to take some time to get that all sorted out."

"I understand. And I wasn't trying to rush you." Josie had charged a high enough rent for the six months to cover herself for taxes, insurance, and utilities for a year. But she was more concerned about the unopened store. It was one thing for most of Main Street to have papered-over storefront windows. Somehow, it seemed worse to have a store full of stuff that no one could buy. Like a bait-and-switch scam.

"Have you heard whether Lyndon's niece, Taylor, has arrived in town yet?" Harry's tone was neutral, but all the same, Josie had a feeling there was no love lost between the two.

"Haven't heard." Should she go for it? Nothing ventured, nothing gained. "You know who *is* in town, though? A television producer." She watched him carefully.

Harry's jaw tensed. He knew something. Finally, he said, "You may as well know. Lyndon had just signed a deal with Norton to star in a new reality show called *Diamond in the Rough*. They were going to film Lyndon traveling around the country, buying antiques directly from people's homes." Harry's voice held more than a touch of bitterness.

"Wow. A reality show? That would be great for your business."

Harry scowled. "That's just it. The producers didn't want the *business*. They wanted Lyndon. And they wanted Taylor, so there'd be a young woman on the show."

It wasn't hard to see where this was going. "And they didn't want you." She immediately regretted her blunt words.

"Correct. I don't have the camera presence, according to Kai Norton. Nor do I have the signing bonus the show was about to give Lyndon. *He* was poised to make a lot of money."

Poor Harry.

Margo returned at that moment. "That was Darrell. He's on his way. They made good progress out at the old Ryder house today. I don't mind telling you I'm more than a little excited about a craft brewery opening up."

"The building is an authentic colonial saltbox," Harry said. "It's lasted three hundred years. It could last another three hundred."

Both women turned to Harry in surprise. "How do you know about the Ryder house?" Margo asked.

"Because Lyndon and I bought the contents of the house. Most of it wasn't worth anything, after tenants had been in there for years, but we found some salvageable things in the attic and out in the barn. Lyndon never got the chance to set anything up at the store." The color drained from Harry's face. "But unless I'm very much mistaken, somebody found something we brought back from there."

"What do you mean?" Josie said. But she thought she knew.

Harry's eyes caught and held Josie's. "We had a box of old farm tools, including a pair of antique sheep shears."

Josie and Harry were silent, each remembering the rusted metal sticking out of Lyndon's chest.

"The murder weapon?" Margo asked.

"We—" Harry gave a barely perceptible gulp. "We bought the thing that killed Lyndon. And I have no idea who could have done such a thing."

Josie motored through the side streets of Dorset Falls on her way out of town. But she wasn't headed back to Eb's farm just yet, though the light was beginning to fade.

Whether he knew it or not, Harry had just given himself a pretty good motive for murdering Lyndon. He stood to inherit Lyndon's half of the business. No telling how valuable it was; according to Harry they had inventory all around the state. If they were also doing some kind of online business, which seemed likely, especially for smaller items like jewelry, coins, silver, or even art, Nutmeg Antiques & Curiosities could have substantial assets.

Means and opportunity were clear as well. He had unquestioned access to the unopened store.

And he was clearly disgruntled about being cut out of the television show. Some of those reality stars made thousands, even multiple thousands, of dollars per episode depending on the popularity of the show. Lyndon and his niece had apparently hit pay dirt.

But Harry's dirt was just . . . plain old dirt.

Josie took a turn onto Ryder Road, just on the outskirts of

town. Should she go to the police, tell Sharla about what Harry had just revealed? But the police had already questioned Harry. And Evelyn had told Sharla about the producer's being in town, so all this stuff was probably already in the police file, or would be soon.

Harry might have been uncharismatic in front of a camera, but he wasn't unintelligent. And he could just as easily have kept the information about the business and the show to himself.

So if Harry hadn't killed Lyndon, which Josie was inclined to believe, who had?

When she spotted the tall hops poles silhouetted against the sky, she slowed the car. This was the place she'd thought it was. A huge rectangle of a house, with white paint peeling off the clapboards, a wooden front door studded in nails, which were blackened by age and weather, and a pitched roof that slanted sharply back from two stories in the front to one in the back. It was a magnificent old place, even though the outside was a bit rundown, and she could understand why someone would want to renovate it.

Who had Bea Ryder been? This was a big old house for one person, though if Bea had grown up here, memories could have filled much of the empty space.

Helen had said Bea just disappeared one day. Perhaps she'd wanted to shake up her life. Move away, without a backward glance. Maybe she'd run off to Europe with a minor prince of some obscure region. Josie liked that story, hoped it was true.

But the far greater likelihood was that Bea had been killed. As romantic as it sounded, the prince scenario was just wishful thinking. People didn't just up and leave their homes, their businesses, their friends.

Josie thought of her box of doilies. Had it come from here? Lyndon had said he'd just bought the box and hadn't had time to sort through them yet, so it seemed likely. She wasn't sure how she felt about that. Comforted, somehow, to have something that had belonged to the probably dead woman? Creeped out? Maybe a little of both.

Josie backed out of the driveway and drove home.

Chapter 10

Eb had been uncharacteristically agreeable when she'd told him she wanted to put up a clothesline and asked where she could find the materials. He'd grunted and told her he'd do it, which was what she'd been hoping for. Not that she couldn't have figured it out herself—setting up a line seemed far easier than knitting—but Eb had been spending a lot of time in his workshop lately. It would be good for him to get outdoors. He might not want her to screw something up—though any harm she could do with a length of rope and a couple of pulleys seemed minute. More likely, he was anticipating a lower electricity bill due to her not using the clothes dryer. Her great-uncle was good with money, she had to give him that.

Josie stood at the counter of Miss Marple Knits, opening the mail that had accumulated over the last couple of days. Other than a box of sample yarns from a new company, there was nothing of importance. Just circulars for the hardware store and supermarket the next town over, a credit card solicitation, and a request for a donation to a charity she'd never heard of.

She placed the paper stuff into the recycling bin, then ran the credit card offer through the shredder in the back.

When she returned to the front of the store, Evelyn and Helen had arrived and were hanging up their jackets. "Hi, Helen," Josie said. "It's been a couple days since you've been in."

"What am I? Garter stitch?" Evelyn said. She and Helen looked at each other and laughed. It must have been some private knitting joke between them, or maybe garter stitch was the equivalent of chopped liver. Who knew?

"You were next on my greetings list, don't worry." Josie carefully sliced open the tape holding the box together. She dumped it out on the counter. Evelyn and Helen crowded round. "I'm glad you're both here, actually. Let's take a look at these samples. Maybe you two could knit up some swatches and tell me if you think we should order anything for the shop."

Evelyn and Helen dove into the pile as though Josie had just emptied a box of hundred-dollar bills in front of them. They each pulled up a skein, rolled the yarn between their fingers, and examined the color and label. It was like watching an Esther Williams movie on the oldies channel—the women were perfectly focused, perfectly synchronized.

Having made their choices, Evelyn and Helen removed themselves to the seating area, one to the couch, one to the armchair, and got to work.

Josie watched them fondly. She'd grown to love these two ladies. And she needed them. Josie armed the sample skeins to one end of the counter, then retrieved the box of doilies from under the counter. She hadn't taken them home last night, after all. She dumped them out and began to sort again. It was either this or clean the tiny bathroom or sweep out the storeroom, so the choice was easy.

Josie laid out each doily, finding several sets of two or three that matched, as Evelyn had predicted. As she sorted, her mind wandered.

Doilies would just look silly in any modern home. But she wasn't going to let someone's hard work go to waste. And they were so pretty.

What if she repurposed them? They could be sewn down on the back of a sweater or jean jacket. She liked this idea so much, if she'd had her jean jacket with her, she would have threaded a needle right then and there.

Josie chose one of the matching sets, then moved around the flat, lacy circles with the palm of her hand, one large and three smaller ones, identical in pattern except for the size, until they made a pleasing arrangement. What if these were tacked onto throw pillows? They could even be framed and hung as art on a wall. Her skin started to tingle, and her mind started to race with possibilities, the reactions she always had when her creative juices were pumping. Could she get more of these? She could sell the home décor items through her future online shop. And charge a nice price for them too.

"Are you playing with those doilies again?" Evelyn said from across the room. "I brought you the dish soap and starch."

"Just brainstorming what to do with them. Eb said he'd put up a clothesline for me today. I'll hang them out when I get home."

"Good idea," Helen piped up. "Hang them out dry. If you hang them out wet, they're liable to shrink, or at the very least get pulled out of shape."

Josie picked up the box, preparing to put them away again for the second time in as many days. They weren't smelling any fresher, and she didn't want the mustiness to spread to her inventory. Which she wished she'd thought of yesterday, but no harm seemed to have been done. There was some writing in black block letters on one side of the box. *Ryder House*. That confirmed it, then. These were Beatrice Ryder's things.

"Helen," Josie said. "Would you like any of these?"

"Whatever for? I mean, thank you, of course, but I still have my mother's put away in the cedar closet. I don't need any more."

"Well, I know Bea Ryder was your friend. And it looks like these came from her house. I thought you might want one as a memento."

Helen made a small sound. "Oh, dear, that is so sweet of you." She set down her knitting and approached the counter. "I wish I could say I recognized any of these." She peered at several of them in turn. "I'm not even sure Bea made them. I never saw her crocheting, only knitting. Though she was older than I was and could have given it up before we became friends." Helen looked over the array on the counter, then picked up the small, odd piece. "What's this?" She held it up to the light. "This piece is knitted, not crocheted like the rest."

"I noticed that one too," Josie said. "To me it looked like a mistake, or a practice swatch. See how the pattern is all off-kilter?"

Helen adjusted her glasses and looked closer. "The pattern may be off," she declared. "But this was made by an expert knitter, which Bea was. Each stitch is perfect."

Helen handed the piece back to Josie. "You can keep these, but again, I thank you. I don't need things to remember Bea. She was special."

Josie began to repack the box. "I'd love to hear about her."

"So would I," Evelyn said. "Let's have tea while we talk." She got up and went behind the counter, then switched on the electric kettle. "Let's try this lemon meringue flavor Lorna concocted."

Josie closed up the box and put it by the front door. When the water was hot, Evelyn poured mugs, and they all sat down,

Evelyn and Helen in their usual spots and Josie in the second armchair. She looked around and smiled. Every day couldn't be like this, of course, but it was awfully nice to be able to take a break when she wanted. Not that she'd worked particularly hard this morning. But that time would come. Business would pick up eventually, as some of the limited advertising she'd done started to pay off and more people from the surrounding area learned about the shop. And with an online component, the sky was really the limit. Maybe she was being overly optimistic, but if she didn't have a positive attitude, who would?

"Now," Evelyn said. "Tell us about Bea." She set her tea down and picked up her knitting again, holding it up and examining it. "I like this new yarn," she said. "It has a nice hand, and it's tightly spun, so it won't pill."

Helen sipped her tea, then turned her head slightly to the side and closed her eyes. "Bea and I met, it must have been forty-five years ago now, though it pains me to say that number. She had her dress shop across the street, had been in business a long time, and I took some dresses in for alterations. She did all her own tailoring. Hems, taking in, letting out, adjusting darts. Clothes were much more fitted back then."

Josie nodded. "Some of those styles are coming back. I love the way they look—so elegant—but I'm not sure how comfortable they are. People now are used to more forgiving fabrics and cuts."

"I know I've gotten used to the stretch. I don't know what I'd do without yoga pants, which are a gift straight from God." Evelyn pulled up an arm's length of yarn and began to stitch again.

"So I took the dresses in, and we started talking. And we got to be friends. Our age difference didn't matter." She smiled at Josie, who smiled back.

"Bea grew up in the old Ryder house, which her family had owned for many years, maybe even a century or more. She never had any brothers or sisters, and according to her, she broke her father's heart and made her mother proud when she joined the WAVES."

"The WAVES? Wasn't that a branch of the military?" Josie didn't know much more than that the women had been volunteers in World War II.

Helen nodded. "I believe it stands for 'Women Accepted for Volunteer Emergency Service.' Basically, it was the women's division of the United States Naval Reserve. She had a college degree already, so she was accepted to officer school and did her training at Smith College, up in Massachusetts."

Josie felt a little swell of pride, even though she'd never met Bea. "She must have been brave—and adventurous."

"She told me stories about when she was stationed in Hawaii, working in radio communications. It sounded as if she had the time of her life. Just before Pearl Harbor, she was reassigned back to the Connecticut shore."

"Which may have saved her life." The rest of Josie's thought she left unsaid, but she knew her friends were thinking the same thing. Bea Ryder had survived active duty in World War II, only to be killed—maybe—in her own hometown.

"Bea—" Helen's voice caught, and she cleared her throat, then sipped her tea before continuing. "Bea came back from the war. But she had left a fiancé in Hawaii. And he didn't come back."

Josie felt tears well up in her own eyes. Evelyn's were dry— she was far less emotional than Josie or Helen—but she might have emitted just the tiniest sound. "Poor Bea. How awful," Josie said.

"When the war ended," Helen said, dabbing at her eyes with a tissue, which she then replaced in her sleeve, "she came back home. Opened the dress shop, and took care of her parents until they died."

"And she never married?"

"No," Helen said. "She never did. Although a good portion of her business was making wedding and bridesmaid and flower girl and mother-of-the-bride or mother-of-the-groom gowns. The irony wasn't lost on her. But war had made her tough, she told me. She couldn't seem to get enough of needlework, whether it was sewing or knitting. She even took up embroidery for a while. I think having her hands constantly busy kept her from thinking too much, if you know what I mean."

"What a story. I wish I'd known her," Evelyn said. "But I'd just moved here when she disappeared. And I always did all my own alterations, or had my sister in Granby do them for me."

"One day, the awnings didn't go up over the shop windows and doors. In all the years I knew her, she never failed to open on time and close on time, Tuesday through Saturday. The WAVES had made her hyperpunctual. So I thought she must be sick. I called, and when I didn't get an answer either at the dress shop or her house, I drove out to Ryder Road in my wood-paneled station wagon. Her car wasn't in the driveway, but I went up and knocked on the door of the house anyway. No answer. No sign of her anywhere."

Helen took a deep breath. "And I never saw her again. Nobody did. She was just . . . gone."

Josie gave Helen a moment, then asked, "Did the police ever find anything?"

Helen shook her head. "Nothing. When they opened up her house, it was as though she'd just teleported out. Food was still in the refrigerator. Her closet was still full. No note, no evidence. The only thing they did find eventually was her car, which had been abandoned on a city street in Bridgeport. By the time the police identified it, vandals had stripped it clean."

Evelyn shook her head emphatically. "Bea didn't just walk away. She didn't commit suicide. She was murdered."

"Why do you think so?" Josie asked.

"Because women would have confided in Bea. When you stand in front of someone in your bra and girdle and trust her to pin fabric around you, touch your body to get a fit just right, you trust her with your secrets. I'd bet money Bea knew something. About someone. And that she was killed because of it."

Chapter 11

The room was silent as Evelyn's words settled around them like snowflakes in April. Cold on the way down, but melting into nothing by the time they hit the ground. Because what was there left to say? Bea's house was being renovated, turned into a new business that, if successful, would bring much-needed revenue and even a few jobs into Dorset Falls. Her business across the street had been closed for as long as she'd been gone.

And she'd been gone for more than forty years, would have been in her nineties if she were still alive. If she had been killed over some secret, chances were good that her killer was long dead too.

So did it matter if she was ever found, or the murder solved? It wouldn't change anything. But Bea had been a real person, with friends, a family. If nothing else, it mattered to Helen. And that was enough for Josie.

Not that there was anything she could do about it. Even if she wanted to help, where could she start? The second best thing she could do would be to honor Bea's memory by doing something useful with these possessions of hers. The first best thing would be to continue to be a friend to Helen. Josie rose and gave Helen a hug.

"Thank you, Josie. Now let me finish this swatch, and you can take a look." She picked up her knitting and began to loop and twist. Josie had seen it before, this ability of knitting to soothe and relax.

"You want a lesson?" Evelyn said. "Now's a good time, while the shop is quiet."

Why was Josie being so stubborn? She couldn't explain the need to figure it out herself *to* herself, let alone to Evelyn. The landline rang. *Saved by the bell.*

"Miss Marple Knits, may I help you?" Josie said when she reached the phone.

The caller inquired about the shop's hours and whether they carried a particular brand of yarn. She promised to come in, in the next few days, and check out the shop. Excellent. Hopefully, she'd bring a friend or two.

The rest of the morning passed quickly. Gwen Simmons came in for a couple of skeins of novelty acrylic to make a spring hat and scarf for her daughter. Evelyn and Helen gave the new yarn they'd tested a thumbs-up, so Josie placed a small order. Just because a yarn tested well didn't mean it would sell, and at this early stage of business ownership she couldn't afford to overbuy.

"You two want lunch?" Josie asked. "I'm going to the g.s."

"You're kidding." Evelyn laughed, and Josie grinned sheepishly.

"I'm that predictable, huh?"

"Well, we do recognize that it's the only place to eat in town. But you go. Helen and I will watch the shop."

Josie didn't have to be told twice. It was a beautiful spring day. She took two extra turns around the block, waving to her friends each time she passed Miss Marple Knits, before heading into the g.s.

Feeling virtuous after getting a modicum of exercise, she ordered a sparkling water and a salad with grilled chicken. Lorna assembled the salad, then asked, "Should I add the toasted walnuts?"

"Load 'er up. They're healthy, right? How are things?"

"Since yesterday? About the same. Say, Josie, I hate to ask. But I need a favor."

"After all the culinary joy you've given me, and the number of evenings you've helped me feed Eb, I probably owe you my firstborn." Not that any firstborns or borns of any kind were going to be appearing anytime in the foreseeable future. Her thoughts bounced to Mitch Woodruff. Which was ridiculous. She barely knew him.

Lorna set the salad and a package of utensils wrapped in a napkin on the tray, then wiped the condensation from a bottle of fizzy water. She glanced in both directions before leaning across the counter. "Dougie wants me to cook a dinner for him and his prep-school buddies at his father's place at the lake. And I could use some help."

Josie hoped her surprise didn't show. Somebody wanted her help cooking? Well, she'd mastered spaghetti, and she wasn't one to back down from a challenge. "Sure. What do you need me to do?"

Lorna laughed. "Don't worry. It's only prime rib for a dozen men. Not that big a deal." For Lorna, maybe. "But I could use some help serving, and clearing dishes and, well—"

"You need some female support in a sea of testosterone. I'll be there."

"It's just, I don't know all these guys, if you know what I mean. I'd feel better if you were there with me."

"Understood. Do you need help prepping the food? I'm willing to learn."

"That would be great. I'll let you know the details."

The door to Dougie's office opened, and out came Dougie,

followed by Rick Steuben. "You're in charge," he said to Lorna. "Don't screw it up."

When they'd gone, Josie said, "Seriously. I will type up your resume myself. Put me in charge of your job search. What an ass."

Lorna smiled. "He is. And he's showing off in front of Rick, who's quite a bit more successful than he is. Of course, when old Alden kicks off, Dougie will be set for the rest of his unnatural life."

A woman came up to the counter with a basket full of items. Josie stepped to the side so Lorna could ring her up. A slip of paper whirred out of the credit card machine. Lorna felt around on the counter for a pen, and, coming up empty, apologized, as the woman felt in her own purse. At the same moment, another customer queued up behind the first. "Josie, would you mind running into Dougie's office and finding me a pen? There should be a cup of them on the desk."

"No problem." Josie hadn't brought a purse, had just put her wallet in the pocket of her coat, so she couldn't offer a pen herself.

Dougie's office was decorated with sports memorabilia. A football jersey, conveniently labeled *Brewster* over the number forty-seven and the words *Collingswood Academy,* was framed and hung behind the desk. An actual football sat on a pedestal on the credenza, next to a leather-bound book labeled *Collingswood.* A yearbook, if Josie had to guess. Dougie must have peaked in high school, since there didn't appear to be any college items. Tempting as it was to poke around, she needed to hurry. Stacks of papers obscured the surface of the desk. It was rather familiar, actually, reminding her of Eb's paper-strewing tendencies. Moving some stacks around, she found the cylindrical container and pulled out two pens, which she quickly tested by scribbling on one of the papers on the desk. He'd probably never notice.

When she returned to the counter, the first woman was gone.

Presumably a pen had been found in Josie's absence. Josie handed the pens to Lorna anyway. "I should go relieve Evelyn. Let me know what you need."

"I will, and thanks. I owe you."

She didn't, but the sentiment was nice.

Josie closed Miss Marple Knits at five o'clock on the dot. She'd finished all her paperwork and sent Evelyn home a half hour ago. Business had been slower than overboiled maple syrup that afternoon.

When Josie got home, Jethro barreled off the porch, once again threatening to knock her over. She tossed him a dog treat, and he ran off to get it, freeing her to make it to the front door. He couldn't have more than a couple or he'd be sick, and they didn't always distract him long enough for her to get into the house, but today luck was with her. He wagged his tail furiously and devoured the treat. She tossed him one more for good measure. He could stay outside for a while, just in case.

The house was quiet when she went in, but the wood stove was blazing. "Eb? I'm home." She set her box of doilies on the kitchen counter, then opened the door to the workshop.

"Clothesline's up," a voice said from somewhere in the depths. "And now that you mention it, I prefer my Fruit of the Looms smelling like fresh air."

"It's my pleasure to serve you," Josie said. "Fresh skivvies coming right up."

There was still an hour of daylight left, so she decided to take advantage of it before starting dinner. She grabbed the box of doilies and headed out the kitchen door.

A line was now looped around the metal pulley attached to the back of the farmhouse. It ran doubled to a similar pulley, which extended from a pole inserted into the ground about twenty feet away. The setup could hold a lot of laundry, which she didn't plan on testing. Ever. She liked to do the minimum of housework to get by. But then again, it had been a very long time since she'd slept in sheets that had been line dried. Like since she'd moved away from her mom's house, more than a decade ago. The memory of that scent rose up, and somehow she didn't blame Eb for the underwear comment, even though he'd said it just to needle her.

A flowered pillowcase had been fashioned into a bag, which was suspended from the line by what appeared to be a coated wire hanger. Whose handiwork had that been? Cora's? The bag wasn't old or faded enough to go back to Eb's mother, Josie's great-grandmother. Whoever had made it, it was useful, full of wooden clothespins. Josie pulled out a couple and began to hang the doilies. It didn't take long to figure out that if she pulled on the top line, the bottom line moved toward the pole.

She was nearly at the bottom of the box when the line refused to move. She gave it another tug, but it was still stuck. The problem appeared to be at the other end, so she headed in that direction. The line had slipped out of the groove in the wheel of the pulley. The weight of the doilies, even though they were dry, made it more difficult to reposition, but she managed to fix the mechanism. She gave the post a little punch. "Behave," she told it. Something wiggled at the top. There was another wire coat hanger stuck into the pole, this one twisted out of shape. If this was one of Eb's thingamajig sculptures, it was one of his less successful ones. Perhaps it represented some of his early work.

The doilies could stay out all night. As long as it didn't rain, the worst that could happen was that they'd be a little damp with dew in the morning. She didn't think that would ruin them.

After dinner, Eb disappeared back into his workshop and shut the door. He was going to have a good-sized inventory, at the rate he was working. Was he planning to open a gallery? Some kind of roadside attraction?

Josie took her tea into the morning-borning room and opened her computer. First, she did a search for ideas for repurposing doilies. As she'd suspected, her ideas hadn't been original—there were only so many things that could be done with the lacy squares and circles, no matter how creative someone was. But with the right marketing spin, she could give them her own brand. Country chic. Modern Victoriana. If nothing else, she could sew them on jewel-colored velvet pillows and call them Christmas décor.

Next was another blog post to write: *Sticks and the Single Girl: My Life in the Country.* If it worked for the Pioneer Woman, it could work for her. She checked her stats. Excellent. They'd increased. Someone from the Ukraine had read her last post, in addition to her friends from Malaysia. Things were looking up.

The yarn and knitting needles sat in the drawer to her left. *Figure me out,* they taunted. But before she could feel guilty, or frustrated, or give the inanimate objects a snappy mental comeback, her cell phone beeped with a text message: *Can you talk? Call me.* The sender was Margo Gray.

"Josie?" Margo said when she picked up. "It was getting late, so I texted rather than called."

"What's up?"

"The police were just here. Harry's been arrested."

Chapter 12

Josie felt her mouth drop open. "Harry? What happened?" She supposed she shouldn't have been surprised, but somehow, she hadn't really considered him a viable suspect.

"Well, of course Mark Denton didn't read off the evidence when he put Harry in handcuffs. But he did say he was taking Harry in on suspicion of murdering Lyndon Bailey."

"I wonder what they have on him," Josie mused. But when she put together what she knew, maybe it added up to enough. Harry now owned the entire antique business, including all the inventory, except for, apparently, some pieces that Lyndon had bought himself, which would presumably go to his heir or heirs. Harry was clearly disgruntled about being cut out of the television show. Had he secretly been so angry that he decided to take matters into his own hands, effectively canceling the show before it even got started?

"Well, I can tell you that he and that television producer, Kai Norton, had a huge argument here around dinnertime. By the time Darrell and I heard the raised voices, it had already escalated to the point where Darrell had to grab Harry to keep him from going after Kai. We only heard part of the argument, but Kai almost seemed to be baiting Harry."

"Baiting him?" What a jerk. Kai didn't want Harry for the reality show, and then was teasing him about it? Josie didn't like her next thought, but it had to be asked. "Uh, he wasn't filming it, was he?"

There was a short silence on the other end of the line. "I never even thought of that. I don't recall seeing a camera, but those things can be pretty small these days. If he filmed me or Darrell, I'll tell you right now we are not signing any releases. Our faces will be blurred out if that footage ever airs."

Josie wasn't sure how she should react to the news of Harry's arrest. Relieved that Lyndon's murderer had been captured? Or enraged that an innocent man was now behind bars?

"And now, to make things especially awkward," Margo continued, "guess who called and asked me to rent her a room?"

Josie ran through the possibilities and said the only name she could think of. "Taylor . . . what's her name. Lyndon's niece?"

"Yup. Taylor Philbin. So what am I supposed to tell her? 'Sure, love to have you. By the way, the guy who's accused of murdering your uncle? Yeah, he could be out on bail and back here any minute.'"

Margo was in a tough spot. It wasn't as if she could turn down business. But on the other hand, she couldn't put these two people under the same roof. *If* Harry came back, which was not at all certain. He might not be granted bail, or he might not be able to raise the money. "So what did you tell her?"

"I told her she could stay tonight, at least. Even if Harry does get out, I'm not sure I can let him stay here. A man is innocent until proven guilty and all that, but there's the safety of myself, my husband, and my guests to think about. Harry's paid through the weekend, so I'll just lock his door and keep the room as is."

"And deal with it if he gets out. Makes sense. Thanks for calling, Margo. And if you hear anything else, let me know."

"I will, and you do the same." Margo disconnected.

Josie leaned back in the office chair and blew out a breath. Coco seemed to know she was needed, as if Josie had flashed the Cat-Signal in the sky, because she jumped up into Josie's lap and began to purr, a feline superhero.

In her gut, Josie didn't think Harry was capable of murder. But what did she know? The first time she'd met him he had been standing over a body. She knew nothing about him, really, or about what kind of relationship he and Lyndon had had, what animosities there could have been between them.

From a practical standpoint, she now owned a building with a shop full of antiques, a shop that didn't look like it was opening anytime soon. If ever. Her thoughts went back to when she'd first arrived in Dorset Falls, with no other tasks than helping Eb recover from his broken leg and closing up Miss Marple Knits. The idea of packing up the inventory of the yarn shop had been daunting enough. What if she had to pack up the inventory of the whole antique store? Of course professionals could be hired, but that would cost a fortune, and there would be storage fees on top of that. There was no guarantee she'd ever get that money back. Even considering she'd been paid six months in advance, storage fees for that amount of stuff would eat up the advance fast. It seemed a little insensitive to think about, when a man was dead, but she had to be practical too.

Coco jumped to the ground when Josie leaned forward and shut the lid of her laptop. "We'll just have to wait and see what happens, I guess." But Coco was already gone.

When Josie delivered her eggs to the general store the next morning, Mitch's grandfather, Roy Woodruff, was sitting at a table by himself. He seemed nervous—his eyes darting around and his fingers drumming on the table. "You okay, Mr. Woodruff?" Josie asked, wondering if she should call Mitch. Which, she had to admit, would not be a chore.

"Huh?" Roy looked up, but didn't seem to recognize her. His flannel shirt hung open over a thermal undershirt and under a red-and-black buffalo-plaid wool jacket. Thick silver-white stubble lined his chin.

"It's me, Josie. Eb's niece? From next door?" Agitation was rolling off the old farmer in waves.

Josie glanced toward Lorna behind the counter. Lorna returned the gaze and inclined her head slightly in a "come here" gesture. "Roy?" Josie said. "You want a glass of water or a coffee or something?" An untouched blueberry muffin sat on a plate in front of him.

"What? Dad-burn it, leave me alone, will you?" He broke open the muffin and jammed some into his mouth.

She knew a thing or two about dealing with cranky old men. Leaving them alone when asked was generally a good strategy, so she approached Lorna and raised an eyebrow in question.

"What's going on with him, do you know? Mitch said he was acting strangely."

Lorna smiled. "So, we've been talking to Mitch, have we? Do tell."

Josie held up a hand. "Nothing to tell, I swear." Though, she rather wished she *had* had something to tell. "And you didn't answer my question."

Lorna leaned over the counter and lowered her voice. "I don't know. It's unusual enough to see him here this time of morning. He's a farmer, so you'd think he'd be doing farm chores, right? But he's been here for an hour, either staring off into space or jumping at every little noise or movement."

The front door opened and in walked—oh joy—Diantha Humphries. It was questionable which was colder, the breeze she let in or the stare she leveled at Josie. What had she ever done to this woman? Other than take over the knitting shop Diantha wanted to buy and send someone she loved to prison, that is.

Diantha made a beeline for Josie. "You—" she spluttered. "You've only been in town a few weeks, and you've already managed to *ruin* it." Her face began to fluoresce into the shade of neon purple Josie knew so well.

Josie was fairly certain she was not personally responsible for the decline and fall of Dorset Falls. Maybe that of Diantha's empire, though. "What can I say? It's a gift."

"You rented a building to a *criminal*." Diantha's breathing was faster than normal.

"Well, sure. It's all part of my master plan. I'll have Dorset Falls under martial law in no time." Josie knew she wasn't her best self when Diantha was around, but the mother of her high-school boyfriend could get under her skin like almost no one else. The woman had some nerve. Or was delusional.

Roy Woodruff chose that moment to abruptly get up. He looked around the store again, then hurried toward the front door. Diantha was saying something, no doubt something nasty, but whatever it was barely registered. Josie's eyes were fixed on Roy. Should she follow him to his truck? Roy's normal was taking care of his farm and pranking Eb. This behavior wasn't normal.

Diantha was still blabbing when Josie cut her off. "Yeah, okay, thanks for letting me know how you feel. I have to get to work. At my *yarn shop*. So much new inventory to unpack, you know." She followed Roy out the door and into the parking lot.

Roy got into his truck and peeled out. Impossible to say where he was going, and she wasn't about to follow him. But she did pull out her cell phone and call Mitch.

Chapter 13

Evelyn and Helen were both at Miss Marple Knits when Josie arrived. Evelyn was running a feather duster over the counter, pausing to straighten things up as she went. Helen was in her favorite armchair, knitting away on a good-sized tubular piece with a complicated pattern of colorwork. If Josie had had to guess, she would have said it was the body of a sweater, sans arms at this point.

Josie set her box of doilies back on the counter. As she'd suspected, they'd picked up some dew from being on the line overnight, but that didn't matter. They were being washed today anyway. She took a deep whiff. Definitely fresher smelling. Sunlight would have helped even more, but she and Evelyn could reevaluate once the washing and drying were done.

She was just hanging up her coat when the shop bells chimed. A twenty-something woman paused in the doorway, then stepped inside. She gave her head a toss, and her glorious mane of dark auburn waves undulated with the movement. Josie felt like an extra in a shampoo commercial. "Welcome to Miss Marple Knits," Josie said.

The woman approached the counter. Her eyes were a deep olive green, and her complexion was creamy. Flawless. Josie amended her prior assessment. Not a shampoo commercial. She half expected the woman to whip out a fiddle and start playing vigorous Celtic music while simultaneously dancing.

"Are you the owner?"

"I am. Josie Blair."

"I need a key to the antique store. Please get me one."

What a snot. "And you are?"

The woman let out a little huff. *Not just a snot. A princess, used to getting her own way.* "Taylor Philbin. That store is mine now, and I want to go in."

If the woman thought she could intimidate Josie, she had another think coming. "Well, Taylor, first off let me say how sorry I am that you've lost your uncle."

"Yeah, it was a shock." Her tone made it sound as though the news of her uncle's being stabbed with a pair of antique sheep shears was anything but shocking.

"But I can't let you in. The lease agreement I signed was with Nutmeg Antiques & Curiosities. So unless you're a partner of some kind, it wouldn't be ethical of me to give you a key." Actually, Josie was no contract lawyer, so she had no idea what Taylor could or couldn't do. But, well, she didn't like the woman's attitude. If Taylor was entitled to entry onto the premises, she would have to prove it.

Taylor eyed Josie, then apparently decided to change tacks. "Look. My uncle is dead. I'm his only heir. Harry Oglethorpe is in jail. So the business is at least half mine. I need to get in there and find the partnership agreement with Harry so I know what my rights are. It wasn't in Uncle Lyndon's apartment, so it must be here. You understand the position I'm in, right?"

Taylor's new girlfriendly tone was lost on Josie. "I do. And you understand the position I'm in, right? Sorry."

From the corner of her eye, Josie could see that Evelyn wasn't even pretending to dust shelves anymore. She and Helen were watching the exchange intently.

Taylor narrowed her eyes into glittering green slits. "That shop is mine now. What do I have to do, get a court order? I can do it, you know, as Lyndon's executrix. So why not just save us all the trouble and give me a key now?"

"You get your court order, and I'll be happy to comply. Now, if there's nothing else, I have a shop to run." Josie pretend-busied herself with straightening up things on the counter that Evelyn had already straightened.

Whereas Josie had the ability to make Diantha Humphries's face go purple, she apparently had a different power over Taylor Philbin, whose face was now the color of a June strawberry.

"There's plenty of rental space in this town, you know. I don't have to stay here." She turned abruptly and stormed off, her spectacular hair swinging as she exited.

"Helen," Evelyn said. "You've got Bea's old shop across the street available. Why don't you chase after her?"

The three women burst out laughing.

Josie was about to suggest that Evelyn show her how to clean the doilies, when the door bells tinkled again. Three women—not regular shop customers, so they must have been out-of-towners—came in. They dispersed to various parts of the shop and began to touch the inventory. One even held a skein of silk/rayon blend up to her cheek and gave a gentle rub. Josie glanced at her watch. The average yarn shop visit, which she'd determined unscientifically by simple observation since she'd opened, was forty-five to sixty minutes. Longer if the customer decided to chat or to look through the pattern books and three-ring binders for inspiration. But the longer they stayed, the more they tended to buy.

Helen continued to knit away, while Evelyn hovered discreetly, ready to make suggestions or answer questions. Josie busied herself at the counter, also keeping an eye on her customers.

By the time the women left, they'd spent a few hundred dollars combined and promised to bring their friends back on a field trip. Josie was pleased. She could now make her student loan payment this month without worrying.

"Come on, then," Evelyn said. "Let's get to work on your doilies."

"I'll help too," Helen said.

They took a half dozen of the lacy squares and circles to the bathroom. Evelyn and Josie crowded in around the sink, while Helen stood in the doorway, ready to let them know if anyone came into the shop. Evelyn tested the running water with her finger. "Lukewarm," she said. "Perfect." She fitted the plug in the drain and let some water accumulate in the bottom before squirting in some white liquid dish soap. "This stuff is mild," she explained. "We'll start with this, then if any stains remain after drying, we'll try some other techniques." Josie handed her the stack of doilies, which she submerged and swished around gently.

"These can sit for a few minutes, then we'll drain and shape them. You're not planning to use them on tables, right? So we don't need to use the starch. But it's here if we ever do want it." She pointed to a can under the sink. Josie couldn't imagine ever wanting spray starch for, well, anything. But Evelyn knew best, and Josie never minded Evelyn's being a little bossy.

"Now," Evelyn continued, "set up that plastic table in the storeroom. We'll lay them out there." When Josie came back after complying, Evelyn showed her how to gently squeeze out the water and roll the wet fabric up in a white cotton towel. They took the whole roll out to the table, and Evelyn laid the doilies out on several templates. "We could pin them, but they'll keep their shape well enough if we don't disturb them."

"So that's it? Just like hand washing a sweater."

"Right. In another hour or two, after some of the moisture has evaporated, we'll put a press cloth over the top and hit them with some heat from the iron I brought. That'll set the shapes. Now go open the back door a crack. We want to get some—but not too much—air circulating in here."

Josie did as she was told. It would take at least twenty-four hours for the doilies to dry, so it was going to be a several-day process to finish them all. But now that she knew how to do it, she could take some home and do a batch there to speed things up.

A fresh breeze blew in as she opened the back door. There was a narrow gravel parking lot along the backs of all the buildings on this side of Main Street, but she'd never seen anyone parking out here. Not that there was much call to. It wasn't like the parking spaces out front were ever filled up. She was surprised to see a person—no, two people—about a hundred yards away, standing in front of a car. They were close together, but it was clear it was a man and woman.

If she wasn't very much mistaken, the man was California-Kai Norton.

And there was no mistaking the burnished mahogany mane of Taylor Philbin.

Josie pulled back from the edge of the door, but if she angled herself just right, she could watch through the crack between the frame and the jamb. Kai stroked Taylor's magnificent hair, then pulled her into an embrace. Josie stepped back inside.

Whoa. What had she just seen? Well, she knew what she'd seen, but what did it mean? That was no casual hug. There was some, uh, feeling behind it. According to Margo, Taylor had checked into the Gray Lady. Kai was also staying there. The question was whether this was a spur-of-the-moment hookup, or whether they'd already known each other and had planned to meet in Dorset Falls all along.

And if this wasn't just a casual encounter, what else were they up to? Harry had said that the television producers wanted Lyndon and his niece for the show, and after seeing her, Josie knew why they wanted Taylor. She was stunning. But no matter which way Josie looked at it, she didn't like it. Lyndon—and Harry—were the losers in that game.

Josie dialed Margo and filled her in. Then she called Sharla and left a message. Josie knew the police already had their culprit in custody, or so they thought. And Kai and Taylor's affair, if that's what it was, should have been their own business. But with Lyndon dead, the situation gave off just enough stink, like the old doilies she'd been working with yesterday and today, to make Josie think she should let Sharla know.

Chapter 14

Lorna lived on the top floor of a big Victorian house a couple of streets over from downtown Dorset Falls. Josie rang the bell, and Lorna met her at the door. "Come on up," she said, leading the way up the stairs.

The apartment was small, but comfortable, consisting of a living room open to a kitchen, with a counter with stools separating the two spaces. Two closed doors presumably led to a bedroom and a bathroom. A lovely abstract painting hung on the wall where Josie would have expected a television.

"Home sweet home," Lorna said. "Thanks for coming. There's a lot to do before the dinner, and you'll be a big help."

Josie shrugged. "If you needed fashion advice, I'd be a big help. But I'm willing to try this."

Lorna poured two glasses of white wine and handed one to Josie. The wine was cold and dry, just the way she liked it, not that she usually kept any at home. Eb liked a beer once in a while, so that's what the Lloyd kitchen contained. "Fill me in on what's happening tomorrow night."

Lorna took a sip and settled back into the couch. "Dougie's class reunion is Saturday, at a restaurant near the school."

"Collingswood Academy," Josie said. "Where is that?"

"It's a super-snooty place a couple of towns away. One of those places that's so exclusive, you've never heard of it? These days celebrities send their kids there. It's close to Greenwich and New Canaan, but not too close, for that optimal prep-school experience."

Josie laughed. "Was Dougie's family that well-off?"

"By Dorset Falls standards, yes. His father, Alden, made money in real estate, not just here but in Florida too. Lots of rental properties. I think Alden wanted Dougie to manage them, but when he didn't have the talent or inclination to do that, his father eventually sold them."

"What about the general store? Is that one of his father's properties too?" Josie took a sip of her wine.

"Yes and no. From what I understand, Alden bought the store decades ago and rented it out. But when Dougie needed something to do, his father gave him the store to run. Which he's not all that good at, as you can see. As far as I know, Alden still owns the store. We manage to stay in business because we're the only show in town."

Josie was pretty sure that the reason they were able to stay in business was Lorna and her culinary talents, and told her so.

"Well, I suppose I might have *something* to do with it. Which is why I'm torn. My dream is to open up a café of my own."

Josie felt like applauding. A few months ago, she would not have understood just how satisfying owning her own business could be. And now, she wanted Lorna to experience the same satisfaction. If that's what her friend wanted. "I think that's a great idea," she said.

"But at the risk of tooting my own horn, I'm afraid that if I leave, Dougie won't be able to keep the store afloat. And Dorset Falls needs the general store."

Josie knew what Lorna meant. "It's not just the things you can buy there. The g.s. is the center the town revolves around."

"Exactly. Not that I think I'm irreplaceable or anything—"

"Other people might disagree with that, but go on," Josie urged.

"But it would take some time to find the right person. And can Dorset Falls support two eateries?"

Josie thought it could. Dorset Falls-ites traveled to other towns to go to dinner. Why shouldn't people from other towns come to Dorset Falls?

"Lorna," Josie said. "I'm not telling you what to do. But the general store will sink or swim on its own. You can't take that kind of responsibility on yourself for the benefit of other people. If your dream is to own your own place, then you should go for it."

Lorna looked grateful. "I know you're right, of course. I have a few more months before I'll have enough money saved to move ahead. And the extra money from doing this dinner will shave another couple of weeks off. But just knowing that I *will* be able to leave makes it possible to put up with Dougie for now."

It occurred to Josie that she might be looking for a tenant in six months if Nutmeg Antiques didn't open, but she kept that to herself for now. It would be awfully convenient not to have to walk a whole block to the g.s. for her tea and lunch. She chastised herself for being mercenary. And lazy.

Lorna rose and headed for the tiny kitchen. "Shall we get to work?"

Josie followed. "Ready, willing, and able."

Lorna began to unload contents from the refrigerator. She set two heads of romaine lettuce on a cutting board. "You want to start with the salad?"

Lettuce. This she could handle, no problem. Lorna handed

her a salad spinner, and Josie got to work. She filled the bowl halfway, then gave the greens a rinse and a spin. Lorna gave Josie a covered plastic container to store her handiwork. "You can make salad a day in advance?" Josie asked.

"As long as you tear, rather than cut, dry it well, and keep it in the fridge, it's fine. Romaine is fairly robust. Some of the other more delicate lettuces you should prepare just before serving."

They worked along companionably. "So who'll be at this dinner?" Josie asked.

"Dougie, his friend Rick Steuben—you saw him at the g.s., I think—Alden, and eight other men, so we're cooking for eleven. The original count was twelve, but I guess somebody dropped out."

"The lake house must be good sized, if it can accommodate that many people."

"All the houses on that end of Lake Warren are huge, and so are the lots they're on, which is why there aren't that many of them. I haven't been there yet, so I don't know what kind of kitchen setup there'll be, but Alden and Dougie assured me there's a double oven and plenty of room to work. Just the same, I'm keeping the menu simple: shrimp cocktail in a sweet chili sauce, green salad with walnuts and bleu cheese, green beans, loaded baked potatoes, and a standing rib roast, with individual chocolate mousses for dessert."

Nothing about that menu sounded simple to Josie. She finished with both heads of lettuce, then moved on to scrubbing and drying a dozen raw potatoes. She might not be an Iron Chef, but she could clean vegetables like a pro.

"I know I've said it before, but I really appreciate your stepping in," Lorna continued. "Dougie said I could do the prep work at the house, but I honestly have no interest in being there alone with him, his father, and their friends any longer than I have to. So the more we get done now, the less time we have to spend there tomorrow." She pulled an enormous hunk of beef out of the refrigerator, unwrapped it from its plastic shroud, and began to pat on a thick layer of a mixture of spices.

"I enjoy learning from a master. Mistress? Whatever. You know what you're doing. You heard about Harry Oglethorpe's being arrested for Lyndon's murder?" Josie washed her last potato and set it on a kitchen towel with the others.

"Once those are dry, you can rub them with this vegetable oil and sprinkle them with salt and pepper, then put them in here." Lorna pointed to a heavy metal pan on top of the stove. She had surprisingly professional equipment in this tiny kitchen. "And yes, I heard about Harry. I didn't get a chance to meet him before he got arrested. Do you think he did it?"

Josie rolled a potato around on the towel, then began to massage oil into the thick brown skin. "Honestly, I don't know. My gut tells me no. But I may not know everything the police do."

"What about that television producer who's in town? He came into the g.s. this morning, asking for fresh-squeezed orange juice and sprouted spelt bread toast. Maybe he didn't like Margo's breakfast." Lorna replaced the plastic wrap, gave it a firm tug to seal it to the roasting pan, and replaced the meat in the refrigerator, where it took up a full shelf.

Josie made the decision not to reveal to Lorna what Harry had told her about being passed over for the show. She wasn't sure if Harry had intended that to be confidential, so it was better to err on the side of caution. "I met him. And I saw him with Lyndon's niece, Taylor." That was definitely not confidential, and Lorna might have some insight.

Lorna poised her knife over the cutting board. She'd moved on to slicing onions. "What do you mean, saw them together? Like talking?"

"More than talking." Josie reached for the next potato. "Kissing."

"Whoa." Lorna recommended chopping her onions.

"Whoa is right."

For a minute there was only the *whap* of Lorna's knife on the cutting board. "The question is, what, if anything, did they stand to gain with Lyndon—and Harry—out of the way?"

"Or, if the police are right, what did Harry have to gain with Lyndon out of the way?"

"If this were a detective show on television," Lorna said, "we'd know the answer in less than an hour."

Wouldn't that be nice?

Chapter 15

When Josie got home from Lorna's, Eb was seated in his armchair, doing one of his crosswords, Jethro at his side and quiet for once. Good. Eb had been spending too much time in his workshop. Although what was the difference, really? Tinkering with his thingamajig sculptures or tinkering with a crossword. It wasn't like she could tell him to go outside and play.

"Did you eat dinner?"

"Leftovers. You're late," he said, not looking up. He penciled in something.

"I called and left you a message. If you're not going to check the answering machine, we're going to have to talk about getting you a cell phone." She shrugged out of her jacket and hung it on a peg next to the front door.

"Talk all you want. Lived my whole life without one. Ain't getting one now." Jethro gave a little whine, as if to underscore Eb's words.

"We'll see. You've got a birthday coming up next month, don't you? A cell phone would make an excellent gift." Josie had no intention of getting Eb a phone, which would likely end up at the bottom of his personally stocked trout pond once the ice completely melted. But she enjoyed their repartee as much as her great-uncle did.

Eb finally looked up, glaring. "Cake. Since you can't bake one, you can buy me one. That's it." He went back to his puzzle.

Josie looked at the clock. She probably could finish washing and shaping the rest of the doilies she'd brought home. Or it could wait till morning after she took care of the chickens. She'd have to clear space somewhere and lay out towels, which seemed like too much work right now. In fact, everything seemed like too much work right now. Fatigue had settled in, almost without her knowing it. An early night was just what she needed.

"G'nite, Eb." Coco appeared at her side, ready to take up her nighttime sentry position sleeping on Josie's legs.

Eb grunted.

The next morning Josie started laundry, accomplished her henhouse chores, and washed out the doilies, all before eight o'clock. The small, Formica-topped table in the kitchen, emptied of its covering of newspapers and boxes of old dishes, turned out to be the perfect spot to lay out the lace on a couple of mismatched bath towels. They'd still be damp by the time she got home, and she could give them a quick set with a hot iron then.

She opened both kitchen windows a crack for cross ventilation—it promised to be a warm spring day—and made a mental note to ask Eb if the china and glassware had belonged to Cora or to some earlier generation of Lloyd women. She was pretty sure Eb had brought these things out, for whatever reason, after Cora died. The kitchen had almost certainly been Cora's domain in the few months she'd lived here, and it seemed unlikely she'd have allowed that kind of mess. There were still plenty of rooms in this house that Josie had never explored, although Coco probably had. Someday, when Josie had some free time—and there wasn't a lot of that these days—she'd take a better look around. Maybe even start helping Eb clear the upstairs—although "help" was probably a relative term. She might end up doing the bulk of the work herself. Her great-uncle had lived this way for so long, there was a good chance he might not see any need to change things.

The old pipes gave their characteristic shudder before spraying out water from the kitchen faucet as she washed her hands. A few minutes later she'd spread some peanut butter on an English muffin and headed out the door with breakfast in hand. She left another muffin in the toaster for Eb, alongside a banana and a pot of coffee—she'd finally mastered the mysteries of the percolator, though she still wished for one of those one-cup-at-a-time machines like she had at the shop. Maybe *that's* what Eb would get for his birthday, though it seemed a bit self-serving.

After delivering the eggs, she pulled up in front of Miss Marple Knits, but left the engine running. *Sharla,* she texted. *Have you checked contract between producer and Lyndon and Taylor? Possible motive?* As tired as she'd been last night, scenarios had played in her head until sleep finally came.

Arrest already made, girl. But I'll look.

Josie was going to look too. Because the more she thought about it, the more she wondered if Harry really was guilty. Maybe. He had a motive. But so did that producer. Would he go as far as murder to hype his new show?

And Lyndon's self-absorbed niece. Maybe Taylor didn't want to share the spotlight with her uncle. Maybe she wanted her inheritance now, and the show all to herself, without having to wait an inconveniently long time for Lyndon's natural death.

Josie replaced her phone in her pocket and pulled out her key ring, then exited the car. The crime-scene tape was down at the antique store, and she had every right, as landlady, to enter the property. So why did she feel as if she were trespassing?

The store was dark, with a smell of old wood overlaid with a faint mustiness. It was probably impossible to get that completely out of upholstery and books. Shivers ran up her arms as she entered. Not that she minded saving some heating costs by having the temperature set low, but she could see her breath. That couldn't be good for antiques.

The thermostat was located on the wall behind the counter, near where Lyndon had died. Back here the scent was of disinfectant, probably from the work of the cleaning crew. There was a noticeably lighter spot on the wood floor where someone had scrubbed it, erasing all traces of Lyndon's body. Josie steeled herself and stepped over the spot. She had to believe Lyndon was in a better place.

There was a cold draft back here, far colder than it should have been. Not being the superstitious type, she was pretty sure it wasn't Lyndon's ghost, and when she looked for the most likely cause, she found it. The back door was ajar. The lock appeared to be damaged, a piece of what might have been a wire coat hanger sticking out of the keyhole.

"Dammit." Josie texted Sharla again, then looked around. She had the same thought she'd had before: It was impossible to tell if anything had been taken, or even disturbed. The boxes had never been fully unpacked, the furniture never fully unwrapped and arranged. And Josie couldn't possibly remember everything she'd seen the last time she was here.

The obvious suspect was Taylor. She'd demanded entry to the shop yesterday, but hadn't gotten her own way. Had she broken in and found what she was looking for, the partnership agreement with Harry? Had it ever been here in the first place?

While Josie waited for Sharla, who'd promised she was en route, she poked around. If there was a partnership agreement here, it could be anywhere.

Of course, there might not even be a paper copy, which would explain, at least partially, why Taylor hadn't found it at

Lyndon's apartment. The agreement might just be in a digital file, in which case it would be on Lyndon's computer. Something to ask Sharla about when she got here, although if a computer had been here at the shop, or back at the Gray Lady, the police presumably already had it.

Josie scanned the store, thinking logically. If she had important papers, she'd keep them here in the back, not in a drawer of one of the antique dressers. There was no filing cabinet, no desk. She tapped a finger on her lower lip. The other option would have been upstairs, where Lyndon's unmoved-into living quarters were. But since she needed to wait for Sharla, she decided to stay where she was.

The counter in this shop was similar to the one next door at Miss Marple Knits. The wood was dark, with deep grooves and scratches here and there attesting to the fact that it had been well used over the years, though not anytime recently. Josie had no idea what this shop had been before it had been abandoned. Evelyn or Helen would know. Not that it probably mattered, but now she was curious.

Under the counter, facing the back wall, were some low shelves set alongside a metal safe painted in 1960s utilitarian green. The safe had not been here when she and her friends had cleaned the store in preparation for Lyndon's arrival, so he must have installed it sometime during the moving-in process. She reached out and tried the handle. It scraped, but only moved a fraction of an inch. Then she jiggled the handle until she heard it engage. The door opened.

Was this how successful safecrackers felt? But she couldn't give herself too much credit. The safe wasn't locked, just had a sticky door. Josie bent down, a little thrill of anticipation running through her. When her eyes adjusted to the relative gloom, she realized, with disappointment, that the safe was empty.

Which only made sense. What had she been thinking? That a safe that had been installed in a building where a murder had taken place would not have been opened and investigated by the police? The shelves next to the safe were empty too. She straightened up. This was a waste of time, and if there was any evidence here of who'd broken in, she'd probably destroyed it. She sat down on a wooden chair to wait for Sharla.

A box of books sat to her left. The top was open, so she looked in. An old *Life* magazine stared back up at her. Or rather, the Max-Factored eyes of Elizabeth Taylor did. She pulled out the magazine and angled it so the light struck it. Yup. Those eyes were violet, or at least they were in this photo. She set the magazine back down into the box on top of a hardbound book. *Collingswood Academy* was embossed on the front.

Why did this look familiar? Right—there'd been a similar one in Dougie's office. She hadn't looked closely enough to remember what year Dougie's yearbook dated from. This one had a shield with *Founded 1878* under the name, so Collingswood had a long history, and there were probably a fair number of these books out there somewhere. Josie replaced the book when she heard the front door open.

"Josie?" Sharla called.

"Behind the counter," Josie answered, rising from her seat to greet the cop.

"You want to show me the back door?" Sharla crossed the floor of the shop quickly. "Just a formality. I've been here before, unfortunately. You okay?"

"I'm fine. This way."

When they reached the door, Sharla pulled out her flashlight, which she shined in a narrow arc around the door frame and the handle. She snapped on a pair of latex gloves, then swung the door the rest of the way open to examine it. "The lock's been jimmied," Sharla declared.

"I figured as much." Josie pointed to the wire. "Is it hard to pick a lock?"

Sharla took hold of the wire in the keyhole and gave a gentle pull. She placed the wire into a plastic evidence bag and sealed it, then filled out some information on the outside of the bag. "I doubt we'll get any usable prints from this. And to answer your question, it's not as easy as it looks on television, that's for sure. This isn't the best tool for the job, either. But this is an old lock—which you might want to consider having replaced with something more modern. With Google access and some persistence, it could be done. Obviously. I don't see any actual damage to the lock."

A memory struck Josie. When the murder had happened in her shop a few weeks ago, someone had had a key. As far as she knew, the only people who had keys to this shop were Lyndon and herself. At least, she'd only been given two sets of keys when Eb signed the building over to her. But Diantha's son Trey had owned this building before Eb bought it. What if there was another set of keys out there?

Lyndon had had a key since he signed the lease. Josie had overnight mailed it to him herself. He could have made any number of copies and given them to anyone he wanted. Harry. His niece, Taylor. "Sharla?"

"Yes?" Sharla shined the flashlight on the floor in front of the door, presumably looking for more evidence.

"Could that piece of wire just be for show? To throw us off the scent?"

Sharla turned to her. "You mean, could this have been staged? I suppose it's possible. But why?"

"What if . . ." Josie took a moment to organize her thoughts. "What if someone had a key, but wanted to make this look like a random break-in? So we wouldn't suspect him. Or her?"

Sharla dropped her gaze to the evidence bag, then looked at Josie. "That's not a bad theory. Why would someone want to get into this shop? The site's already been investigated, and we have a suspect in custody."

"I can only think of two reasons," Josie said. "One, some random burglar realized that the police were done with their investigation and decided to break in and see if he could make off with some antiques. Though how we'd know if anything is missing, I have no idea. The place is full."

"Or two," Sharla continued, "someone connected with the murder—not Harry Oglethorpe, obviously—was looking for something, but didn't want anyone to know about it." Sharla set down the evidence bag and pulled out a small spiral-bound notebook and a pen and made a few notes.

"Which brings us back to the reason I texted you earlier. Taylor Philbin stopped by the yarn shop yesterday, demanding to be let into this building. She said she was looking for a copy of Lyndon's partnership agreement with Harry."

Sharla looked thoughtful. "I'm thinking a visit to Taylor might be in order."

Josie thought so too.

Chapter 16

Evelyn already had Miss Marple Knits open and was waiting on a customer when Josie arrived from next door. *Where've you been?* Evelyn mouthed while the customer was signing her credit-card slip.

Josie had to smile. Evelyn was like her second mom, and Josie didn't mind at all.

"Stop in again," Evelyn said. "And bring your friends!"

"I will," the woman said, placing a knit hat over her straight dark hair. "Do you have a mailing list?"

"We sure do," Josie said. Evelyn slid a clipboard across the counter. "Just write your name here and your e-mail address here," she said, pointing. Josie could almost, but not quite, hear Evelyn's foot tapping in anticipation. Evelyn loved her gossip.

The woman wrote down her information and left. "Marilyn Deni, from way up near the Massachusetts border. That's good. We're attracting customers from a bigger area." Evelyn put her hands on her hips. "Well? What's going on? Sharla's cruiser is parked next door. That customer came in, and I couldn't go out to see for myself."

Josie took off the heavy sweater she'd been wearing—another of Cora's beautiful handmade garments. This one was made of a bulky wool and knit with a heavily patterned yoke, cuffs, and waist in shades of gray.

Evelyn's eyes softened. "I remember Cora knitting that sweater. It's a traditional Icelandic pattern. If you look around the house, you'll probably find a matching hat and mittens. I remember her making those too. The set hung in the shop a few years ago."

"I will." Josie pulled the crocheted cozy off the teapot behind the counter and poured herself a cup, then inhaled the fragrance. "Is this chocolate mint? That's a tea flavor whose time has come."

Evelyn pursed up her lips. "Yes, it's another of Lorna's creations. Now stop stalling. What in the world is going on?"

Josie took the couch, and Evelyn chose the wingback chair. "The antique shop was broken into," Josie said.

"What? Why?" Evelyn demanded. Josie told her what she knew, which didn't seem like much when she laid it out.

Evelyn sipped her tea. Her mug read *Knit Happens*. She set it down and picked up her knitting. It was a large piece, perhaps a lap throw or even a full-sized afghan. A few stitches later, she spoke. "What would someone want over there? It's full of antiques, of course, but unless the items being taken were small, there'd be little chance of getting anything valuable out of there without being seen. Without having a truck. Dead as this downtown is"—Josie winced at Evelyn's choice of words—"the police do patrol the street out back and Main Street."

Josie saw no reason not to tell Evelyn her suspicions about Taylor, and did so.

"Makes sense," Evelyn said. "That girl doesn't seem all that broken up about her uncle's death." She gave a vigorous stab into the knitted fabric and wrapped the yarn around the end of the needle before pulling it back through the loop.

"No, she doesn't." Josie watched Evelyn's hands as she worked. The rhythm was soothing, even if Josie wasn't doing the work herself. Since her ill-fated attempt the other night, she hadn't picked up her own needles. It hadn't been deliberate avoidance, but it was avoidance nonetheless. She was off the hook for tonight, though. Dougie's dinner party was scheduled to start at seven, but Lorna needed Josie at five. It was a toss-up which was less appealing: failing at knitting, or spending an evening with Dougie and his prep-school friends. But she'd promised to help Lorna, and help she would. At least she'd be in the kitchen for the most part.

"Speak of the devil," Evelyn said. "Look who's here."

Josie owled her head around to look out the front window. She could just see a slice of dark red hair. "Taylor. Is she coming in or not?"

The bells over the door chimed as Taylor finally entered Miss Marple Knits. Taylor seemed momentarily flummoxed, staring at the counter, before she finally spotted Josie and Evelyn. She strode over, picking up speed as she neared the sit-and-knit area. "You want to tell me why I just got a phone call from the police? What kind of a landlord are you, anyway? Didn't you have an alarm next door?"

Taylor was quickly working herself into a froth. There were a number of reasons why she'd be so upset about a simple break-in, when she'd barely registered a single emotion over her uncle's death. One, she'd been awakened from her beauty sleep and was not a morning person. Two, she considered the contents of the antique shop hers now, and was angry over what might have been taken. Three, she'd broken into the shop herself, and was putting on a good show for Josie's benefit. Or four, she hadn't broken into the shop, and was now kicking herself for not taking advantage of the open back door to look for Lyndon's partnership agreement with Harry.

Josie's years in the New York fashion industry had armed

her with plenty of experience dealing with temperamental types. Best thing was not to feed into Taylor's snit, but to be firm. "Settle down, Taylor. You want a cup of coffee? Tea?" *Say no,* Josie willed her.

Taylor shook her head so that her glorious Celtic curls bounced around her shoulders. "What I want is for you to tell me why I've been called down to the police station. I don't have time for this. I have to meet with the funeral home today about Lyndon's ashes, and I don't even know the town it's located in."

Josie resisted the urge to roll her eyes. All four of her ideas still seemed equally likely. "I found the back door open this morning, and I called the police. End of my part in this story. What's your part?" She took a calm sip of her tea, which seemed to infuriate Taylor more. Taylor's eyes narrowed into those catlike slits Josie had seen before.

"Are you accusing me of breaking in? To my own shop?" She glared at Josie, her face turning that shade of strawberry Josie had seen before.

"I'm not accusing you of anything." And it wasn't Taylor's shop now, and maybe never would be. According to Harry, the shop and its inventory were now his except for Lyndon's personal stash of antiques scattered all over Connecticut. Which was certainly going to throw a monkey wrench into a couple of peoples' reality-show plans.

"See that you don't," Taylor said, her voice better controlled now, crisp and precise. "Because as it happens I have an alibi. An *all-night* alibi."

"Don't tell me." Josie really didn't need to know any more than she already did about Taylor's love life, but was still interested in the information. Taylor had to be talking about Kai, whether it was true or not. "Tell it to the police."

"I will. And my . . . friend will back me up. So you can stop looking at me like you think I did this."

"If you didn't do it, who do you think did?" Evelyn piped up. Good old Evelyn. Josie had been about to ask the same thing.

"How should I know? It was probably some random theft. Though who'd want any of that junk except to resell it is beyond me." Josie hoped Taylor would be a good actress if that reality show actually happened. The woman didn't seem to have antiques *or* curiosities in her blood. "Why don't you let me in now, so I can take a look around and see if anything's missing?"

Nice try, Taylor. Dollars to donuts she'd tried both doors of the antique store and found them locked up before she came into the knitting shop. "Taylor, you know I can't let you in." *And there's no possible way you could know if anything was missing—unless you took it yourself.* "So you should probably head on over to the police station and give your statement."

Taylor gave that hair a toss over her shoulders. "You might want to be nice to me. Think about your own business. You'll get some free advertising—national advertising—when my show happens. *If* we decide to base it out of the store next door."

Tempting, but not quite tempting enough. Especially considering that, if what Harry said was true, Taylor had no claim to the business. Harry might be in jail, but he hadn't been convicted yet. And if—when—he got out, he didn't owe Taylor anything. She might be completely out of luck.

"Thanks for the advice." Josie's cell phone buzzed in her pocket. "I have to take this call." It was really a text, but Taylor didn't need to know that.

"Fine. I'm leaving anyway. But think about what I said. And FYI, I'm meeting with a lawyer later today. About Lyndon's estate. So I'll have that court order letting me into the shop shortly. Have a set of keys ready." Taylor turned and left.

"Good luck with that," Evelyn said, giving Josie a smile. "Today's Friday, and I happen to know that the closest probate judge is opening her cottage at Old Saybrook this weekend. Not a chance Taylor is getting any kind of order before next week."

"If she can at all," Josie said. "I don't know how the process works, whether Lyndon's will will have to be probated here where he died, or where his permanent residence was, assuming he hadn't changed that yet."

"Me neither," Evelyn said. "My second husband's estate was done here. I don't remember about the first one, honestly. I'd have to think about it."

Someday Josie would ask Evelyn about her husbands, but right now Josie pulled her cell phone out of her pocket and looked at the display. Margo had sent her a text. *Saw Taylor leaving Kai's room this morning. Don't know if she was there all night. Heard about the break-in. U OK?*

Josie responded. *All's well. Thanks for update. Police will probably contact you.*

Already done, Margo texted back. *Sharla worked fast.*

Chapter 17

Josie looked at her watch. "Close enough to lunchtime," she said. "It's clam chowder day at the g.s. You want some?" Josie couldn't pay Evelyn a lot, but she could spring for lunch most days they didn't brown bag.

Evelyn, who had resumed her knitting, nodded. "In a bread bowl," she said. "Can you have Lorna sprinkle on some extra pepper? I'm feeling spicy today, after our last visitor."

Josie laughed. "Coming right up. You want to walk over with me?"

"Go on ahead. I'm almost at the end of my pattern repeat, and I want to finish these last couple of rows. It'll be a nice stopping point before I begin the lace panel."

Josie was a long way from any kind of repeating patterns or panels of anything. Guilt, or fear, or some other emotion she couldn't quite identify prodded at her again. *Shut up*, she told it. *I'll learn.*

The sky was a brilliant blue over the rows of mostly vacant three-story brick buildings lining either side of Main Street when she stepped outside. Just as the local weather guy on Channel 8 had predicted, the day had turned out warm and sunny. Josie's mood instantly lifted as she breathed in the spring air, then took a little dive as she passed Nutmeg Antiques & Curiosities. If she could even call it that, since the store had never officially opened for business.

Poor Lyndon. She'd barely gotten to know him before he died, but had a feeling he would have been a great addition to Dorset Falls, both as a downtown business owner and a member of the community. And there was Harry, sitting in jail for a crime he might or might not have committed. The police clearly had enough evidence to arrest him, but did they have the right guy? Even if he did manage to get himself cleared, would he want to stay here? If she were in the same position, she wasn't sure what she'd do. Just being arrested might be enough to taint the town and make her want to leave.

But no. If she'd been in the same situation, she'd be determined to stay and prove everyone wrong. Which she had to admit was sort of, kind of what she was doing by moving back to Dorset Falls and running Cora's yarn shop. Was Harry made of the same stuff? She knew even less about him than she did about Lyndon.

The tables at Dougie's General Store were mostly full, which was to say there were about a dozen people sitting at them, and another three standing in line at the counter. Josie took her place behind Darrell Gray, Margo's husband. He turned. "Hey, Josie."

"Hi, Darrell. How are things?"

The woman at the front of the line raised her voice. "There's only one piece of bread in here," she said, huffy.

"Lady," Darrell said over the head of the person in front of him. "She's busy. It doesn't take any more effort to be nice, you know." The woman glared at him. Lorna shot Darrell a grateful look and dropped another roll into the bag. One piece of bread *was* the norm, but Lorna probably just wanted to get rid of the woman.

Darrell turned back to Josie. "Can't complain. The bed-and-breakfast and the construction businesses are both doing well." He dropped his voice. "And the lovebirds kept it quiet last night, so I slept well."

Josie smiled. There wasn't much else she could say in public about that subject, so she changed it. "How's the work coming on the old Ryder house? Have you met the new owners?"

"Good, and yes, though they haven't moved to town yet. It's a lot easier now that we don't have to work around all the contents of the house and barns. That's all been cleared out."

"At least some of the items are in the shop next door to mine." Josie thought about the box of doilies she'd bought, the contents currently drying in the storeroom of Miss Marple Knits and on the kitchen table back home. And the sheep shears she'd seen sticking out of Lyndon's chest. She swallowed hard, then had a thought. "When did the barns get cleared out?"

"Let's see. Maybe a couple of weeks ago? I was there putting together an estimate when the antique store van came. It wasn't Lyndon who was driving it. It was Harry Oglethorpe. Why do you want to know?" Darrell turned toward the counter and took a step forward, since the line had moved up, then turned back toward Josie.

"Just curious, I guess." She didn't really know why she'd asked the question. Harry would have had access to the shears anytime during those two weeks, but so would any number of other people who might have been onsite before the barns were emptied. And the shears didn't seem like a thing someone would use for premeditated murder. *Ooh, lookie! Rusty antique sheep shears. I know just who I'll kill with these.* Had Lyndon's murder been committed on impulse? Perhaps there'd been an argument and the murderer had used whatever was handy? That made more sense.

Darrell turned around again and ordered. "Ham and cheese on pumpernickel, lettuce, tomato, pickles, yellow mustard. And a can of root beer," he told Lorna. Josie peeked around Darrell. Lorna was looking a bit frazzled. Not surprising, considering she was working both the register and the prep counter singlehanded. A loud guffaw came from the direction of Dougie's office. There were at least two of them in there, based on the volume of the laughter.

What a jerk. Too cheap to hire Lorna some help, and too lazy to come out and help himself. It would serve him right if this place went under. But then Lorna would be out of a job. Which might not be a bad thing. She'd said she was close to having enough money saved to start a little restaurant of her own. Josie wouldn't be able to help her. Cora's yarn shop had been losing money while Cora was alive, and Cora had been keeping it afloat with her own money. Not great business sense, but it had been her money to spend how she wanted, and she'd apparently loved the place. Josie was turning a profit, but barely. Fortunately, her expenses were low, living with Eb. But there wasn't any extra. Eb, though, had a nice nest egg thanks to Cora's insurance and the proceeds from selling her house. If it came down to it, Josie would ask Eb to invest in Lorna. Lorna was a great cook, and it would benefit Eb—or at least Eb's stomach—to keep her in business.

While Darrell was waiting for his lunch and checking out, Josie surveyed the store. The Charity Knitters Association table was looking a bit forlorn. Not surprising, now that Diantha Humphries was the only member of the association. Josie didn't know if Helen Crawford and Evelyn had quit officially, but it seemed pretty clear that no one was knitting new stock for the group. There were only a couple of pairs of mittens, a couple of scarves, and a stack of knitted squares wrapped in a ribbon, which Josie assumed were coasters. She felt a little stab of guilt, then squelched it. It wasn't her fault the Charity Knitters were in trouble. Diantha Humphries could heap that blame squarely on her own shoulders. Maybe, when Josie finally learned to knit, they could do some projects at the shop to donate . . . wherever such things got donated. Evelyn and Helen would know.

Josie glanced around the tables. Roy Woodruff was sitting by himself again, a cup of coffee in front of him. He wasn't drinking it, just staring at the plastic lid. Based on the increased length of the stubble on his jaw, he hadn't shaved since the last time she'd seen him. He started when the front door opened. Josie had only met him a few times, but she'd never known him to be so jumpy.

"See you around, Josie," Darrell said, paper bag in hand. "I've got to get back to work."

"Bye." She stepped forward, gave another glance at Roy, then faced Lorna. "Hey, friend. How're you holding up?"

Lorna blew at a strand of hair that had escaped her ponytail. "It's Friday. We're always busy—or at least busy by Dorset Falls's standards. What'll you have?"

"Two clam chowders in bread bowls, one with extra pepper, to go. I know you've got other things to do, but have you noticed Roy Woodruff? He's . . . not well."

"You mean, he's acting paranoid? Yeah, I noticed that too." She leaned closer and whispered, "Rumor is that he thinks he's been hearing aliens."

Whatever Josie had expected Lorna to say, that hadn't been it. Josie made sure no one was in earshot before speaking again. "Aliens? Like little green men? You're kidding, right?"

Lorna sliced the tops off two boules, releasing the lovely fragrance of warm yeast bread, then scooped some of the insides out and placed the innards into a bowl that was already mounded up. "For bread pudding later," she said. "I wish I was kidding. He says they've been communicating with him. And he's been talking back. On his short-wave radio." She set each bread bowl into its own deep to-go container, then ladled in two scoops of thick, creamy chowder. She placed the lids, then put both containers into a small box. "This'll be easier to transport. I heard him telling Rusty Simmons about it. Not sure what he thought Rusty could do."

Josie wondered that too. "Maybe he spoke to Rusty because Rusty's in the volunteer fire department? Or because he runs the auto repair shop, so he knows about machinery. Does Mitch know? I wonder if Roy's medication is off or something." She looked back over at him. He was twisting a piece of paper, perhaps a straw wrapper, into a tight rope, then untwisting it.

Lorna smiled. "You should probably call Mitch. He's gone to New Haven for something or other. He stopped in for a coffee before he left. Roy came in a half hour later and hasn't left."

"Doesn't want to be alone out at the farm? I don't blame him, if he's really afraid of aliens. You've seen the movies. That's where people always get abducted from."

Lorna gave a little snicker. They shouldn't laugh. The poor man was obviously ill. But aliens? Still, it would be a good excuse—er, reason—to call Mitch.

Josie paid Lorna, dropping a five-dollar bill into the tip cup when Lorna's eyes were on the cash drawer. Josie took her change and the box. "I'll meet you at five at your place, then we can load up and head over to Dougie's father's lake house for the dinner tonight?"

"See you then."

Chapter 18

From outside the general store, Josie could see a couple of figures standing on the street near Miss Marple Knits. That was unusual enough, but there also seemed to be people congregated on the other, more vacant side of Main Street. She quickened her steps—not too fast, or she'd spill her lunch, and it smelled too good to risk that—until she was close enough to see what was going on.

Kai Norton stood outside Nutmeg Antiques, holding a camera, which he had trained on Taylor Philbin. He was talking, and she was responding, so it appeared to be an interview. Josie moved closer so she could hear the conversation.

"I don't know what to do," Taylor said, dabbing at her eyes with a tissue. "First my uncle dying here, and then a break-in. It's like the place is"—she looked directly at the camera—"cursed." A collective gasp went up from the small crowd that had gathered.

Oh for the love of Prada. What was going on in this town? First aliens, now a manufactured curse. Designed, no doubt, to make the show more interesting. Was this going to be their angle? Cursed antiques, or a cursed store? Josie's opinion of Kai and Taylor, not high to begin with, took a dive. And if people actually believed this curse business, how would Josie ever attract a new tenant?

The other question was, could Kai and Taylor somehow be responsible for Roy's condition? Could they have singled him out for some reason and managed to make him think there were aliens here? It wasn't outside the realm of possibility, and it made a kind of sick sense. The rumor was that Roy was hearing or talking to extraterrestrials, not that, according to Lorna, he'd seen any. Kai had sound and recording equipment with him. It would probably be easy for him to rig up something he could use to torment Roy. Take one cursed antique shop, throw in a dash of crazy townspeople, and you might have the makings of a hit show.

"I'm thinking of calling in a priest," Taylor went on. "But at the moment the woman who owns the shop won't let me in. I just can't stand to think of poor Uncle Lyndon's soul trapped inside this awful building." She worked up some more tears.

You'll never get in that shop now as long as I have something to say about it, Josie thought. Even if Taylor eventually produced some kind of order, Josie would have it scrutinized by her own lawyer. She could—and would—make Taylor wait a long time.

"Perfect, baby," Kai said. "That's a wrap for now."

Taylor smiled, her grief and fear clearly forgotten. "I can't wait to see how I look on camera." She didn't seem to care that other people were listening. The crowd—well, by Dorset Falls's standards it was a crowd—dispersed. Josie walked up to the filmer and the filmee.

"Did you get good footage at the expense of your dead uncle?" Josie knew she shouldn't bait Taylor, but she was angry and couldn't help herself.

"Hello, Josie," Kai said, answering for Taylor. "Do you

want to be in this segment? I can get my camera back out." His self-satisfied smile was insufferable. Taylor's was even worse, if that were possible.

"I wonder how the police will feel when I tell them to look into this. It's awfully convenient, the shop's getting broken into just before you two decide to start filming."

Taylor shot Josie a withering look. "We've both already been to the police station today, thank you very much. Why don't you do something useful, like put an alarm on the doors? Or go knit something." Taylor and Diantha Humphries, though not related as far as Josie knew, were cut from the same cloth.

Her words hit the mark, even though Josie was pretty sure Taylor didn't know about Josie's temporary inability to master the craft on which she based her livelihood.

Kai tapped into the tag-team ring. "We don't really need this shop, you know. We can just say the priest got here and refused to go in, and this outside footage will be enough until we get Taylor a home base. It could be any of these stores." He swept his hand down Main Street. "Or we could go to some other town."

As much as Josie wanted, even needed new enterprises to open in Dorset Falls, she couldn't quite see these two as members of the chamber of commerce. Not that Dorset Falls had one, since there were only a handful of businesses. "Suit yourselves," Josie said. "But if I find out you two deliberately broke in to give yourselves material for the show—if there really is a show—I'll send the repair bill to you, Kai, since you were nice enough to give me a card with your address on it." She strode past them and entered Miss Marple Knits.

She set the tray with the soup on one end of the sales counter. She'd be doubly angry if her lunch was cold after her encounter with those two.

"What's happening out there?" Evelyn asked. "I was going

to go out and see, but a customer called and kept me on the phone."

Josie filled her in.

"That ungrateful little witch," Evelyn said. "And poor Lyndon barely cold yet."

"That's what I thought too. Here, let's eat. I lost my appetite for a while there, but now I'm starving again."

Josie unwrapped her spoon, then took the lid off the container and stuck the spoon in. The handle stood straight up. That was the way New England chowder was supposed to be, she'd found since she moved here. She spooned up a piece of clam coated in thick cream and scored a chunk of potato in the process. Heaven. A few more bites, and Josie felt substantially better. Which probably meant she had some kind of psychological issues with food. Or maybe her blood sugar had just been low.

"Lorna does make some delicious soup," Evelyn said. "The clams seem extra tender today." She broke a piece off her bread bowl and dipped it into the liquid.

"She does. So who called?" Josie said when she came up for air.

"Someone from Litchfield. Wanted to know if we had a Sunday drop-in."

Josie followed suit and tried her own bread. It was whole wheat, slightly sweet, and the perfect accompaniment to the salty clams. "Do we?" She wasn't quite sure what a Sunday drop-in was.

Evelyn laughed. "Not exactly, but we might want to start one. We could open the shop for a couple hours on Sunday afternoons. Customers can drop in to chat and knit—and shop."

"Just for a couple of hours?" Josie wasn't all that enthused about opening on Sundays. She already worked a lot of hours every week, and she needed Sundays to catch up and relax.

"Yes. Most yarn shops have a Sunday drop-in. It would be

similar to the informal circle we've been having, just with regular hours. I wouldn't mind coming in after church. I knit every day anyway, and I can do it just as well here as at home. You'd only have to be here if you want to."

Josie did a quick calculation. She'd need to pay Evelyn, but if these drop-in people also made purchases, opening the shop would pay for itself. "Let's try it out. Take this Sunday off, and we'll start next week."

"Deal."

Josie gave her soup a stir, then took another bite. Lorna had thoughtfully included a couple of pats of butter. Josie opened one and spread some on a chunk of the bread bowl, then dropped the rest on top of the soup, where it melted into a luxurious yellow pool. She clamped down on her clamoring conscience. Weren't the experts now saying butter was good for you? If she looked hard enough, she could probably find one.

"Evelyn, have you heard anything around town about Roy Woodruff?"

Her friend set down her own lunch and eyed Josie. "Heard anything? Like what?"

"He's been acting . . . odd."

Evelyn wiped her lips with the paper napkin included in her lunch sack and put the top back on her soup. "I'll save the rest of this for tomorrow's lunch. Now that you mention it, I did hear a rumor that he wasn't feeling well. I was planning to take a casserole out to him. You want to come? You could talk to Mitch while I evaluate Roy." Evelyn's tone was all innocence, but her eyes sparkled behind her glasses.

"You're not trying to play matchmaker, are you?" Josie didn't need any help figuring out that Mitch Woodruff was the kind of man a woman could settle down with. She just wasn't quite sure yet whether she was the kind of woman who wanted to be settled down with. Her life had done a one-eighty in the last few months. It was too soon to think about anything like a serious relationship. But she had to admit, if she were in the market, Mitch would be a serious contender.

"I wouldn't dream of it," Evelyn said. "Now, I can tell you've heard something about Roy. What is it?"

There was no reason not to tell her what Lorna had said. If Evelyn didn't hear it from Josie, she'd hear it from someone else, so it made sense to cut out the middleman. Or middlewoman. "I just heard at the g.s. that Roy thinks he's been communicating with aliens."

Evelyn stared for a moment, then burst out laughing. It took her a moment to get herself back under control. "That's the funniest thing I've heard in a long time." Her face grew serious. "Does Mitch know about this? Roy's not getting any younger. Could he be having some episodes of dementia? I'm sorry I laughed. That could be extremely serious."

Evelyn fixed her gaze on the back wall where the movie still of an elderly Miss Jane Marple hung. Was Evelyn thinking about a friend or family member who had suffered the same fate, intellect and consciousness and free will wasting away while the body hung on longer? Or was she thinking about her own mortality? Evelyn, too, was not getting any younger.

Josie thought about giving Evelyn a hug to comfort her, no matter where her thoughts were, but refrained. Evelyn was a no-nonsense woman who didn't care much for overt displays of affection. "I don't know if Mitch knows the specifics. He knows Roy's not acting like himself."

"Well," Evelyn declared. "Tomorrow's our half day. I'll make a casserole, and you and I will both take it over there tomorrow afternoon." It apparently didn't occur to Evelyn that Josie might have had other plans for her half day off. Not that she *did* have any other plans, but still. "Sometimes when people are close to a situation, like Mitch is, they don't recognize when professional help is needed. I'll talk to Roy myself, then I'll be able to make a recommendation to Mitch." Good old Evelyn.

She was not only an expert knitter, she apparently thought she had medical qualifications. Still, she had a point. Another set—or two—of eyes on Roy couldn't hurt.

Josie closed up her soup, marked the top with a *J*, and replaced it in the tray. She put Evelyn's next to it. "I guess my eyes were bigger than my stomach. I'll go put these in the fridge for tomorrow."

"Yes, and why don't you head home? I can handle the shop by myself this afternoon, and you have a long evening in front of you."

Josie felt guilt and gratitude at the same time. It would be so nice to go home and maybe take a short nap before the dinner party. "Are you sure?"

"I'm sure," Evelyn said decisively. "In fact, I'll put away the soup myself. Now go."

Josie did as she was told.

Chapter 19

When Josie had lived in New York, she hadn't had much—okay, any—opportunity to drive just for the joy of it. Driving was just a way to get from one place to another, and frankly it was nearly always easier to just walk or take a cab or even the subway rather than compete with the traffic. Let alone find a legal place to park. So now that she had an unexpectedly free afternoon, she decided to take advantage of it.

She drove to the end of Main Street, past the g.s. and the town hall, and out into the countryside, which was blooming with early spring flowers. She made a mental note to ask Evelyn or Helen about putting in some bulbs at the farmhouse this fall. Some nice cheerful daffodils and little purple crocuses. Maybe she'd even try some tulips. How hard could it be?

She almost laughed at herself, making plans for next spring. Was that her subconscious telling her she was planning to stay in Dorset Falls, even if the information hadn't quite caught up to her brain yet? Maybe.

And here might be another indication her subconscious was working overtime, though she didn't know what it meant. The sign on the pole up ahead read RYDER ROAD. Well, she was here. She might as well take a look and see how the construction was going. She rolled to a stop in the driveway, which had been paved all the way to the house, then opened up into a new parking lot she hadn't noticed before. It spanned the distance from the old Ryder house to the large barn on the right.

Since she'd last been here, a sign had been placed in the front yard. Made of carved and painted wood with some dull gold metallic accents, the sign featured two hands, crossed at the wrists, each holding an old-fashioned tankard. ETHAN ALLEN BREWERY was written under the logo. Josie had thought Ethan Allen was a Vermonter, so she had to wonder why he was lending his name to a tavern in Western Connecticut. Yankee was Yankee, she supposed.

The ancient clapboards encasing the house had received a fresh coat of white paint, and the front door and shutters were now a glossy black. A banner, probably made of some kind of vinyl, was tacked up to the left of the door. OPENING IN MAY, it proclaimed. Josie wondered if that was wishful thinking. It was March now, and that didn't leave a whole lot of time to get this place up and running. Late May, maybe.

The barn was made of weathered dark wood that had a faint, rich glow. Based on the chemical scent that was now drifting toward her, it had recently been stained or sealed. A sign, smaller and simpler than the main sign out front, hung over the door. BREW HOUSE, it said. This must be where the beer-making equipment was going. Though it was possible the new owners were going to brew their own beer somewhere else. She'd been in brewpubs in New York that did not have on-premises vats and tanks and whatever else it took to produce the beverage.

The sound of tires on gravel made Josie crane her head. She probably wasn't supposed to be here. *DLG Construction* was painted on the door of the truck that had pulled up next to her on the other lane of the driveway. Darrell Gray got out and came to her door.

"Long time no see," he said with a grin. "What brings you out here?"

Josie breathed a little sigh of relief. She wasn't in trouble. "Evelyn's minding the shop this afternoon, and I'm headed home early, but I thought I'd swing by and see how things were going here."

Darrell gave her an assessing look. "Yeah, Margo and I are excited about a new business coming to town too. You want to come in and have a look around?"

"I do," she said. "How'd you know?" She got out of the car and planted her feet on the driveway. The sun was warm on her face, and the breeze smelled fresh and clean, now that she was upwind of the freshly coated barn.

"This is one of the oldest houses in Litchfield County. Pre-Revolutionary War." He closed her door behind her. "If I hadn't already seen the inside, I'd want to. Come on." Darrell led the way over two thick, worn slabs of rock that served as steps, over the threshold, and inside.

Josie found herself standing in a foyer, facing a set of steep stairs lined with a delicate wood balustrade. Doorways framed in simple painted woodwork lay to her right and left. "This," Darrell said, gesturing to one doorway, "will be the bar. And on the opposite side will be the dining room. We're not taking down any walls. The new owners want to preserve as much of the house's integrity as they can."

Josie liked them already. "Who are they? I haven't heard anything about them."

"They're from somewhere near Boston, I think. He's an architect; she's an engineer of some kind. They retired early and decided to come out here and open a brewery. Probably hoping to hobnob with some celebrities."

Josie had heard Litchfield County was home to a fair number of famous actors and musicians, who liked the country life, but needed to be within a couple of hours drive to New York City, but she had yet to meet any. Maybe she *should* hire Evelyn to give private knitting lessons. That might draw some in to the shop.

Darrell led Josie through the dining room door. Another room of approximately the same dimensions lay through a wide archway, so there appeared there'd be plenty of indoor seating, possibly some outdoors in the nice weather, if the owners were smart and put in a covered patio. Each room had its own fireplace complete with wooden mantel carved with a shell design. Josie closed her eyes, then opened them again to take a fresh view of the rooms. This front room was probably where Bea had spent most of her time, knitting, crocheting, reading perhaps. Josie had no idea what Bea had looked like, but she could picture her anyway. The farther room had probably been the dining room, or maybe a second parlor. She wondered if there was a borning room, like she had back at Eb's farm.

Josie didn't believe in woo-woo, but this house seemed peaceful, even though it must have seen its share of death and tragedy over the centuries of its existence. Bea hadn't died here, Josie was almost sure of it. How she knew, she couldn't say.

Darrell led her through to the back of the house, where an enormous hole lined with stones took up an entire wall. "Original beehive oven," he said. "There aren't too many of these left outside of houses that have been turned into museums. The last owner's lucky his tenants didn't destroy it."

"Oven? Women used to cook in these things? That must have taken some skill." The opposite wall was lined with knotty pine cabinets topped with yellow countertops with a turquoise-blue boomerang design. Fifties era, if Josie had to guess. There was a deep white porcelain sink and an electric range. Had Bea stood at this stove, preparing simple, single-person meals? It was impossible to tell.

"They did, using cast-iron pots. I understand there were a lot of burn injuries, which only makes sense. We're putting on an addition off this room. Restaurant kitchen and updated restrooms. It's going to be nice."

"I'll bet it will. Thanks for showing me." Josie turned to go back the way they'd come.

"Do you want to see upstairs? The owners are going to use that as office and storage space. There are just some bedrooms up there, nothing really to see. Once the brewery build is done, we're breaking ground on a new house for the owners on the far side of the property. They designed it themselves, and it's going to be a showplace."

Josie was tempted, but she'd already burned through any extra time she had. "Thanks. I have to get home. I can't wait to come out here for dinner and a drink."

"I don't know if they'll make May, but they'll be open by midsummer."

A few minutes later Josie was back in her more or less trusty Saab and headed for home. Bea Ryder seemed to have replaced Lyndon, Taylor, and Kai in her thoughts. The Ryder property seemed fairly large, and there were a number of other outbuildings besides the barns. Was Bea's body somewhere inside her house? Inside that enormous oven? Or buried somewhere on her own property? Surely that would have been the first place the decades-ago police would have looked. Of course technology wasn't as good then as it was now. But maybe they hadn't needed technology. Josie was pretty sure the police were using trained dogs back then. And if they had used dogs, wouldn't the dogs have found Bea?

Clearly, they hadn't. And Josie was fresh out of ideas of where Bea might be.

Chapter 20

Eb's truck was gone from the driveway when Josie pulled in. She opened the front door cautiously and peeked in before entering. Jethro didn't greet her, so the dog was either sleeping or had gone with Eb. She looked around. No note on the dining room table. Not that she'd expected one. Eb had been keeping his own schedule and not answering to anyone for most of his life. He was unlikely to start now just because Josie had moved in. Her great-uncle would come back when he was good and ready. No sense worrying about him.

Josie headed for the kitchen, shrugging out of her heavy sweater on the way. She draped it over the back of a chair. It was tempting to go take that nap before getting ready to go help Lorna. But it was equally tempting to see how the doilies she'd washed out were faring.

They appeared to be as she'd left them, laid out on bath towels on the kitchen table. She placed her palm on one. *Bea,* she thought. *What happened to you?* The doilies didn't answer, of course. She almost wished they would. Her hand came away damp, but not soaking wet. Now was the perfect time to set their shapes with a hot iron.

Josie hadn't actually ironed anything since she'd lived in Dorset Falls. None of the clothes she wore now required it, nor could she say she missed it. She recalled seeing an iron in the oversized bathroom closet, which was where everything from antacids to extra pillows were stored. She retrieved it. The appliance looked relatively new, and she was virtually certain Eb had never ironed anything in his life, so she assumed this had been something Cora had brought into the house.

Back in the kitchen, she plugged it in and waited for it to heat. In the meantime, she took a clean white kitchen towel, dampened it, and wrung it out, then laid it on top of the first doily. She went back to the sink. There were a couple of coffee mugs in the sink, so she washed those out and put them in the dish drainer. As she turned to go back to her project, the door to Eb's workshop creaked open, probably set in motion by the movement of one of the old floorboards under her feet.

Josie looked inside. Eb had a good-sized inventory of his thingamajigs stacked several deep in front of the worktable. He'd been in some kind of artistic frenzy the past few weeks, but didn't seem to have any clear plan for his work. Eventually he'd have to do something with his sculptures, otherwise he might box himself in some day and not be able to get out, like a hoarder on that television show.

A coffee mug sat precariously on top of one of the piles of rusty metal on the workbench. She went in to retrieve it. Who knew how long it had been in there? It was probably growing a new—alien?—life form within its depths by now. She stretched out her arm over some of the finished sculptures.

And knocked over a pile of junk onto the workbench, where it fell with a nerve-jangling clatter of metal.

"Great." There was no way she'd be able to put things back

the way they were, so she wouldn't even bother to try. She made a preemptive apology to Coco. Her cat was about to take the blame—and take one for the team.

But no. There was no point in not being honest with Eb when he got home. She was a big girl, and it had been an accident. She moved around to the other side of the worktable and sat down. So this, minus the toppled pile of cogs and springs and gears and whatever else this stuff was that was now spread all over the surface, was what Eb was looking at when he worked on his thingamajigs. Josie wasn't claustrophobic, but it was a tight space. She gathered as much of the detritus as she could into a pile. Her foot bumped something. It didn't hurt, but it surprised her. She looked down.

Holding up one leg of the table, probably to keep it level on the crooked floor of the workshop, was a book. Josie craned her head to look at it. *Official Manual of the U.S. Coast Guard: Semaphore and Morse Code.* Eb didn't seem to keep any other books here in the workshop, or anywhere else in the house for that matter, so she wondered where it came from. He could have gotten it anywhere, she supposed. Perhaps his father or uncle or grandfather had been in the coast guard. She knew little about her ancestors other than the fact that they'd lived in this house.

She picked up the coffee mug, which did indeed have a dry dark ring around the inside. At least Eb drank his coffee black. Cream and sugar would have been much nastier at this stage. Josie closed the workshop door behind her, making sure it was securely latched, and deposited the cup into the sink. A good soak in hot water with a generous squirt of soap should do the trick.

The ready light glowed orange from the iron. Josie dried her hands, then went to work. Placing the soleplate of the iron on the damp press cloth, she applied gentle pressure as a hiss of steam wafted up. She moved the iron until she had pressed the entire doily, the way Evelyn had shown her. When Josie removed the cloth, which was now essentially dry, the doily underneath was set in its shape. Now when it dried completely, it would be ready to use.

Wetting and wringing the press cloth again, Josie repeated the process with the other doilies. Once she found her rhythm, it didn't take long to finish them all. She straightened, stretched out her lower back, unplugged the iron, then glanced at the kitchen clock. It was well after three. She needed to clean up before she went to meet Lorna.

Less than an hour later, showered, shampooed, and dressed in black pants and a white T-shirt as Lorna had instructed her, Josie pulled up and parked in front of Lorna's apartment. They'd be taking Lorna's car, which had a larger back area than Josie's Saab. Josie locked up and was about to ring the bell when Lorna appeared at the door. Her arms were full. Josie opened the door for her, then reached out to take the top box from the stack that her friend was carrying. "Let me help you with that," she said.

"Thanks. I shouldn't have tried to carry two boxes at once. It's asking for a disaster." Lorna walked to her car, then set the box on the crisp brown grass of the lawn while she found her keys and opened the trunk. "At least we don't have to bring dishes or table linens. Dougie says they have those at the house and we should use them."

It took three trips to bring everything down the stairs, including a picnic cooler that Josie assumed held the perishables. She would have thought the stuff would have been okay for the twenty-minute drive to the lake, but Lorna was the food professional, and Josie deferred to her judgment. Each holding one end, they bumped the cooler down the stairs and wrangled it into the car. After they shifted some items around, the trunk lid finally closed.

"That's everything," Lorna said. "You ready to go?"

"Ready as I'll ever be," Josie replied. "Do I need to move my car?"

Lorna eyed the Saab. "Nope, it should be fine there."

"I hope you know the way. I don't think I ever went to the lake when I lived here as a kid."

"It's not far." Lorna got into her SUV, and Josie followed suit. "A few miles from town. No public beach, so it's no surprise we never went there back in the day." Once they were buckled up, Lorna pulled away from the curb.

As they drove, Josie gave Lorna a rundown on what had gone on earlier in town.

"I heard that there was filming going on in front of the antique store," Lorna said. "But not about some made-up curse. That's pretty low, exploiting Lyndon's death for a television show that doesn't actually exist yet."

"Or for any show. Or any reason." The more she thought about it, the angrier Josie got. Taylor and Kai were pieces of work, as her mother would have said if she were here.

Josie decided to change the subject. It was going to be a long evening, and it would go better for everyone if she could play her part with a smile on her face. "So who'll be at this dinner party tonight? What will you have me doing?"

Lorna put on her blinker and made a left turn to head west. "To answer your questions out of order, all the prep work is done, thanks to your coming over the other night. So we'll throw the potatoes and the roast into the oven. Closer to serving time, we'll cook the vegetable and whip the cream for the dessert. But it'll mostly be assembly. Are you comfortable with serving? It'll be more efficient with two of us."

Josie had somehow missed the obligatory table-waiting gig while living in New York. Most everyone she knew had worked in a restaurant at some point during his or her residence in the

Big Apple. But she'd eaten at enough establishments that she thought she knew more or less how it was done. She hoped. "Zero experience in that department, but I can follow your lead."

Lorna laughed. "Just remember to serve, pour, and clear from the right of the guest, and you'll be fine." Josie would be extra fine if she didn't dump dinner into anyone's lap.

"To answer your other question, Dougie didn't give me a guest list, and we're not doing a formal seating arrangement. But I know it will be him, his father, and his friend Rick Steuben, plus eight other men. Their official Collingswood reunion is tomorrow afternoon."

"I guess as long as we keep the food and alcohol coming, they'll be happy."

"That's what I'm counting on," Lorna said. "Meat, potatoes, and liquor." She pulled off the pavement onto a gravel road. Even with her trusty GPS unit, whose Italian-accented voice she had named Antonio, Josie wasn't sure she could have found this place. There was no sign, just a space between trees on a heavily wooded stretch of road.

The trees formed a dense canopy overhead. There was still daylight left, but it barely filtered down through the leaves. Was this old-growth forest? If it wasn't, Josie was willing to bet it was on its way to reclaiming that designation.

Gravel crunched under the tires as they rolled along at a whopping speed of fifteen miles an hour. "It's about half a mile up this road," Lorna said. "So sit back and enjoy the drive."

"As long as we don't get attacked by bears, I'm happy." Josie, not a nature girl, wondered what other kind of animals lived in these woods.

"Keep your eyes open. Maybe you'll even see a moose."

"You're kidding, right? Aren't those in Maine?" Josie had never seen a live moose and was curious.

"We've got them here, too. They're huge. Keep your distance if you ever come across one. Although sightings are pretty rare. They're dangerous."

People can be like that too, Josie thought. *Dangerous.* Her thoughts went back to Lyndon lying dead on the floor of his shop. He'd faced the ultimate danger and lost.

Chapter 21

Within a few minutes Lorna had pulled the car to a stop. They were in a cleared area on a gravel driveway. Ahead of them loomed a broad expanse of wall, covered in dark wood shakes, punctuated by a few white-trimmed windows. To the right of the house were more woods. To the left, Josie could just see water in the near distance. Even from this vantage, it was clear that the front of the house had a million-dollar view of Lake Warren.

"This is the kitchen entrance," Lorna said. "We'll unload, then get started." She popped open her trunk, and she and Josie exited the vehicle.

"Aren't there some liveried servants who could help us?" Josie was sort of, but not quite kidding. Some servants would definitely be nice.

Lorna laughed. "Unfortunately, no. Alden is cheap, which is probably how he's stayed so rich over the years. He has a woman come in and clean for him every other week, and she brings him basic groceries. I pack up meals for him when he comes in to the g.s. or when Dougie's going out to visit. I don't know how Alden manages while he's in Florida during the cold months, but I imagine he has a similar arrangement."

"I guess we're pack mules again. Load me up." Josie took hold of a box, Lorna did the same, and they headed for the back door of Alden Brewster's lake house.

For a house of this size, the kitchen was fairly small, not to mention fairly outdated. It wasn't quite as retro as the kitchen at Bea Ryder's house *cum* brewery, but probably dated to the 1980s based on the white laminate cabinets and sage green countertops. Despite the obvious age, the surfaces were in pristine condition, which made sense if, as Lorna had indicated, this wasn't a kitchen that got used much.

They set their boxes on the counter, which was thankfully clear except for an inexpensive coffee maker and a toaster, then went back out for the rest.

When everything had been transferred to the kitchen, Lorna took charge in earnest. She handed Josie a black apron, then pulled out her phone, made a few swipes and taps with her thumb, and studied the display. "Okay, first item on my list is to get the roast and potatoes into the oven. Can you pull the potatoes out of the cooler and arrange them in this baking pan? Line it with foil and our cleanup will be easier." Lorna took a pan out of one of the boxes and handed it to Josie, who was all for easier cleanup. Lorna turned on one of the ovens to preheat. "I'll deal with the meat. Dougie assured me both of these ovens worked. He'd better be right."

Josie lined the shallow pan with foil, then placed the potatoes, the same ones she'd scrubbed and oiled previously, inside it in a single layer. Lorna instructed her to sprinkle more coarse salt on the skins. "Not that any of these guys is probably allowed to have salt. They're probably all hypertensive. But since nobody gave me any dietary restrictions, we'll make these babies taste good."

"Should I put them in the oven?"

"Go ahead. It's not critical that it be up to temperature to start the potatoes."

They worked steadily and companionably for the next half hour, Lorna giving instructions and Josie gladly following them. She was just placing plastic wrap over the tops of two crystal bowls filled with rich sour cream and topped with a generous sprinkling of chopped dill, parsley, and chives when the kitchen door opened.

Dougie Brewster held the door ajar while his father rolled in, in his motorized wheelchair, and circled to a stop in front of Lorna. "Our guests are starting to arrive. Did you fill the ice bucket in the living room? Why does it look like a tornado hit here?" Alden Brewster had that classic old-man Yankee charm.

Lorna smiled. "Everything's under control, Mr. Brewster. I have a cheese and charcuterie platter ready to put out as soon as your first guest gets here, to be followed by tropical shrimp cocktails. I also have your bar garnishes ready, and plenty of ice."

Dougie frowned. "Shar-coot-a-what? If I can't pronounce it, I don't want to eat it."

"Charcuterie," Lorna said. "It's a selection of sausages and dry-cured meats. You'll love it." She offered the platter to Dougie, then to Alden.

"Well, I do like sausage, so I guess it'll be okay." Dougie waved the toothpick containing his chunk of meat in Josie's direction. "What's she doing here? Did she talk you into making something with eggs so she could sell more to you?"

Josie would have quite liked to dump the sour cream she'd just prepared on his head. The four dozen eggs she delivered to the general store most mornings netted her and Eb just about enough to pay for chicken feed, and prevented Dorset Falls-ites from having to go all the way into Kent for basic groceries. She wasn't gouging anyone. She smiled sweetly instead. "Hi, Dougie. Lorna needed help, so I offered. We want everything to run smoothly for you tonight."

Alden Brewster looked at Josie appraisingly, then at Lorna, and nodded. "Very good. Efficient. Smart." He turned his gaze on his son. "Which is why I hired this out to her." He pressed a button on his wheelchair, which whirred to life. "Come on. I need a drink before your cronies get here." He wheeled through the swinging door into the main part of the house, Dougie following.

Not daring to say anything for fear of being overheard while Dougie and Alden made their way to the bar, Josie just looked at Lorna. *It's only one night,* Josie mouthed. Lorna smiled.

"Josie, would you take that sausage platter into the living room? It's right through that door, you can't miss it. There's a buffet table covered in a white cloth set up in front of the bay window. I had the cleaning lady get it ready."

"Aye-aye, skipper. Maybe they'll be happier if they eat." Josie hefted up the tray, bumped the swinging door open with her hip, and entered the main house.

The room was large and open, with a more or less full wall of glass windows overlooking Lake Warren. Even from this far away, Josie could see that the water was calm and blue, with an overlay of rosy silver shimmering from the early evening sun. The view was nothing short of spectacular. She must have emitted some small noise, because Alden and Dougie, who were at the bar, turned to look at her.

"Sorry to bother you," she said. "But I'm just admiring your view. It's stunning."

Alden sat up a little straighter. "Yeah, and I bought when land here went for nothing. It's worth a small fortune now. Not sure who I'm going to will it to when I die." He shot a look at Dougie. As poorly as Dougie treated Lorna, Josie almost felt sorry for him. It couldn't be easy to have a rich, successful, controlling father who had no respect for you. She squelched her tender feelings. Her first loyalty was to Lorna.

Josie set the tray down on the table, adjusted the stack of small plates and napkins so they looked balanced, then headed back for the kitchen. A formal dining area took up one end of the room, but was open to the seating areas, which were furnished, predictably for a single man with lots of money and a no-nonsense style, with lots of dark leather and simple wooden coffee and occasional tables topped with smoky glass. She noticed a book sitting on one of the tables as she passed. There was no mistaking the Collingswood Academy logo emblazoned on the leather cover. Well, this was a reunion. People would probably be looking at the book and reminiscing tonight.

When Josie returned to the kitchen, Lorna was checking on the beef. "So far, so good," Lorna said, nodding toward the oven dials. "They both seem to be heating."

Josie kept her voice low. "There's no love lost between those two." She inclined her head toward the door.

"Nope. I'm not sure Alden even attended Collingswood. Maybe. It might not have been as exclusive back then. But Dougie needs his father to support him, so he does what his father wants. And frankly, I think deep down, even as old as he is, Dougie is still a little boy who craves his father's approval." She started pulling the salad ingredients out of the refrigerator. "Here, you can start putting these together. The plates are right here."

As they continued to work, the relative silence was punctuated by the metallic clunk of car doors opening and closing. Dougie's friends must have started arriving.

"They're not coming through the kitchen, so how are they getting in?" Josie asked.

"There's another road that services all the big cottages on this side of the lake, and another driveway. The one we came in on is only for this house."

Made sense. Wouldn't want the servants entering through

the same doors as guests, and vice versa. This property must be enormous if it had a private driveway. They'd come a long way through those woods.

"Whew." Lorna used her forearm to smooth back a strand of hair that had escaped her ponytail. "Those salads look good. Just before we serve them we'll drizzle on the dressing. And the shrimp cocktails are ready to go as the first course. So we can take a little break now."

"You don't have to ask me twice," Josie said. "Catering is hard work. Honestly, I had no idea."

Lorna laughed and handed Josie a bottle of water, then twisted off the top on one of her own. "That's because when it's done well, it seems effortless to the person being catered to." She took a long swig, and Josie followed suit. The water was icy cold and tasted wonderful.

"We haven't talked about this," Lorna continued, "and I'm not sure when I'll get paid. But I want to pay *you* for assisting me. This was so much easier with you helping."

Josie had no intention of taking any money for tonight, and told Lorna so. "Consider this an investment." She glanced toward the door to the living room. "You know what I mean."

Lorna opened her mouth as though to argue, but then closed it up again. "Thanks," she said. "I'm so glad you came back to Dorset Falls, and we found each other again. That's probably selfish of me. You probably miss the excitement of New York."

Josie thought for a moment. "Well, I have to admit I didn't stick my hands into the nests of live chickens in the neighborhood I lived in, and the town didn't roll up the streets at six o'clock. But I like it here. It's a different kind of life, one I never thought was for me, if I gave it any thought at all. Yet here I am. I've got my shop, which I love, and I've got great friends, whom I also love. I've even got Uncle Eb and his dog. It's a pretty good deal."

A crash sounded from the living room, causing Josie and Lorna to start. Dougie burst through the kitchen door a moment later, moving faster than Josie would have given him credit for being capable of. "Lorna, come help. Somebody knocked over a beer glass, and it broke on the floor."

"I'll see if I can find a broom and a dustpan," Josie said.

"And I'll take the paper towels in and get started. Thanks." Lorna grabbed the roll from the counter and followed Dougie.

Josie located a small closet and pulled out the broom and dustpan, which she took into the living room. There were now five or six other men there in addition to the Brewsters. Four of them, now including Dougie, were wearing football jerseys that looked a bit, or, in Dougie's case, more than a bit, tight around the middle. She glanced around again. It was like being transported to some high-school party in an alternate dimension. She hurried to where Lorna was squatting near one of the side tables.

Lorna looked up. "We're in luck," she said. "It broke on the hardwood, not the carpet, so it'll be much easier to clean up."

A man stood nearby, grinning sheepishly. "Sorry, honey. We were reminiscing about the championship game our senior year, and I got a little animated I guess. You want me to help with that?"

"We've got this, but thanks," Lorna said. She mopped at the mess, placed the big pieces of glass in the dustpan Josie dutifully held out, then applied some fresh paper towels to the remaining liquid. She stood. "I'll go throw this away, then come back with some cleaner. Josie, can you sweep up the small pieces?" Josie nodded and set down the dustpan, carefully so as not to dump the shards already collected back onto the floor.

"I haven't seen you around," the man said. "Trevor Mason. I manage the third largest hedge fund in Connecticut." *Big whoop,* Josie thought. *If it was the first largest, maybe the second, then I'd be impressed.* Did he know how big Connecticut was? Or more accurately, how big it wasn't? Josie began to sweep. But she supposed she had to answer.

"Josie Blair. I haven't been in town long." She poked the broom under the leather chair and pulled a few pieces of glass out from under it.

He rubbed his fingers over his well-barbered gray goatee. "Is this your job? You a caterer?"

"Uh, no. I own the yarn shop downtown. I'm just helping out a friend tonight." She made a few more passes with the broom, then swept everything she'd collected into the dustpan. It was the best she could do.

The man was staring at her. "The yarn shop? Isn't that next to the antique store? I saw it as I drove into town." Every head turned.

Dougie shot him a look. "Yeah, it is," he said quickly. "And apparently it's not doing very well if its owner is chopping salads and cleaning up after us."

Jerk. She wished she could tell him off, but this was important to Lorna, so Josie kept her mouth shut. And what was that all about, anyway? Why had Trevor stared at her like that? And why had Dougie cut him off, unless it was just to put her in her place? Or the place he thought she belonged in, anyway? She picked up her broom with one hand and her dustpan with the other and made her way back to the kitchen. One of the men was gentleman enough to hold the door open for her as she passed. It wasn't Dougie. Josie wasn't surprised.

Chapter 22

Over the next hour, the noise level from the living room increased. There was a lot of good-natured shouting, and what even sounded like a bit of roughhousing. Josie remained in the kitchen while Lorna braved the fray to restock the bar—which Josie guessed was pretty depleted at this point—and check on the platter of cheese and crackers. Josie was making garnishes consisting of a lime wedge wrapped in a basil leaf and skewered with a toothpick for the shrimp cocktails. When she finished the eleventh one, she stood back to admire her handiwork. They looked pretty good, two shades of green and fresh. She placed one in each of eleven martini glasses, which were filled with shredded basil and stacked high with fat pink shrimp glistening with Lorna's sauce. There were two extra glasses of shrimp. Josie assumed those were backups and made two more garnishes.

When Lorna returned, she was carrying a box of empty beer bottles. "Nobody wants wine," she said. "They're just going to drink beer with their dinner, which means less work for us. Refilling wineglasses all night is a pain."

"Has everyone arrived?"

Lorna nodded. "Alden said to start serving the first course in ten minutes. Those shrimp cocktails look delicious, by the way. We can load them up on this tray. I'll carry them in, since I'm experienced. It's not as easy as you might think to walk while balancing a tray full of food on your shoulder and the palm of your hand."

Josie had never thought that was easy. Getting the tray down from the shoulder without creating a disaster seemed even harder. She cleaned up her garnish-making supplies and washed her hands for at least the tenth time this evening, then smoothed them over her apron. It was still clean enough to serve in.

Lorna filled two small dishes with extra sauce and put them on the tray. "Ready?" she asked. "You go in first and set up the tray stand. Then I'll set down the tray. You'll serve one end of the table, and I'll serve the other."

"Sounds easy enough."

"It will be." Lorna hefted the tray onto her shoulder, and Josie followed her into the dining area.

Alden or Dougie must have corralled their guests, because eleven men now sat around the big table. Josie recognized Rick Steuben, whom she'd seen at the general store. Alden's mechanical steed sat empty, off to one side. Its former occupant now sat at the head of the table nearest the windows. Perhaps Dougie, or one or more of the others, had helped him into the dining chair or perhaps he was able to move short distances on his own. The men continued to chat while they waited to be served.

Josie retrieved two glasses of shrimp from the tray and set one down in front of Alden, mentally patting herself on the back for remembering to do it from his right side. She set the other in front of Trevor. "Thanks, honey," he said. Josie steeled herself. She hated being called that. *You're doing this for Lorna.*

Suck it up. He probably doesn't mean anything by it anyway, so don't be so sensitive.

Josie delivered the rest of her appetizers. Lorna had already finished her end of the table and was now pouring glasses of water for everyone. "Will there be anything else right now?" she asked Alden. He shoved a shrimp into his mouth and shook his head. Lorna and Josie retreated to the kitchen.

"That wasn't so bad," Josie said, taking another long sip of her bottled water.

"Yeah, when you put food in front of them, people tend not to notice you so much." She handed one of the extra shrimp cocktails to Josie. "Chef's treat," she said.

Josie realized she was starving. She popped a shrimp into her mouth. It was perfectly cooked, tender, and the sauce was sweet and spicy at the same time. In short, delicious. Not that Josie was surprised. Lorna had a talent for cooking and a talent for identifying delicious recipes—unless she'd invented this one herself, in which case her gifts were all the more impressive. "This. Is. Amazing."

Lorna smiled. "I don't have time to fuss with things like this at the g.s. Too many other duties. But it is fun to put together some fancy food once in a while." They finished up, washed their hands again, and prepared for the salad course.

Josie was just setting a salad in front of her new friend Trevor when he stood up abruptly. She managed not to drop the plate and to step back without falling over.

Trevor raised his beer, his arm perpendicular to his body, and cleared his throat. "Collingswood Cougars, I'd like to propose a toast." His speech was just slightly slurred. Twelve heads, including Josie's and Lorna's, turned toward him. Ten hands gripped around a glass or bottle, and ten men waited expectantly.

"To the greatest team, and greatest group of friends, a running back could have." He lifted his glass a little higher, then took a sip and sat down.

"Hear, hear," someone said, and drinks were taken all around.

Someone on the other side of the table rose. "To all those who couldn't be here tonight. Bunch of losers." A laugh went up around the table, and glasses were raised again.

There was a pause. Lorna nodded to Josie, and they each set down the salads they'd been holding. They picked up the last of the plates, preparing to deliver them.

Dougie stood up, then pulled his too-tight football jersey down to cover his waistband. Beer bottle in hand, he looked at Rick Steuben, whose eyes were fixed on Dougie's face, or something right behind him. "And especially to those who've gone before us. God speed, Beelzebub. You're running with the angels instead of the devil now." He drained his glass.

Rick continued to stare at Dougie. A small muscle ticked in his jaw. Who was this Beelzebub? It appeared that he and Rick had some kind of history, and, based on Rick's expression, it might not be good.

"To Bub," the voices said in unison.

"Fastest SOB I ever saw," somebody added.

"Didn't he steal that cheerleader you liked right out from under your nose, Rick?" somebody said with a laugh.

Dougie sat down. His father looked at him, then down at his plate, which he seemed to find much more interesting. Alden dug in. Josie and Lorna delivered the remaining salads, then went back to their temporary domain.

Lorna began slicing the roast beef, which she'd removed from the oven twenty or so minutes ago and had left resting on the counter. She placed the slices on a platter in the oven to keep warm until it was time to plate them. "You can go ahead and get the potatoes out of the other oven," she said. "They'll stay hot."

Josie put on some oven mitts and retrieved her potatoes. She'd made these herself, start to finish, so she was feeling a little proprietary toward them as she placed one on each plate. "What do you suppose that was all about?" Josie said. "I don't know who this Beelzebub was, but did you see the look on Rick Steuben's face?"

"I couldn't from where I was standing," Lorna admitted. "But I did see Dougie. That was no simple toast." She took the plastic wrap off the dishes of sour cream and placed them on a tray, then went to a sauté pan she had going on the stove. Dropping in a generous cube of butter, which sizzled when it hit the heat, she placed some partially cooked bright green beans on top of the butter and gave them a toss. A delicious garlicky fragrance drifted over to Josie's nostrils. She wondered if any of the men in the other room truly appreciated the meal they were being served.

"There must have been something between this Bub and Rick," Josie mused. "No one else seemed to have a problem."

"You heard what that guy said about the girl. Or maybe they competed for the same position on the team. Could be anything. Grudges, even if they're based on something stupid, can run deep."

"Don't I know it," Josie said. "Look at Eb and Roy Woodruff."

"Or you and Diantha," Lorna added. "Sorry." She gave a little giggle.

"Don't be," Josie said. "It's her problem, not mine. You think they're done with their salads?"

Lorna checked her watch. "Bring me the dishes of bacon bits and pats of butter, then go peek in and see. These guys don't seem like the type to linger too long over salads when there's rare roast beef in the offing."

Josie did as Lorna asked. "They look like they're done," she said. "Want me to go clear the dishes?"

"Would you? Then I can start plating the main courses. We'll have to deliver these in batches."

Josie made her way back to the dining room table for the umpteenth time. And there would be more to come. She started with Alden and worked her way counterclockwise around the table, picking up salad plates and silverware and stacking them as she went along. When she reached the tray stand, she deposited the dishes, then started around the other side of the table.

Despite Lorna's prediction, the men had done a pretty good job with the salads. The only exception was Rick, who'd barely touched his. When she asked if he was finished, he looked her in the eye. "I guess so. Take it away." Josie could see Dougie watching the exchange. He seemed to almost be enjoying himself. Which was odd. When she'd seen Rick in the general store, he and Dougie had seemed to be old friends. Clearly, they had had some falling out since then.

When she'd cleared the table, Josie picked up the full tray. She didn't dare try to shoulder it, but the salad plates were small and not too heavy, so she carried it in front of her. Awkward, yes. But she managed.

Lorna had the plating nearly finished and was just adding some sprigs of parsley to each plate. The meat was a perfect pink surrounded by a delectable-looking darker crust. "Let's get these delivered, then we can start cleaning up. We're in the home stretch."

It only took a few moments to set out the main courses and return to the kitchen. Josie found the dishwasher—thank goodness the kitchen, though dated, was modern enough to have one—and began rinsing and loading. Lorna stored the leftovers in disposable containers and put them in the fridge for Alden and Dougie. She put three containers aside. "For me, you, and Eb," she said. "Trust me. Tomorrow you'll be so tired you won't want to cook. And what Alden and Dougie don't know won't hurt them." She wrapped a huge meaty bone in some foil. "For Jethro."

Josie didn't know who'd appreciate the dinner more—dog or master.

As Josie worked on the dishes, her mind wandered. It had been a long, long day. First the break-in next door, then Taylor and Kai and the fake curse, and now something going on between Dougie and his friend Rick.

And then there was Harry, still in the county lockup unless he'd been transferred somewhere more secure. He had reason to be angry at his partner, who had gotten a television deal that didn't include him. And he had no alibi.

Taylor had a couple of reasons to want her uncle dead. With him out of the way, she could have the television show all to herself. Not only that, but she stood to inherit Lyndon's estate, depending on how he'd structured his will.

Kai Norton was using Lyndon's death to his advantage too. He was getting his jollies on with Taylor, as well as sensationalist material for his show. No matter how you looked at it, Kai had more to gain with Lyndon dead than alive.

Josie started in on the pots and pans. Mercifully, there were only a few: the pan she'd baked the potatoes on, which only needed a light wash thanks to the foil, the sauté pan for the green beans, also a breeze, and then the big roaster. When she turned around, she realized Lorna wasn't there. She'd started to feel guilty about being wrapped up in her own thoughts, but now she could go back to them.

She squirted some fresh dish soap into the sink and ran some hotter water. Much as she wanted Lyndon's murder solved conclusively, it was Bea Ryder who stuck in her head.

Poor Bea. She was dead. Josie was sure of it somehow. And the injustice of it had been eating away at her, ever since she'd been to the house today. Bea deserved to be found, even if her killer was never identified. But short of renting a cadaver dog and running it in a grid pattern around Bea's property and the rest of Dorset Falls, Josie had no idea how to accomplish that. It was clear Jethro would not be up to that task.

"That roasting pan is as shiny as the day I bought it," Lorna said, coming to stand next to her.

Josie looked down. She'd been scrubbing the same spot for a while now. She gave the pan a rinse and put it in the dish drainer. "Sorry," she said. "Just lost in thought. Where'd you go?"

"Bathroom. You should see it. The wallpaper actually has a raised fuzzy design. Not that I wanted to feel it. I'm not sure how you'd clean something like that, and it's bound to be crawling with bacteria. Now let's get coffee and dessert served so we can get out of here."

Chapter 23

The individual chocolate mousse desserts topped with home-made cinnamon whipped cream were rich but small, so it didn't take long for the men to finish. Lorna poured coffee all around, while Josie collected empty beer bottles and cocktail glasses. She put the bottles into a box and set them by the back door, then tackled the dessert dishes. All that would be left now were the coffee cups. Even if they wouldn't fit in the dishwasher, they'd be easy enough to wash out by hand.

Josie grabbed Lorna's keys from one end of the counter and took the box out to the car. She popped the trunk and shoved the bottles as far back as she could. She supposed she could have left them here, but at a nickel a piece, they could add a few dollars to Lorna's kitty. As she closed the trunk, Josie saw movement off to her left. In the moonlight, she could see two figures. If she wasn't mistaken, one of the figures was Dougie. The other might have been Rick Steuben. They must have slipped out sometime after dessert.

She hadn't exactly been quiet, but they didn't seem to notice her, and in any event they were at least fifty yards away. They appeared to be arguing. A wind was blowing up off the lake, and it carried a few words her way.

"What . . . doing?!"

". . . agreement."

The figure who might have been Rick put out both hands and gave a hard push on Dougie's chest. Dougie grabbed on to Rick's football jersey and held on, keeping himself from falling. They tussled for a moment, then broke apart. Dougie took a moment, maybe to catch his breath, then headed back toward the house. Rick went in the opposite direction. She heard a car start up and the crunch of tires on gravel.

What had she just witnessed? Now she knew there was something going on between these two, but short of coming out and asking one of them, she'd probably never find out what it was.

It was nearly ten o'clock by the time she and Lorna got back to Lorna's apartment and unloaded. Fortunately, the boxes and cooler were much lighter this time around. Toting them all downstairs had been bad enough. Taking them back up, filled, would have been torturous.

"You want a drink?" Lorna asked when they were finally done. "Or a chocolate mousse? I've got extra."

Chocolate was always tempting, but Josie shook her head. "I'm wiped. And I've got to work tomorrow. Time for me to head home."

"I can't deny I'm ready for bed myself," Lorna said. "Thank you so much for your help tonight. If there's ever anything I can do for you, you only have to ask."

"I will. But I had fun, even though it was hard work. And I learned some stuff too. So we're good."

"Good night, and thanks again."

Josie gave her a hug. "I'll see you in town tomorrow."

As she drove home, she thought about the altercation between Dougie and his friend Rick Steuben. It was too bad she'd only heard snippets of their conversation. It would almost have been better not to have heard anything. Then she wouldn't have to wonder what else had been said. Rick had said "agreement" in a way that made her think Dougie had somehow broken whatever it was.

She turned on the radio. More static than music, as usual, but it might serve to push out the thoughts that were competing for space in her tired mind.

It worked. Because by the time she got home, Josie's only thought was to crawl into bed.

The sun shining through her bedroom window woke Josie the next morning. She snuggled deeper under the handmade quilt that covered her bed. Coco had been sleeping on the other pillow by her head and woke up when Josie moved. Coco gave her a look, walked across her stomach, her little white paws sinking into the bedding, then jumped off the bed and strolled out the door.

Josie stretched out under the covers. Yup, every muscle in her body was sore. Catering was hard work.

She looked at her bedside clock. Ten minutes before her usual wake-up time. *Be realistic, Blair. Ten minutes isn't enough time to go back to sleep. You might as well get up.* She sighed and threw off the covers.

A faint odor of food wafted into her nostrils. Not exactly unpleasant, but not exactly fresh, either. Probably her hair. She should have taken a shower last night. Well, the sheets needed washing anyway. She stripped the bed, carried her bundle to the downstairs bathroom, and dropped the load into the washer.

Eb was in the kitchen when she came in to put on the coffee. He wore his half-moon reading glasses, so he must have either been working in his shop or preparing to do one of his crosswords, though it seemed a little early for either of those. Eb liked his routines.

"You want wheat flakes for breakfast? That's what I'm having," Josie said as she set up the old-fashioned percolator and turned on the burner underneath. The contraption had baffled her when she first came to live here, but once she'd gotten the hang of it, she had to admit it made pretty good coffee.

"Yup. Put some blueberries in."

"I was planning to." Josie made two bowls of cereal, added milk and the requisite blueberries, and stuck in two spoons. "Let's eat at the table," she said.

For once he didn't give her an argument, but followed her into the dining room and sat down. She pushed aside his stack of newspapers to clear a surface and set down the bowls. Eb ate a few bites of cereal, then said, "How come my workshop's a mess?"

She almost spit out a blueberry. "Uh, Eb? Look around you." But she knew what he meant. "Sorry about your worktable, though. I was getting your dirty coffee mug and accidentally knocked some things over."

"I expected you'd blame it on the cat." He'd almost, but not quite, busted her.

"Yeah, well, sorry. What are you going to do with all your thingamajigs? The workshop's pretty full."

Her great-uncle stirred his cereal around before answering. "I could bring some out here. Decorate." He looked her full in the face, which she knew was registering some degree of horror. They didn't need one more thing to maneuver around. Or dust. Then he guffawed. "Gotcha."

All right, so she wouldn't have to dust. But he still hadn't answered her question. And knowing Eb, if he hadn't done so by now, he wasn't about to.

In the kitchen, the percolator was emitting the rhythmic *blurp, blurp* sound that meant it was almost done. She'd give it a couple more minutes.

"Eb, do you remember Bea Ryder?"

He didn't look up from his breakfast. "Owned the dress shop in town. Lived out on Ryder Road. Disappeared. Probably dead."

Mr. Sensitivity. "Were there any rumors? Any clues at all as to what happened to her?"

"Why do you care?" He went back to his cereal.

How could she make Eb understand when she barely understood it herself? "I heard about it and was curious, that's all."

"Don't go snooping into things that'll get you in trouble. They never caught who did it."

Wow. Was there concern hidden in those words? She went back to the kitchen, then brought out two mugs of hot coffee and the container of half and half. She poured some into her coffee and gave it a stir with her cereal spoon. "I'm not snooping. What are you doing today?"

He eyed her. "Last I knew, I didn't report to you."

"Just making conversation."

"Well, don't. But if you have to know, I'm driving over to Tractor Supply, then to the feed store. Taking my dog with me."

That would make Coco happy. She and Jethro had an armed—or perhaps a better word would be *clawed*—truce.

"Save room for dinner. I've got roast beef from last night."

"Yup," was all Eb said.

Chapter 24

Josie sat in front of a computer screen at the Dorset Falls Free Library. Before she left the house, she'd taken a look at her doilies. Correction: Bea Ryder's doilies. They looked good. They were going to look even better once she tacked them down on some accent pillows. But for now she'd left them on the kitchen table. Some of them were still ever so slightly damp, and one more day of drying wouldn't hurt them. The ones in the storeroom of Miss Marple Knits should be ready by now. She'd nearly forgotten about them.

But she hadn't forgotten about Bea Ryder. The librarian, one of two who staffed the library, made some keystrokes and, with a couple of clicks of her mouse, pulled up a screen. "You're in luck. The *Dorset Falls Tribune* has been digitized through the 1970s, so we have the right time period. It's even searchable. Not too long ago, we would have had to hunt through rolls and rolls of microfiche to find what you're looking for."

Josie had called Evelyn and asked her to open for her this morning. She didn't expect to be here long. Wasn't even really sure what she was looking for, just that she needed to know more about Bea's disappearance.

"Here you go," the librarian said. "There are only a few hits."

"I guess that makes sense." A woman's disappearance, without evidence of foul play, was not likely to spawn a lot of follow-up articles in a small-town newspaper.

"Let me know if you need anything else. I'll be at the circulation desk."

Josie read the first article.

LOCAL WOMAN DISAPPEARS

Miss Beatrice Ryder, of Ryder Road, age 51, has been reported missing by her friends. Anyone with information is requested to call the Connecticut State Police.

Well, that told Josie exactly nothing. She moved on to the next article.

MISSING WOMAN'S CAR FOUND

The car of Miss Beatrice Ryder, who has been missing for the last two weeks, has been located in a city south of here. The state police are investigating all leads. Anyone with information is requested to call the Connecticut State Police.

Skunked again. Josie sat back, drumming her fingers on the arm of the chair. She went back to the first article. What else had been going on in Dorset Falls around the time of the disappearance? It was worth a look.

Josie scanned through the other articles on the front page:

County Dairy Princess Named. New Stoplight Installed on Main Street. Dorset Falls Bijou to Show Double Feature this Saturday. Local Football Team Beats Collingswood Academy.

Collingswood. She was seeing that name everywhere. She read the article.

> The Dorset Falls Falcons scored an upset victory over last year's state champions, the Collingswood Academy Cougars. In a nail-biting overtime game, the Falcons scored a final touchdown to end the game with a score of 21-14. Outstanding performances were given by Douglas Brewster for the Cougars and Timothy Wagner for the Falcons.

Dougie? He was playing high school football at the same time Bea disappeared? That meant the other men who had dinner at the lake last night, with the exception of Alden Brewster, had also been on the team.

Was there a connection? It didn't seem likely. Josie scanned the text of the rest of the articles. Her eyes passed over, then went back, to a name in the dairy princess feature. Richard Steuben. *Mayor Richard Steuben presented Miss Jennifer Scott with the Dorset Falls Dairy Princess crown last Saturday.*

Richard Steuben. That had to be Rick Steuben's . . . father. So he'd been mayor of Dorset Falls when Bea disappeared. This was significant, it had to be, but Josie didn't know how the pieces fit. Her thoughts turned to the argument Dougie and Rick had had last night, and she wondered again what their "agreement" could have been.

On a whim, she pulled up an Internet browser and typed in "Collingswood Academy." A website appeared, showing photos of venerable-looking ivy-covered buildings surrounded by beautiful landscaping and beautiful teenagers with perfect teeth and artfully casual haircuts.

She clicked on the *Events* tab. A calendar appeared, populated with a month's worth of activities. She read through them, then read through again.

There was no mention of any reunion.

So the gathering of men at Alden Brewster's lake house was a private reunion. Why would Dougie arrange a get-together of his old football pals now?

Bea Ryder's house had been bought, and renovations were being made to it, potentially bringing her disappearance—and probable murder—back into the light.

There was only one explanation that made sense. Some, or all, of the members of that year's Collingswood Cougars knew something about Bea Ryder, and were meeting to figure out what to do. Josie would bet on it.

Chapter 25

Josie drove to Miss Marple Knits and parked out front. She replayed everything she knew and kept coming back to the same conclusion. It was no coincidence that the football team was back in town.

When Josie got inside, Evelyn was seated in her favorite chair, knitting on the same big project she'd been working on yesterday. It had grown by another several inches, so she must have been working on it last night. "Everything all right?" Evelyn asked. "Or did you just have a late night?" She pulled up some yarn from the ball somewhere inside her cavernous purse and made a few stitches.

"I'm fine, and yes, it was a late night." Josie poured herself a cup of tea and sat down. "Ev, do you remember anything about Dorset Falls when you first moved here?"

"What do you mean by 'anything'?" Evelyn looked her in the eye. "What's this really about?"

Josie blew out a breath. "It's this Bea Ryder mystery. Every time I look at or think about her doilies, I think about her. What could have happened to her. Why she never came back."

Evelyn nodded. "I understand. But we should really talk to Helen. She'll remember."

"Where is Helen, anyway? She hasn't been around in a few days. I hope she's not sick or anything?"

"Nope. She's just spending some time with her niece over in Westchester County. She'll be back tomorrow. I texted her and made her promise to come to our knitting drop-in."

Josie had forgotten about that. Maybe she *would* come after all. Especially if Helen was going to be there.

The bells rang, and Josie and Evelyn both looked up. Four women came in. They each grabbed a basket and dispersed around the shop. Based on the yarn lust Josie could see written on each face, it was going to be a lucrative morning.

The women were as good as their yarn lust promised. By the time they left, Miss Marple Knits was a couple hundred dollars richer.

Evelyn looked at her watch. "We close in thirty minutes. Do you mind if I run home now and pick up the casserole I made for Roy?"

The casserole. Right. She and Evelyn had planned to go see him. Josie felt a little flutter in her stomach. She hoped Mitch would be home.

"Go on ahead. We should each take our own car. That way I can go home after you do your evaluation."

"I'll have you know, my powers of observation are very keen." Evelyn put her project into her bag and snapped the top closed.

"I know that better than most, Evelyn. Now go. Whenever you get back, we'll close up and go."

While she waited for Evelyn, Josie went back into the storeroom. The doilies were as she had left them. She picked one up. It smelled nice and fresh, and when she held it to the light, she could see that the thread had a faint sheen. Very pretty. She pictured it sewn onto a white pillow, for a tone-on-tone look that was popular. It would also look wonderful against a black background—very contemporary, despite the age of the embellishment. She set the doily back down on the table, then gathered all the rest into a stack, which she carried out into the main shop and placed on the counter. *Oh, Bea. I wish you could talk to me.*

Evelyn didn't waste any time getting back, parking out front and honking her horn. Casseroles waited for no one, Josie supposed. She grabbed her purse and sweater and locked up behind herself.

Josie got into her Saab, then waited for Evelyn's Buick to pull away from the curb. The drive to the Woodruff farm was just a little bit shorter than going home, since the farm was closer to town. Evelyn turned into the driveway, shut off her engine, and got out. Josie did the same.

The Woodruff farmhouse was about the same vintage as Eb's, which was to say about Civil War era. Josie had never actually been inside, but she'd been to the alpaca paddock several times. New porch floorboards, identifiable because they were of light-colored wood that had not yet been painted, were interspersed with old ones, and a new railing had been installed around the perimeter of the porch. The Woodruffs had been busy.

"Do you think we should have called first?" Josie said. Back in New York, no one ever just popped in unannounced.

"Hold this." Evelyn handed Josie the foil-wrapped casserole. A small, square paper was taped to the top. "Chicken Divan" was written in Evelyn's perfect penmanship on the paper, along with simple heating instructions. Evelyn rang the bell. "Nonsense," she said to Josie. "We're neighbors—at least you are—and this is the neighborly thing to do."

Josie glanced toward the barn. Mitch's SUV was parked there. Roy's truck was nowhere to be seen.

Evelyn rang the bell again, frowning. "I can't just leave this here on the table. Where do you suppose they could be?" She reached out toward the doorknob. Evelyn had some moxie, but would it extend to walking into someone's home uninvited?

They didn't have to find out. The door opened, and Mitch Woodruff's face broke into a broad grin when he saw them.

"Mrs. Graves, Josie, come in. I was out in the backyard garden, checking on the asparagus."

"Mitchell Woodruff, you call me Evelyn. And the minute that asparagus shoots up, you let me know."

Mitch's grin got wider. "Yes, ma'am. There's going to be a lot this year, looks like. And we don't eat that much, so I'll be glad to give some away in a couple weeks." He held the door open for them, and Evelyn marched inside. Josie followed. Mitch brushed her arm with his own as she passed. "Sorry," he said, looking anything but. Josie wasn't exactly sorry either, but the contact would have been a lot more interesting if they each hadn't been wearing several layers of clothes. "What have you got there?"

"That is a casserole," Evelyn declared. "We heard Roy was ... not quite himself." She craned her neck around, not even trying to be discreet. "Is he here?"

Mitch took the casserole from Josie. "That's very nice of you," he said. "Dinner delivered by two beautiful women. What more could a couple of bachelor farmers want?" He held Josie's gaze a moment longer, then turned to Evelyn. "Just go on into the living room and make yourselves comfortable while I put this into the fridge."

Evelyn led the way, obviously having been here before on one of her casserole distribution runs. Josie unwound the scarf from around her neck and sat down on the loveseat. Evelyn took an armchair. She waved her hand at Josie. "Move over," she whispered.

"Why?" Josie whispered back, complying automatically. But before Evelyn could answer, Mitch came in. He strode over and sat down next to Josie. The corners of Evelyn's mouth turned up in a self-satisfied smile. For the love of Worth, was Josie that pathetic that she needed help in the maybe-possibly-gonna-date-someday department? Apparently so.

"Now," Evelyn said, back to business. "Where's Roy?"

Mitch settled back into the loveseat. Josie tried to relax, but couldn't. "He's gone to the hardware store in Torrington. What's this really about, ladies?" He said "ladies," but his eyes were on Evelyn.

Evelyn finally unzipped her knitted sweater-jacket and looked Mitch in the eye. "I'll get straight to the point," she said. "Roy's been seen in town acting strangely. So we came out here to see what's what. Now when will he be back?"

From where she sat, Josie could see a little muscle twitch below Mitch's ear. He hadn't shaved this morning and had a cute dark stubble covering his strong jawline and chin.

"What do you mean by 'strangely'?" he asked.

"Just what I said, right, Josie?" Evelyn folded her hands in her lap. She must have left her giant purse containing her knitting in the car, because it was nowhere in sight. Her hands looked fidgety, as though she needed a yarn fix.

"Josie?" Mitch turned to look at her.

How did you tell a person his grandfather had gone off the deep end? She thought about what she'd want if they were talking about Eb instead of Roy and decided to be frank. "There's a rumor going around town that Roy is talking to aliens." There. She'd said it.

Mitch continued to regard her. "That gossip's made it to the general store, eh?" He stood. "Come on, ladies. Let me show you something." He headed for the living room door. Evelyn looked at Josie and nodded. They followed him through the house and out the kitchen door.

"This used to be a tool shed," Mitch said, leading them to a building about eight feet square on a side. A large antenna was mounted on top, along with a satellite dish. "Roy converted it a few months ago to a kind of private radio station. He had all this amateur radio stuff left over from when he was a kid, and he set it all up out here."

Mitch opened the door, and they all stepped inside. A long table was covered with all kinds of ancient-looking equipment: speakers, boxes with knobs and dials, antennas on a smaller scale than the one on the roof. An old metal office chair upholstered in green vinyl sat behind the table, and positioned on the table in front of the chair was a microphone on a stand.

"What is amateur radio?" Josie asked. Nothing about this setup looked remotely fun, and weren't hobbies supposed to be fun? But to each his own, she supposed.

"Without going into too much detail," Mitch said, "amateur, or ham, radio operators with the proper equipment can tune in and talk to people all over the world. It's sort of a proto-Skype or FaceTime, except all you need is the equipment to harness the electromagnetic radio waves to make it work. No cell or Internet service. It's been around for a long time now."

Evelyn's foot began to tap, ever so slightly. "So this is where it's happening?"

Mitch nodded. "A couple weeks ago, Roy came back into the house after being out here all night. He was agitated, and not just from lack of sleep. I handed him a cup of coffee—and, yeah, caffeine probably wasn't the best thing to give him at that point, but I had to make a choice between making him even more jittery or giving him a rip-roaring headache from lack of coffee."

"I need my coffee in the morning too," Josie said. "Go on."

"Well, he said he'd been hailed the last few nights by someone who didn't speak English."

"So?" Evelyn said. "I'd venture to say that most people participating in this . . . sport don't speak English."

Mitch grinned. "True. But whoever this was, he was very insistent. Would come on at strange times of the day, but mostly in the evenings. And when whoever it was couldn't make Roy understand, he started communicating with clicks and taps."

"Clicks and taps—like a dolphin?" Josie amended quickly. "Not that I think he's talking to a dolphin."

"I'm willing to bet *that* never occurred to him," Mitch said. "But he's got it in his head that he's talking to some extraterrestrial and that the clicks and taps are some kind of code. Personally, I think he's misinterpreting some kind of static or something. But he says there's a regular pattern to it. He even wrote down one of the transmissions." Mitch pawed around on the table. "Here it is."

He held up a piece of paper that contained a series of *X*s and Os, written in pencil. It was like some kind of binary code.

Josie had a nagging feeling about this. She looked up at Mitch. "Can I take this?"

He handed the paper to her. "Sure. But why?"

"I happen to know someone who's very good at puzzles. I wonder if he's very good at codes too."

Evelyn, who'd been silent for a while, spoke up. "You don't think . . ."

Mitch shook his head. "I can't believe this didn't occur to me. If you're right, Eb's really raised the bar."

Chapter 26

On the short drive home, Josie rolled the whole thing over in her mind. The more she thought about it, the more she knew Eb was involved. She couldn't help being a little bit impressed. This was a prank that, as Mitch said, really raised the bar. But she was also a little bit angry. Eb had gone beyond just annoying Roy. Messing with his truck or signing him up for an online dating service was one thing. Messing with a man's head was another.

Eb's truck was gone when she pulled in. That suited her just fine.

She was about to do some snooping.

Coco must have heard the Saab pull up because she greeted Josie at the door, twining around her feet until Josie set down her keys and bag and reached out to give her kitty some love. Coco was not the kind of animal that liked to be picked up and carried or held. But she did love to have her throat and the top of her head scratched. "Come on, girl. Let's go get you some dinner."

The cat followed Josie to the kitchen. Josie opened a fresh

can of food and scooped a spoonful into a clean bowl, then retrieved the bowls of dry food and water from atop the refrigerator, which was the only place she'd found that Jethro couldn't get to, and set them on the floor. When Coco had finished, Josie replaced the bowls and rinsed out the wet food bowl. Coco purred contentedly and sauntered off to her small, soft bed in the corner by the window, where she did her customary few spins, then settled down for a nap.

"No time like the present," Josie said aloud. She dried her hands, then headed for Eb's workshop.

Her great-uncle had cleaned up the mess Josie had made on his worktable by piling everything up in one corner. She wasn't exactly sure what she was looking for. Some kind of radio, a transmitter, a device that could be sending signals to Roy Woodruff. Lately Eb had been adding wire curlicues to his thingamajigs, and she saw a spool of wire on the workbench. Could he be hooking that up somehow? She wished she knew more about how radio worked.

She sat back in the chair and looked up. A loose piece of wire hung more or less perpendicular to the ceiling. She followed it with her eyes. It was tacked up on the ceiling and ran all the way to the outside door, which Josie opened. The wire continued along the side of the house, then took a jog out across the yard.

And ran the full length of her clothesline, suspended about a foot above it. It ended at the pole that held up the far end of the clothesline. Josie didn't need a ladder to know that the wire was attached to the wire coat hanger sticking up and out from the top of the pole. The wire she'd thought was one of Eb's less artistic sculptures.

Gotcha, she thought. Now what was she going to do about it? She and Mitch had an unspoken agreement to stay out of the feud between Eb and Roy. Well, no need to make a decision yet. Mitch was keeping an eye on his grandfather, would watch to make sure he was only shaken up, not being seriously harmed. But she wasn't going to let this go on too much longer.

Josie went back inside through the workshop door, closing it behind her. She took another look at the worktable. He could have hidden the transmitter, even taken it with him. The point seemed moot now. The wire was enough to convict him. She looked down. There was that coast guard manual that was shoring up one leg of the table. *Semaphore and Morse Code.*

Clicks and taps.

*X*s and *O*s.

Dots and dashes? She found a piece of wood about the same thickness as the book, placed it under the table leg, and took the book with her.

It took only a minute to traverse the house, then settle herself in the morning-borning room at the desk. She found paper and a pen, then pulled out the notes Roy had made.

Morse code was a simple combination of long dashes and short dots. There was nothing cryptic about it, nothing that left room for interpretation. The only thing she didn't know was whether Roy had recorded the longs as *X*s and the shorts as *O*s, or vice versa. But it was simple enough to figure out. If one didn't produce a comprehensible document, the other would, as long as this really *was* Morse code.

Dot. Dot. Dash-dash-dot-dash. Her first attempt at translation made no sense at all, the letters combining into unreadable words. But the second attempt produced better results.

W-O-O-D-R-U-F-F. Y-O-U. D-O-P-E.

It turned out that Eb simply repeated that phrase, six times. Or at least, six was as many times as Roy wrote it down.

Josie had to hand it to Eb. He'd outdone himself this time. She pulled out her cell phone and dialed Mitch, then told him she'd confirmed what they suspected.

Mitch gave a low whistle. "Good detective work. Now the question is, do you and I get involved?"

You and I. She liked the sound of that. But there were other things to think about now. "You know these two better than I do. What do you think?" Josie reached into the bottom drawer of her desk. The yarn and knitting needles were there. She pulled them out and set them on the desk, running her hand back and forth over the yarn.

"Well . . . I don't see any way around this but to put them together in a room and see if we can get Eb to confess. I've got to tell Roy."

"I agree," Josie said. Stroking the yarn was calming her, the same way stroking Coco's black-and-white fur would have done. "Roy's got to be told before he's affected psychologically any more than he already is. And Eb's got to understand that he went a little too far this time." She wasn't actually so sure Eb would understand anything, but the effort had to be made.

"We should be there when it happens," Mitch said. "Roy is going to be humiliated, then he's going to go ballistic. Better that happens when we're there to mitigate any damage."

"You doing anything tonight? Let's get this over with. Lorna packed up two roast beef dinners last night, but there's more than enough for all of us. Bring Roy over around seven." Josie caught her lower lip between her teeth. She'd just asked Mitch over for dinner. *Don't be a dope, Blair. It's not a date. It's a business meeting.*

There was a short silence on the other end of the line before Mitch spoke. "The promise of one of Lorna's dinners might just be the only way to get Gramps over there. See you at seven. I'll tie Gramps to the bumper if I have to. And Josie? I'm looking forward to it. Well, not the impending nuclear explosion, but seeing you twice in one day will make it worth it."

He rang off before she had to respond.

She took the book back to Eb's workshop and replaced it

under the table leg. Eb should be home soon—he never stayed out much past six—but there was no need making him suspicious or getting him riled up before the main attraction.

The dining room table, as usual, was covered with Eb's stuff. There wouldn't be time to do more than a dash and stash job on it, though it was tempting to just take everything into Eb's workshop and dump it there. The kitchen table was smaller, but it would seat four comfortably, and it only had Bea's doilies on it.

She felt one. Dry. She pulled a plastic storage box out of a cabinet and stacked the doilies inside, then set the box on the counter out of the way. She only needed to drag the boxes of old dishes out from underneath the table and put them in the corner, then wipe down the table.

When that was done and the table was set, she pulled the to-go containers from the fridge. There was plenty there. The skins of the baked potatoes would probably crisp back up if she put them in the oven. The green beans and beef would only need a quick reheat so they didn't get overcooked. Dessert? It wasn't going to be anything fancy, that was for sure. Where was Evelyn or Helen with some home-baked cookies when you needed her? A fresh package of Nutter Butters she remembered was in the cupboard, plus coffee, would have to do.

Josie was just closing the oven door on the potatoes when Eb came in. She quickly checked to make sure the beef was back in the refrigerator, because she could hear Jethro's nails clicking on the hardwood floor, getting closer.

Eb took one look at the set table and scowled. "What's this?"

"We're having company for dinner. Go wash up."

Eb raised a hairy eyebrow. He wasn't used to being told what to do. But he also didn't ask who was coming over, for which Josie was grateful.

"I'll be doing my crossword," he said. "With my dirty hands. Tell me when dinner's ready." He went back out to the dining room and sat down in his velour recliner near the front window. Eb was crankier than usual. Perhaps things hadn't gone well at Tractor Supply. Or maybe he had some kind of sixth sense about what was going to happen tonight. Well, it was his own fault. He wasn't going to get any sympathy from her.

A couple of minutes after seven, a knock sounded at the front door. There was a pause, and then another knock. Josie came out of the kitchen. "You're three feet from that door. You think you could open it?"

Eb glared at her. "That's Woodruff's vehicle, which I don't mind. The boy's all right. But why's that bastard Roy Woodruff with him?"

Josie didn't answer, but opened the door. Eb was about to find out.

Chapter 27

Mitch came in first. He greeted Eb and Josie. Roy stood still in the doorway. Mitch took his arm and guided him inside.

"Glad you could make it, Mr. Woodruff," Josie said. "You can hang your coat here." She indicated a row of hooks on the wall to the right of the door. "Come right on out to the kitchen. Dinner's almost ready."

Eb's glare had been replaced by a smug look. "Hey, Woodruff. How's the radio going?"

Roy turned sharply. "How do you know about that?" he ground out.

"Let's eat. Josie's gone to a lot of trouble," Mitch said. "Come on, Gramps, Eb. We don't want it to get cold."

"You mean Lorna went to a lot of trouble," Eb said.

"Yeah, well, I made the potatoes. You can let me know how I did." Josie led the way to the kitchen.

Mitch sat Roy down at one end of the table. Eb sat at the other. They could look directly at each other, but they weren't quite in touching distance, which was good. Mitch walked over to Josie at the counter. "It wasn't easy, but I did it," he said, his voice low. Then louder, he said, "What do you want me to carry?"

Josie handed him a platter containing the meat and potatoes. "You can put this on the table." She brought the green beans and the gravy boat. Thank goodness the cupboard had also yielded a jar of premade gravy, which always had a soothing effect on Eb. Left to his own devices, he'd put gravy on chocolate cake.

They ate, Mitch and Josie supplying the only conversation. Eb and Roy refused to look at the other, each keeping his eyes on his own plate. When they'd finished, and the dishes had been cleared and coffee and cookies put out, Mitch spoke.

"Eb. Gramps. Josie and I want to talk to you about something."

"You want our blessing?" Eb said. Josie's cheeks burned. The man had an uncanny ability to home in on the exact thing that would cause you the most embarrassment. She supposed it was a gift.

"That might come later," Mitch said, giving Josie a smile. The heat in her cheeks was now accompanied by a little warm tingle in her chest. "But tonight," Mitch continued, "we're going to talk about the two of you."

Eb grunted. "Nope."

Roy gave a grunt of solidarity. "For once I agree with you, Lloyd." He reached for a cookie, then dunked it in his coffee.

"Yes," Josie said. "We are." She turned to Eb. "Now suppose you explain why Mr. Woodruff here—"

"Mister? What is this, the Waldorf?" Eb interjected.

Josie shot him a look, which didn't register because Eb was twisting a cookie apart, probably in preparation for eating the frosting out of the middle. He had a habit of doing that. "Why Mr. Woodruff here has been getting some strange messages on his radio."

Eb looked at Roy. "Strange messages for a strange man." He

used his butter knife to scrape the frosting off the cookie, which he transferred to his plate in a peanut-buttery pile.

Understanding dawned on Roy's face, transforming quickly to relief, then rage. "You, you, you!" he spluttered, apparently unable to put any more coherent words together. Mitch tensed, ready to step in if things got physical. According to Mitch, Eb and Roy always stopped short of physically hurting each other. But that didn't mean it would always be that way.

Eb went to work on another cookie, adding the frosting to the pile on his plate. He took one of the denuded peanut-shaped desserts and dipped it into the frosting before taking a bite. Talk about strange men. "All's fair," was all he said.

Roy's face had gone purple. "Fair? You're gonna pay for this, Lloyd. You wait and see." Josie wasn't so sure. From what she'd seen in the last few weeks, her great-uncle was a more imaginative prankster than their neighbor. Had a better command of the subtleties.

"Go for it," Eb said. Roy made a sudden movement in Eb's direction. Mitch checked him and sat him back down.

"Now," Mitch said, in an authoritative tone. "I want to know what it is between you two. I've heard about the feud between the Woodruffs and the Lloyds my entire life. And I want to know what caused it." He returned to his chair, but kept an eye on his grandfather.

Josie was impressed. She was dying to know the source of the animosity too. "Eb?" she prompted. "Why don't you start, since you're the reason we're here tonight."

Eb sat there silent, dipping his bare cookies into the small amount of frosting each had yielded.

"Gramps?" Mitch said, after it became clear Eb wasn't talking.

Roy's jaw was set hard, and his mouth was compressed into a line so thin his lips were invisible. He, also, apparently wasn't talking.

Mitch looked at Josie. She knew what he was probably thinking. *What do we do now?*

She remembered something Mitch had said when they first met. She'd dismissed it at the time, but it came to the forefront now. "You two don't know how this all started, do you?" Neither looked up. Neither spoke.

Mitch picked up where she had left off. "Just how far back does this go? Gramps?"

Josie had had about as much as she could take. "Eben Lloyd, you answer or I will never bring you dinner—or any meal—from Lorna ever again. And you'll be back to taking care of your own chickens and washing your own dishes."

Eb finally looked up, his gaze meeting Josie's. They'd bickered and sparred over the weeks she'd been here, but she'd never given him a direct order like this. The question was, would he obey it?

He did.

"Don't know. Always been this way. Always will be."

Mitch caught Josie's eye. They were on the same wavelength. If they had anything to do about it, the feud, whatever had started it, ended with their generation

With them.

"Our fathers fought. Theirs before too," Roy said.

"And you just blindly went along with it, for no reason?" Mitch said, exasperated.

"Yup." Eb and Roy answered together.

Josie looked at Eb, then at Roy. The feud would never end for them. These two old bachelors didn't want it to end. It was all they knew.

"Well, this particular prank is over now, got it? When someone's health is at risk, you've gone too far. Don't cross that line again, either of you." She got up and topped off the four coffee cups.

She felt a little—just a little—bit bad about coming down so hard on Eb. She was pretty sure he couldn't have known Roy would react the way he did. Eb had probably thought Roy would have figured it out long ago instead of jumping to crazy conclusions. Josie began to clear the table. Mitch jumped up to help.

"No leftovers. That's good," Josie said. "Less cleanup." Mitch replaced the lid on the butter container, then put it into the fridge. Mitch came to stand beside her. It felt right having him here. But now was the wrong time to think about it.

She ran hot water into the sink, squirted in some soap, and began to wash plates, glasses, and silverware, which she stacked in the drainer. Mitch dried almost as fast as she could stack, and they were done in minutes. Eb and Roy sat at the table drinking their coffee, not talking and not looking at each other, at least that Josie could tell.

Josie and Mitch returned to the table. "Now what?" Josie said. "What do people do in the country anyway?" She'd been working a lot of hours in the few weeks she'd been here. But there didn't seem to be a lot going on in town—or anywhere—anyway.

"We could play cards," Mitch said.

"We could go home," Roy said, draining his cup. "Josie, I thank you for the meal. But we're done here." He rose.

Mitch took a long draught of his coffee and stood. "I suppose he's right. I'll be in town for a while tomorrow. Maybe I'll see you?"

"Maybe," she said. The word came out coy, and she hadn't meant it to. Not really.

"Evelyn and I are opening the shop for a couple of hours tomorrow."

Mitch grinned. "On Sunday? Dorset Falls has never seen such a thing."

"Out with the old, in with the new."

"Sounds like it's worth a try. Come on, Gramps. Time for your beauty sleep." Mitch and Roy left.

When they heard the car leaving the driveway, Eb rose. "Time for my show." He went off to the living room, leaving Josie to clean up the coffee cups and put away the cream and sugar. She thought about trying to talk to him some more, but she decided she'd be wasting her breath. He was clearly done for the night.

And so was she. It had been another long day.

But, on second thought, she wasn't quite done. It had been a few days since she had updated her blog. Eb was watching *Fish or Cut Bait*, his favorite show. He said nothing as she passed on her way to the morning-borning room, didn't even acknowledge her presence. Oh, well. He'd get over it eventually. Maybe.

At her desk, she booted up her computer and began a new blog post. She stared at the screen. Normally she had no trouble thinking of a topic for her dozen or so readers, but tonight nothing jumped out at her. Well, maybe she could postpone this—it wasn't as if she was going to disappoint anyone who was desperate for new content. Maybe tomorrow's drop-in session would provide some material.

The knitting? No, it was too late, and she was too tired. She'd just make a bigger botch of it than usual.

Maybe she should just make an early night of it again. Back in the city, she'd just be going out for dinner at this time, then to a show or a club. She wouldn't be getting to bed before three a.m.

But then, back in the city, she hadn't had morning chores to do. Although she sometimes missed the excitement of New York, she had to admit it wasn't bad here in Dorset Falls. She closed the lid of her laptop.

Eb's show was still on, but he'd dozed off on the couch. Josie covered him with an afghan, turned off the television and the lights, and went to bed.

Chapter 28

Josie slept an hour later than usual the next morning, but couldn't afford to sleep anymore. The ladies of the henhouse needed her. With a sigh, she rolled out of bed, put on her barn clothes, and headed outside.

When she returned, Eb was up and sitting in his dining room armchair, newspaper folded out to the crossword. He appeared to still be wearing the same utilitarian pants and shirt he'd worn yesterday, but then most of his clothes looked alike, so it was impossible to tell, really. "Coffee," he grunted.

"Yeah, I'd like some too. Is it ready?"

Eb grunted.

"What did you do before I moved in?" He was still sort of in the doghouse, so she wasn't going to let him off so easily.

"Made my own. Yours is better."

"Flattery will get you nowhere, Eb, and you know it."

"Worth a try."

She supposed it was, gave in, and started the percolator, then prepared two bowls of cereal. Bananas this time, instead of blueberries. She took hers to the kitchen table and sat down. "Breakfast is ready, Eb," she called into the dining room.

He didn't answer, and he didn't come. Well, she wasn't a waitress. He could come and get it when he was ready.

She ate her own breakfast, scrolling through her e-mails as she did so. Since she'd moved to the country, her daily in-box was considerably less full, despite the fact that she was running her own business. There was nothing of interest there. When had she gotten on so many mailing lists?

When you did all that shopping, her internal voice said. *Remember?*

She did remember. Designer clothes bought at sample sales, on deep clearance, or at a discount from the Haus of Heinrich where she'd worked. Weekly trips to the nail salon. Monthly trips to the hair stylist. It took a lot of time and money to look good. To stay up to the arbitrary standards of her job in the fashion industry. And now? Eating breakfast in this country house, the same one her ancestors had eaten breakfast in for generations, wearing a sweater and jeans, her hair pulled back into a ponytail . . . Suddenly those city days seemed very far away. And maybe, just maybe, not all that appealing.

Josie took her cereal bowl to the sink and rinsed it out. Her eyes fell on the box of doilies she'd cleared from the table last night. Today, while the other people were knitting, she could get to work repurposing these. She'd need to either make a trip to a fabric store or place an order online if she wanted to make throw pillows, then sew on the doilies for her fledgling Neo-Victorian Chic collection. It was a silly name, but she thought it would fly, especially if she shortened it. NeoVicChic, maybe.

And she did have her denim jean jacket upstairs. She could hand sew a doily onto the back—maybe two or three, layering them on in a pattern. If it came out the way she pictured it, she could make these all day long. And they'd go for a nice price if she found the right market.

She set the box on the kitchen table, then headed upstairs to find the jacket.

When she returned, showered, shampooed, and denim in hand, Eb was at the table, eating his breakfast and still working on his crossword. Though he might have moved on to one of the other word puzzles by now. Jethro sat at his feet, panting slightly and staring at Eb's cereal bowl. The fact that Jethro had a full bowl of food and water not ten feet away was apparently lost on him. Eb reached down, scratched him between the ears, and set the cereal bowl, which was still half full of milk, down in front of him. The dog began to lap madly, slopping milk over the side of the bowl and onto the linoleum. Ugh. Josie wondered how many bowls she'd eaten from that the dog had also. This one, at least, she'd spend some extra time washing.

Josie topped off her own coffee and held the pot out to Eb. "You want some more?" Her uncle didn't look up, but held his mug out expectantly. She rolled her eyes and poured. Maybe she *was* a servant. She sat down at the table.

"What are you up to today?" Josie asked. "I'm going to open the shop for a couple hours, remember? Evelyn thinks it will be good for business."

He flinched, almost imperceptibly, when Josie said Evelyn's name. Evelyn had made no attempt to conceal the fact that she was interested in Eb. Of course, Eb was Dorset Falls's Most Eligible Senior Bachelor, due to the fact that he had inherited a good amount of money from his late wife, Cora.

"She-coyote," he said. Josie rather thought Evelyn would like that term.

"So what are you doing today?" Josie repeated. "What do you want for dinner? It'll have to be something I can pick up at the g.s. I don't think I have the energy to go into Kent to the real grocery store today."

He stared at her over the tops of his cheaters. "Taking down my antenna. Thanks to you."

"Don't blame me because you—"

Coco chose that moment to race through the kitchen. Jethro jumped, knocking over the cereal bowl in the process and spilling milk onto his snout. Before Josie realized what was happening, Eb reached for the box of doilies and began to wipe Jethro's face with one of them. He finished, then dropped it to the floor into the pool of milk. Josie jumped up, grabbing paper towels and bringing them back.

"Eb, seriously? Do you know what it takes to clean those things? Now I'll have to do that one all over." She blotted up the rest of the liquid, then placed her milky, doggy doily inside another paper towel, and carried the whole mess over to the sink. She threw away all the paper towels, then turned on the water to rinse out her doily.

It turned out to be the odd piece. The one with the random pattern of holes and ridges. She rinsed it, then spread it out on a towel. She could bring the special soap back to the shop with her this afternoon and clean it properly. Though really, what was the point? Even though someone—probably Bea Ryder—had put some effort into making the piece, it just wasn't very attractive. Josie couldn't see herself using it for anything saleable.

Maybe she should just toss it. Then she wouldn't have to think about it anymore.

But suddenly, this little scrap of knotted string was all she *could* think about. She smoothed it out on the counter and gave it a little stretch into a more or less square shape.

Josie ran a finger over the ridges, put the tip of the same finger into one of the eyelets, and let it bump along the pattern.

Eyelets and ridges.

*X*s and *O*s.

Clicks and Taps.

Eyelets and ridges.

Dots and dashes.

She stared at the piece of knitted lace in her hand. It couldn't be. But what if it could?

Josie crossed the floor and flung open the door to Eb's workshop. "What the—" she heard Eb yell, as if from a great distance even though it was only a few feet. She retrieved the Morse code manual and set it down on the kitchen table.

"I told you," Eb said, clearly exasperated. "I'm taking the thing down today."

"Yeah, good," Josie said, her mind elsewhere. She found a pen and paper and got to work translating: eyelets for dots, and ridges for dashes.

When she wrote down the last letter of the first word, Josie let out a gasp. There was no mistaking it:

H-E-L-E-N

Bea and Helen Crawford had been friends, despite their age difference. Had Bea been making this as a gift? Josie went back to translating, and this time she didn't stop until she'd written down every word.

HELEN. THREATS AGAINST ME. MAYOR STEUBEN.

BEATS WIFE. SAW BRUISES. BEA.

Josie sat back in her chair, taking in a deep, long breath to replace what she'd been holding. She hadn't realized it, but sometime in the process Eb had come to stand next to her, reading over her shoulder.

"Damn," was all he said.

Bea Ryder had owned a dress shop. What was it Evelyn or Helen had said a few days ago? Dressmakers know secrets. Of course Bea could have seen bruises on Mrs. Steuben. It required no leap at all to think that Mayor Steuben had found out that his wife had been to see the dressmaker—he could have seen her go into the shop, looked at a bill, found out any number of ways. And to keep Bea quiet, he killed her.

And now the mayor's son, Rick, was in town. Josie thought back to the dinner party. Suddenly, it was easy to imagine what kind of "agreement" Rick and Dougie might have had. Rick must have told Dougie about the murder. Even if Rick didn't know for sure, he could have suspected his father was involved. And they'd been keeping it quiet all these years.

"Eb," Josie said, looking up. "Do you remember Mayor Steuben?"

"He was an ass." Not exactly helpful. Eb thought pretty much everyone was an ass.

"Okay. What do you remember about him?"

Eb's prodigious eyebrows drew together. "Thought he was better than the rest of us. Sent his little brats to that prep school. Somehow kept getting elected."

"Whatever happened to him?" Josie fingered the wet doily again. *Bea. I think we're gonna get you some justice.*

"Dead. Heart attack maybe ten, fifteen years ago. Wife's dead too."

Chapter 29

So, as Josie had suspected all along, both Bea and Bea's killer were long dead. Mayor Richard Steuben was beyond prosecution, but it was satisfying to have a name she could take to the police. No question, she was giving this one to Sharla. Josie put the damp doily into a plastic zip bag and put it into her pocket. That thing was not leaving her sight until she'd turned it over to Sharla.

They still didn't have a body, but at least Helen, and anyone else who remembered Bea, would have some measure of closure. It would have to do.

Unless . . . Rick Steuben knew where his father had dumped her. Suddenly, it all made sense. Bea had to be buried on her own property somewhere. Was Rick afraid of what the construction crews at the old Ryder house were going to find? Josie would give that information to Sharla too, though it was a bit more tenuous. But the police could check it out.

Josie pulled her cell phone out of her other pocket and dialed Evelyn. "Emergency meeting of the Bond girls at Miss

Marple Knits. Skip church and meet me there in twenty minutes. Bring Helen."

Evelyn's excitement was nearly palpable through the receiver. "We'll be there. The sermon today looks boring anyway."

Josie parked in front of Nutmeg Antiques & Curiosities, leaving the spaces directly in front of Miss Marple Knits for Evelyn and Helen. Inside her store, she filled the electric kettle with fresh water and set it to heat. There'd be some tea drunk here this morning, that was for sure. Then she pulled the doily out of her pocket and out of its bag and laid it out on the counter.

It was only a matter of moments before both Helen and Evelyn came in. Josie could see Evelyn's big Buick out front, so she must have picked up Helen. They bustled in, eyes sparkling. "What have you got?" Evelyn said. "New evidence in Lyndon's murder?"

Helen set down a small round tray covered in plastic wrap. "I made these for fellowship hour after church, but I imagine they won't miss them."

"Take off your coats and come on back here to the counter," Josie said. "Oh, before you do that, Evelyn, would you lock the front door and make sure the CLOSED sign is turned out?"

Evelyn eyed her. "This must be good." She did as she was asked, then met the other two women at the counter. Evelyn frowned when she spotted the doily. "That old thing? They're so old-fashioned. You," she admonished, "got our hopes up for nothing."

Helen looked at Josie expectantly. "That's one of Bea's. I remember examining it a few days ago. Is that what this is about?" At least Helen was polite about it.

"Hear me out," Josie said. She explained what she'd discovered. When she gave the two women the translation, Evelyn seemed fascinated. Helen went pale.

"You mean, this was meant for me?" Helen whispered. Evelyn took one look at her friend, then grabbed her arm and marched her to the couch and sat her down. "Bring her tea," she ordered Josie.

Josie complied, bringing three mugs of steaming Cherry Almond. She set them down in front of her friends and took one for herself as she sat down.

"I don't understand," Evelyn said. "Why wouldn't she just call you? Or send you a note?"

Helen sniffled, and Evelyn handed her a tissue. "Well, a lot of us had party lines back then, though I don't remember if she did at home or at the shop. But remember, she'd been a radio operator in the war. She knew how easily communications could be intercepted, because she'd done it herself. And if Richard Steuben was threatening her, she already knew she was in danger."

"So she wasn't taking any chances," Josie said. "She spoke to you in a code she knew you'd understand: knitting."

"She was taking a pretty big chance," Helen said. "I didn't know Morse code then, and I don't know it now. The chances of my deciphering this were pretty slim."

Evelyn looked thoughtful. "But she did send you a subtle clue. Bea was an expert knitter. She would never, ever mess up a lace pattern this badly and keep the project. As soon as she figured out it was too gone to fix, she'd frog it and start over."

"Frog it?" Josie had no idea what the term meant.

"It means pull the stitches off the needle and undo your work. It's a method of last resort. And it's a pain in the butt," Evelyn said.

"And you knew she'd been a WAVE," Josie said. "It was reasonable for her to think that you'd be able to figure out she'd done it in Morse code."

"I think," Helen said, thoughtful. "I think this was meant to be an 'If anything happens to me' message. Because otherwise, why wouldn't she just go to the police?"

"I know why," Evelyn said. "Because you remember, Helen, Mayor Steuben and the chief of police back then were tight. Makes you wonder what else Steuben got away with."

"We have to give this to Sharla," Josie said. "It's a cold case, but she could still make some points with the higher-ups by solving it."

Evelyn frowned. "This doesn't really *prove* anything, of course. It's just circumstantial."

"It's good enough for me," Helen said.

"Me too," Evelyn agreed.

"And me as well," Josie said. "So what do we do now?"

"I'll text Sharla to come over," Evelyn said. "I think she's working today anyway."

So they had Bea's killer. Josie should have felt satisfied, happy even, that she'd had a part in solving the old mystery. So why did she feel uneasy? When she thought about it, she knew. Dougie Brewster, and Rick Steuben, and all their football cronies were in town. What would happen when the information they—or at least some of them—had been hiding all these years came to light? When Sharla got here, Josie would tell her about the unsanctioned reunion and what she'd heard at the lake house. It was all she could do.

Or was it? She knew the names of four of the men who'd been at the dinner party: Alden, Dougie, Rick, and Trevor. That left seven unidentified. Seven who might know something, be able to lead the police to conclusive evidence. Maybe even lead them to Bea's body. There'd been no guest list, at least not one that had been shared with her and Lorna. Some of the men had had numbers on their too-small football jerseys, but that wasn't helpful without . . .

A yearbook. Dougie had had a yearbook in his office at the g.s. It might, or might not, have been the same one that she'd seen on the end table at the lake house. She could hardly go over to Dougie's office and start snooping around, though it was tempting.

But she'd seen another yearbook recently, hadn't she? In the antique store next door. She had no idea if it was from the same year, but it was worth a try. She couldn't remember the numbers the guys had worn at the party, but the names would give Sharla somewhere to start.

Evelyn and Helen were staring at Josie when she looked up. "You've been lost in thought," Evelyn said. "What else have you got?"

"Uh, nothing yet. Maybe something that will help Sharla. Can you two watch the shop for a few minutes? I need to go check something out. I'll only be five minutes."

Evelyn and Helen looked disappointed. "Okay. Five minutes. We're timing you."

Josie put on her sweater and grabbed her keys. She unlocked the front door and headed to Nutmeg Antiques & Curiosities.

Chapter 30

Josie entered the antique store, which was dark and gloomy. It didn't get as much natural light through its big front windows as Miss Marple Knits did, being located in the middle of the block of brick buildings, whereas the yarn shop was on a corner.

The yearbook she'd seen had been in a box of other books in front of the bookcases in the back, waiting to be shelved. She threaded her way through the makeshift aisle and quickly located the box. The yearbook was there, and she retrieved it, now wishing she'd brought a bag of some kind. Even though Main Street was generally deserted, and even more so on a Sunday, why advertise what she was doing? She looked under the counter until she found an empty flat box with a lid, which would do. She loaded up the yearbook and headed for the front. If she had to guess, she'd say she was at about the three-minute mark. Not bad.

Before she could make her escape, a figure darkened the doorway.

Kai Norton, holding a camera. And right behind him, Taylor Philbin. Kai turned to Taylor and aimed the camera at her. She let out a dramatic gasp as her creamy white hand flew to her mouth. "What are you doing here?" she said.

Josie stood up straighter. She had every right to be here. She *didn't* have every right to be taking a book, or a box for that matter. But since she hadn't actually left the premises, she didn't think it would count as theft. Yet. "I could ask you the same question," Josie said.

"Go ahead," Kai said, defiant. "We were about to shoot some more scenes outside when we saw you go in. The door was open, so we followed. Now we can get some interior shots."

Taylor gave her magnificent hair a toss. "What have you got there?" she asked, pointing to the box.

"Whatever it is, it isn't yours," Josie said.

"What are you, a probate lawyer now?" This woman was insufferable. Josie *had* planned to just take the yearbook and return it later. But now she had an audience.

"Kai, you can stop filming *right now*. I'm not giving you permission to show my face on your show, so there's no point."

He grinned, showing huge, perfectly straight teeth that looked extra white against his tanned skin. "If I don't show your face, I don't have to have you sign a release. But I can show the rest of you without one." Jerk.

"Well, how's this?" Josie said. "I own this building, and neither of my lessees are in a position to give you permission to be on the premises. So you can leave right now, or I can call the police. Your choice." Josie's stomach tightened. She could talk a good tough-girl game, but her body sometimes didn't feel quite so fearless.

"I—" Taylor began.

Josie pulled out her cell phone and ran her hand up and down the screen, as if scrolling through her contacts list. She didn't really have the Dorset Falls PD on her speed dial, though she did have Sharla's personal number.

"Come on, Taylor," Kai said. "I've got enough that I can put together something here. Let's go finish filming outside, the way we rehearsed."

He took her arm and led her outside. They'd given up awfully easily. But Josie didn't have time to worry about them right now. She took the box back to the sales counter, in the deepest, darkest corner of the store, removed the book, and opened it.

It didn't take long to find the pages containing the sports teams. In those days, Collingswood had only been open to boys—she had no idea whether girls were now admitted, but it seemed likely—and there had been only a few teams. Baseball. Basketball. Football. Swimming.

She located the football team and let her eyes run over the photo. These were just kids, and she didn't recognize any of them. It was possible that none of them had grown into the men she'd met at the lake house. She had no idea what year this book was from.

She moved on to the names underneath. Bingo. Douglas Brewster. Richard "Rick" Steuben, Jr. Matching the names with the faces, she realized that she could just barely see the resemblances to their decades-later selves. Was Trevor there? Yup.

Josie couldn't believe her luck. What were the odds that Lyndon would have a Collingswood yearbook in his stash of old books, and that it would be from the exact year that she needed?

It was a big, fat coincidence.

That's all it could be. Or was it?

She read on in the list of names. Two entries from the end, the coincidence was explained.

Suddenly, everything she thought she had figured out about Bea Ryder's disappearance and death spun on its axis.

Josie looked at the photo again. She could see the resemblance, just barely. Her eyes returned to the list of names.

Lyndon "Beelzebub" Bailey.

Chapter 31

Josie's thoughts reeled. She snapped a couple of pictures of the photo with her phone, then buried the yearbook deep under the other books in the box where she'd found it.

She needed to get out of here, and she needed to talk to Sharla, like now.

Lyndon's death had to be connected to the Bea Ryder murder. By all reports, Lyndon had wanted to move back to his childhood hometown. That seemed reasonable enough.

But then, at more or less the same time, Bea Ryder's house was undergoing renovations to turn it into a brewery. Two new businesses in Dorset Falls was big news, at least in this town. Josie kept going back to the idea that Bea had to be buried on her own property, and that Rick Steuben was afraid that, at the very least, the publicity surrounding the opening of the brewery would stir up memories of the murder. And at the worst, the construction would result in Bea's body being found.

Josie opened the door, stepped out, and locked it behind her. Kai and Taylor were outside, as she'd expected them to be. "Find what you were looking for?" Taylor said.

Josie ignored them and kept walking. Let them film her backside, for all she cared. Well, she might care a little. But that meant nothing now.

When she got back to her shop, Evelyn and Helen looked at her expectantly. Josie must have looked as rattled as she felt, because both women rushed over to her, each taking an arm, and sat her down on the couch.

"Josie!" Evelyn said. "Where've you been? What's going on? It was more than five minutes, you know."

"Evelyn," Josie said when she'd recovered a bit. "I need to find Sharla right now. Do you know where she is?"

"She didn't answer my text," Evelyn said. "But I saw her cruiser go down Main Street toward the general store just a few minutes ago."

Josie had been so absorbed in the yearbook, she hadn't even noticed. "Hold down the fort for me, will you?" She stood up, intending to go to the g.s. and find Sharla, even if it meant she'd have to walk past Taylor and Kai again.

Evelyn stood and put a firm hand on Josie's arm. "We will not."

Huh? Evelyn had never refused to do something Josie had asked. "Evelyn, it's important. Please."

Helen spoke up. "Obviously it's important. Which is why we're not letting you do it alone. Now come on. We'll close up, and we'll all go find Sharla together."

Josie looked from one to the other. Helen and Evelyn's minds were made up, and they were certainly capable of making their own decisions. And she supposed if they were going to accompany her, she should fill them in. She grabbed the lace off the counter and shoved it back into her pocket, then told her friends what she knew. Or thought she knew.

Helen looked stricken. Evelyn's mouth hung open. It took some doing to ruffle her, but Josie had done it.

"Let's think about this for a minute before we go," Evelyn

said when she recovered. "Let's put this story together for Sharla. Lyndon, Rick Steuben, and Dougie Brewster all played football together. From the message in the lace, we know that Rick's father, Mayor Steuben, had been threatening Bea because she'd seen bruises on his wife's body."

"Right," Josie said. "And there was some kind of agreement between Rick and Dougie. Dougie was taunting him about it the night of the party."

"The agreement was almost certainly about Bea Ryder, a pact to keep quiet about the fact that Richard Steuben had murdered her," Helen added. "Perhaps Rick told Dougie. One of them, or both, may have told other members of the team."

"Lorna told me there were originally supposed to be twelve men at the party, but then Dougie told her one couldn't make it so there'd only be eleven. Lyndon Bailey had to have been the twelfth man. But he was killed before the party." Josie's brain was furiously trying to fit all the pieces together.

Evelyn looked thoughtful. "But why did Rick Steuben kill Lyndon after all these years? Why now?"

"The only thing I can think of," Josie said, "is that Lyndon was about to break the agreement. Maybe his conscience was getting to him. Maybe he wanted to make a clean breast of it before he moved back to Dorset Falls."

"And Rick had to stop him," Helen finished. "But why? Old Richard Steuben has been dead for years. He's beyond prosecution, so what difference would it make now?"

Josie had been wondering the same thing. "What if Rick Steuben was involved with Bea's murder somehow? His father might be beyond prosecution, but Rick Steuben is not."

The three women exchanged looks. "Come on, then," Evelyn said. "Let's go find Sharla."

Kai and Taylor were gone when Josie, Evelyn, and Helen made their way toward the general store. Something was definitely going on there. Two cruisers, light bars flashing, were parked near the front doors.

Margo Gray stood about ten feet from the cruisers. The women congregated around her. "What's going on?" Josie asked.

"Oh, hey, Josie. Evelyn, Helen," Margo tipped her head toward each woman in turn in greeting. "I came here to buy milk and eggs, and I'm debating whether to go in or not. Dougie's having an argument with someone, and somebody called the police."

Lorna. Was she all right? "Are they actually keeping people out?" Josie asked.

"I don't think so," Margo said. "I've seen people go in and out. More going in, honestly, probably to see what's happening."

"I'm going to check on Lorna," Josie said. "You can come with me or stay outside if you feel safer, girls."

Evelyn huffed. "Nonsense. If it's safe enough for you, it's safe enough for us. Come on, Helen. Let's lead the way." They started off across the parking lot. Josie had to hustle to keep up with the pace Evelyn set.

The store was full of people when they entered. Sharla stood near the food counter talking to Dougie. His face was beet red, and he looked as though he were about to have a stroke. Officer Denton was conversing with Rick Steuben, who was in about the same state as Dougie. *Murderer.* Lorna had been right. These guys were probably hypertensive.

And where was Lorna? She wasn't behind the counter. Josie scanned the room and found her sitting at one of the tables. Josie sat down and joined her.

"Hey, Josie. Come to see all the excitement?" Lorna seemed okay. Tired, maybe. Which wasn't surprising since she'd been running this place singlehandedly while Dougie's friends were in town.

"I came to see if you were okay. I know Dougie's been

tough on you lately." Josie reached out and put her hand on Lorna's arm. Lorna smiled gratefully.

"I am. Dougie's problem today is with Rick, not me. Or I should say, Rick's got a problem with Dougie. Rick came in here this morning guns ablazing. They'd been at it for at least an hour when Rick shoved Dougie in the chest. Rusty Simmons was in here, and he called the police so I wouldn't have to."

Josie's knowledge was burning a hole in her brain. She needed to unburden herself to Sharla and soon. She might be preventing another murder. Rick had killed Lyndon to keep him quiet. Who was to say he wouldn't work his way through his entire Collingswood football team? Starting with Dougie.

But Sharla was busy, and might be for a while. Who knew how long the talk-down would take? There was nothing for it but to wait. She wanted Sharla to get the credit for what Josie had found.

Knowing what she knew, should Josie try to get people out of there? What if Rick was armed? But Officer Denton seemed to have him well under control, and Sharla had Dougie calmed down as well.

Josie scanned the room. She should have known. Standing over by what was left of the Charity Knitters table were Kai and Taylor. Kai made no secret of the fact that he was filming. Taylor stood there, looking beautiful. Periodically Kai turned the camera on her. Josie couldn't hear what she was saying, which was probably just as well. Josie would only get angry instead of just repulsed.

Denton glanced toward Kai and Taylor. "Shut off the camera," he said.

"Free country," Kai called.

Josie turned to Lorna. "Did you hear what they were fighting about?"

"Not really. They were inside the office most of the time, so their voices were muffled. It was only when we heard furniture falling over that we called the police. When Sharla opened the office door, with Officer Denton as backup, all I heard was a lot of unimaginative swearing."

At that moment, a faint whirring noise sounded from somewhere in the vicinity of the front door. The whirring got closer, and the crowd parted to make a path for Alden Brewster. He wheeled himself up to the counter and actually banged on the flat surface with his fist.

"What the hell is going on here?"

Chapter 32

Every head, including those of Sharla and Officer Denton, turned toward the octogenarian. The two cops quickly returned their attention to their charges.

"Well?" Alden demanded. "This is my store, and that's my son. Somebody answer me."

Sharla took the lead. "Mr. Brewster, there's been an altercation between your son and Mr. Steuben. The situation is under control. So if you'd just step—er, move back, someone will talk to you shortly."

Alden pressed the joystick on the arm of his chair forward and maneuvered toward the flip-up opening in the counter. "No one tells me what to do or not to do in my own store. If no laws have been broken here, you can both leave. Now, officers."

Sharla's face hardened. "Mr. Brewster. Officer Denton or I will let you know when we're finished. So you can move back on your own, or I'll have you forcibly removed from the premises." Go, Sharla.

Alden whipped out a cell phone. "I'm calling my lawyer,

young lady. You're going to regret the day you set foot in the police academy." He punched in some numbers.

"Wait, Dad." Dougie stood up to his full height. I saw Sharla's hand go to the butt of her service revolver, where it rested, presumably ready for whatever was about to transpire. "It's time. I can't live this lie anymore."

The room was silent, waiting for whatever Dougie was about to confess.

"Shut up!" Rick Steuben lunged for Dougie. Officer Denton was much closer to his own football days than Rick was to his, and he wrapped Rick in a bear hug from the front. Sharla whipped the cuffs from her belt, yanked Rick's wrists around to his back, and snapped the cuffs on. Officer Denton forced Rick down into a chair, secured him to it, and pulled out his radio, calling for backup.

Dougie stared at Rick. He lifted his hand and pointed. "That man is a murderer."

A murmur went up from the crowd. "Shut the hell up!" Rick said. Restrained as he was, words were all he had.

Sharla pulled out a notebook and pen. "Suppose you tell us what you mean by that, Mr. Brewster."

Alden stared at his son with something like admiration. Based on what Josie had seen of their relationship, she was willing to bet there had not been too many times Alden had been proud of Dougie.

Dougie cleared his throat. "Not only is he a murderer, so was his father." Another gasp from the crowd.

"Explain, Mr. Brewster," Sharla said.

"Douglas," Alden said. "Don't say anything that will incriminate yourself."

Dougie looked at his father. "Dad. I've been living with this since I was a teenager. I'm done. If there are consequences, I'm ready to take them."

"Mr. Brewster," Sharla said, "you may wish to wait until your attorney is present."

"Thanks," he said. "But I'm ready to talk now, in front of all these people."

Alden's face was stony, impossible to read. He gave an almost imperceptible nod to his son. Dougie continued.

"Rick Steuben and I went to Collingswood and played football there together."

"Go Cougars," someone said, not too loud, but loud enough that a few people heard and chuckled. Nothing about this was a laughing matter, but it did serve to break the tension somewhat. The tension ratcheted up again almost immediately.

"We also played with Lyndon Bailey, the fastest runner I ever saw, God rest his soul. That man"—Dougie pointed at Rick—"killed Lyndon in his own shop."

Rick made an attempt to stand, but couldn't. He must have known the attempt was futile, because he didn't resist when Officer Denton put a hand on his shoulder and pressed him back down.

"His boyhood friend. *Killed him.* And all because Lyndon was about to tell the truth about what happened when we were teenagers. Lyndon can't speak for himself anymore. But I can, by God." Dougie paused, took a deep breath, and went on.

"Richard Steuben, the mayor of this town for years, Rick's father, killed Beatrice Ryder."

If Dougie's previous statements had raised gasps from the crowd, this latest one caused a positive tornado. Josie glanced around. Many of the younger people in the room looked confused, probably because they didn't know the story of the old murder. Evelyn sat stoic. Helen sniffled, pulled a tissue from her purse, and dabbed at her eyes. Evelyn patted her arm.

Lorna's jaw dropped open. "Is this for real? I've wondered about that poor woman for years. My grandmother used to tell me about her." She eyed Josie. "You knew, didn't you? I can tell by the look on your face."

"I just figured it all out, I swear, or I would have told you. I was on my way here to find Sharla to tell her everything."

"Rick knew," Dougie said, "that his father had killed Miss Ryder, who was about to go to the authorities. Rick's father, Mayor Steuben, beat his wife. And Miss Ryder knew."

Rick Steuben hung his head, all the fight gone out of him.

Sharla continued to make notes. She was going to have one heck of a report to write later. "So what are you saying, Mr. Brewster?" she said. "What's your part in all this?"

Dougie hung his own head, then raised it to look at the crowd. "Rick told us—me and Lyndon—that he knew his father had done it. How Rick had seen bruises on his mother, even though she tried to cover them up. How he'd heard his parents arguing about Bea Ryder and how to keep her quiet. And none of us ever went to the police. We covered it up, all these years."

Sharla exchanged glances with Denton. "How old were you when you were told about the murder?" she said, her voice kind.

"Seventeen," Dougie said. "And I've regretted not telling the authorities every day of my life since."

"Mr. Brewster," Sharla said. "I'm no lawyer. But if all you knew was what another kid told you, and you had nothing to do with the commission of the crime itself, you had no legal obligation to report anything to the authorities." She nodded toward Rick Steuben. "And unless he helped his father somehow, neither did he."

The enormity of what Sharla had just said hit Rick hard. His face went white, probably with the realization that he had killed Lyndon for no real reason. Even if Lyndon had gone to the police, it sounded as though there would have been no possible charges against Rick.

Dougie looked stunned, the weight of decades of guilt suddenly lifted from his shoulders. But then his face hardened. "Maybe not a legal obligation. But a moral one."

Josie didn't know about that. If Dougie had no real evidence, only what Rick had told him, was he morally obligated to pass on what he'd been told? The point was moot now. It was all out in the open.

"You have the right to remain silent..." Officer Denton read Rick Steuben his rights, then released him from the chair and helped him to a standing position. Sharla stood on the other side of Rick, and they escorted him out the door to one of the two waiting cruisers.

Josie stole a glance at Kai and Taylor. She had a feeling Rick Steuben wasn't going to fight the murder charge very hard. He'd looked defeated. Broken. And that meant that Harry would be released as soon as his lawyer could get the charges dropped. What that meant for Kai and Taylor's show was anyone's guess.

Dougie came out from behind the counter and stood in front of his father. "Son," Alden Brewster said. "I'm proud of you."

Chapter 33

Josie reached into her pocket and felt Bea's knitted lace. It was still damp from its soaking this morning, but Josie didn't mind. *Well, Bea. I did my best for you. But Dougie Brewster beat me to the punch.*

Now neither Sharla nor Josie would get the credit for solving Bea's murder, or Lyndon's. But justice had been done, and that was all that mattered.

"Lorna!" Dougie's voice boomed out, all traces of the humility he'd just shown gone. "Back behind the counter. We're losing money."

Lorna cut her eyes to Josie. "Duty calls. I'll catch up with you later. I want to hear all about how you figured everything out." She went to work.

Sharla came back inside and headed straight for the counter. "Mr. Brewster? Dougie? We'll need you to come down to the station and give a statement."

Dougie nodded. "I probably won't press charges against Rick, even though he hit me. He's got bigger problems now."

Josie approached Sharla. "I know it's a little late to be giving you this. If I'd figured it out sooner, I would have." She handed Sharla the scrap of lace. "I know this is going to sound crazy, but Bea Ryder knitted the name of her killer into this doily. In Morse code."

Sharla looked at the lace. "I can't wait to hear how you managed to figure this out," she said, grinning.

Dougie stared. "You've got to be kidding. And it's just turning up now?"

"It's a long story, but it all makes sense. Bea felt threatened and intended to give this to Helen Crawford all those years ago," Josie said. She turned to Sharla. "I know you have to follow Officer Denton down to the station. But it's driving me crazy. Do you think Bea's body will ever be found? My guess is she's buried somewhere on her property. But who knows?"

"I don't know," Sharla said. "I'm not sure if the investigation will be opened back up, since the killer is now dead himself. It might be pointless." She handed the lace back to Josie. "Keep this for now. I'll talk to Detective Potts and see what he wants to do." She headed for the front door.

Evelyn and Helen appeared at Josie's side as she was replacing the doily into her pocket.

"Drop-in knitting time," Evelyn said efficiently. "Let's get back to the shop. There are enough people downtown, some may stop in."

Josie, Evelyn, and Helen made their way back to Miss Marple Knits and opened up. After putting on a fresh kettle of water to boil, Evelyn and Helen immediately sat down and pulled out their knitting. Josie threaded a needle with white thread, laid out her denim jacket on the sales counter, and pinned on the doily she'd chosen for the project. Then she sat down with her friends and began to sew.

Evelyn frowned. "Josephine Blair."

Josie looked up. "Yes?" She knew what was coming.

"This doily repurposing project is all very well and good. But don't you think it's time you let me teach you to knit?"

The shop bells rang, like an angel in response to an unspoken prayer. Gwen Simmons and Margo Gray came in, found seats, and pulled up strands of yarn from the depths of their bags. "Now," Gwen said. "I missed all the excitement at the g.s. I want to hear all the details."

"And I want to relive it," Margo said.

Josie let Evelyn and Helen tell the story while Josie placed tiny stitches into the doily and through the thick denim of her jacket. She used the tip of her thumb to push the needle in and out. It had been a long time since Josie had done any hand sewing—probably since she completed her master's thesis—and she wished she had a thimble. They were old-fashioned things, but they worked. Her finger would be raw if she kept going.

Evelyn had finished her account of Dougie's confession. "Can you imagine carrying that around all these years, only to find out your guilt had no foundation?"

"Well," Margo said, "I'm just glad that Dougie won't be arrested and taken away. This town would dry up and blow away without the general store." She made some twisty motions with her right hand and added a few stitches to her crocheting project.

"And *I'd* dry up and blow away if I didn't have Lorna's cooking to rely on a few times a week," Gwen added. "The kids love her macaroni and cheese."

"Change of subject," Josie said. "Does anyone have a thimble in her bag? My finger's killing me, and I still have a lot of sewing to do here."

Gwen and Margo both shook their heads. Evelyn pawed around in the depths of her bag and came up with a small plastic container, which she opened and examined. "Nope," she said.

"Plenty of buttons, stitch markers, and stitch holders, though. I'm sure I have one in my sewing box back home. Though that won't help you now."

Helen shook her head. "I don't have one here either. Not much call for sewing through thick materials in knitted items, unless you add some leather accents to a sweater or something. Wait," she said. "In my building across the street I have some of Bea's dressmaking supplies." Her eyes misted over. "I couldn't bear to throw or give it all away when I bought the building. It just seemed disrespectful."

Evelyn reached over and patted Helen's arm, then handed her a tissue she pulled from the pocket of her cardigan. "You were—and are—a good friend, Helen Crawford."

Helen smiled sadly. "Thanks." She cleared her throat. "I'll just run over and get you your thimble. I could use some fresh air anyway."

"Would you like one of us to go with you?" Josie said. "I should, since you're doing me a favor."

Helen shook her head. "No, I'll do it. I wouldn't mind a few minutes alone with Bea's things, honestly. Maybe it's time to let it all go now."

"Closure," Evelyn said, sagely. "You'll let us help, when the time comes."

"I will." Helen got up and put on her jacket. "Back in a few minutes," she said, and left.

Josie got up and watched Helen walk across the street, put her key in the lock, and open the door to Bea Ryder's old dress shop. *It would be so nice to have another business open up there,* she thought. Maybe now, with Bea's murder solved and no longer hanging over its head, the shop would attract a new tenant. Josie mentally shook her head. It was nuts, thinking these old buildings had souls of their own. And yet, she couldn't deny that's what she thought about Miss Marple Knits.

With Cora's death, her yarn shop could easily be suffering

the same fate as almost every storefront on Main Street right now—it could have been empty. But something had called to Josie when she had first arrived here. Oh, it wasn't anything as obvious—or spooky—as hearing voices or being touched on the arm by an unseen presence. It was more a feeling she got whenever she was here. A feeling of being home. A feeling of being exactly where she was supposed to be.

She sat back down on the couch, picked up one of the knitting magazines, and began to thumb through it. A little prick of guilt stuck her. Again. So many beautiful projects, and she couldn't make them herself. Her friends were yarning away. Maybe she *was* just being stubborn, making excuses for not asking for help.

Decision made, she opened her mouth, about to tell Evelyn she was ready for lessons.

But Evelyn spoke first. "Ladies. We have some decisions to make." Her tone was dead serious. "Not that we can make any without Helen. But we can talk about them now."

All heads turned toward Evelyn. "What kind of decisions?" Margo asked.

"First off," Evelyn said, setting her knitting in her lap and reaching for her tea. "The Charity Knitters Association will have to disband come November, when the by-laws say elections must be held. I'll be resigning, and Helen said she will be too. That means the organization won't be able to seat a board, with Diantha Humphries as the only member."

"That's kind of too bad," Gwen said. "I never joined, but you all did good work."

"We did," Evelyn agreed. "But honestly, I think our time had come anyway. Even when Cora was at the helm, we were winding down. There are only so many charities, and a lot of people out there who knit for them. Our intentions were good."

"Of course they were," Margo said.

Evelyn continued. "But it was starting to feel as if it was all about numbers. Who could knit more hats. Whose mittens sold better at the general store. Who could come up with the most obscure charity to donate to. It had begun to be . . . not fun."

Josie thought she understood. "And it wasn't supposed to be a competition. It was supposed to be about friendship."

"Exactly," Evelyn said. She waved her hand around the group. "This is what it's supposed to be about. Friends getting together to talk, and laugh, and share their lives. Doing a thing they love—needlework—with people they love."

This was, without a doubt, the touchiest, feeliest thing Josie had ever heard Evelyn say. And she couldn't agree more.

"Then let's keep doing it, just like this," Josie declared. "Sunday afternoon drop-ins. Just a couple of hours a week when we can get together and just . . . be friends. And maybe welcome new ones too. We'll call ourselves the 'Yarned and Dangerous Gang.'" She'd just committed to working more hours. But this wasn't exactly work.

Evelyn smiled, clearly satisfied. "That's exactly what I was going to suggest. And I quite like the name of our new club. Now, on to the second thing."

Josie had no idea what was coming next.

"Josie, remember when you, Helen, and I talked about going to see a show in New York? Well, Helen and I have discussed it, and we think it's a great idea. So let's pick one and get ourselves some tickets. We'll reserve Rodrigo and the limo and go down in the morning, so we'll have time to check out some of the yarn shops in Brooklyn. Strictly for research purposes."

"Margo, Gwen, you in?" Josie asked.

"Are you kidding?" Gwen said. "I've got three kids in elementary school and two dogs. Rodrigo, take me away for a day."

"Oh, yeah," Margo said. "Oh, yeah."

Josie smiled. "Let's bring Lorna too. She needs a day off. Desperately. I'll call in sick for her if I have to."

Evelyn nodded. "Quite right. In fact, I think it's high time I had a chat with Alden Brewster. He needs to loosen up the purse strings, promote Lorna to manager of the store, and hire her some help."

If anyone could bring Alden Brewster to heel, it was Evelyn Graves. But Josie knew that might not be what Lorna wanted. Lorna wanted the freedom that owning her own place would give, a want that Josie understood completely. Lorna's own little café was still a little ways off, according to Lorna, though she didn't seem to mind. The journey, maybe, was just as important as the destination.

New York. Was Josie ready to return, even if only for a day? It would be tempting to go into the Haus of Heinrich and give Otto Heinrich a piece of her mind. He'd refused to let her advance in the company, made passes at her, told her designs were no good, and stolen those very designs. But now she was finding it hard to work up much in the way of anger. Well, she wouldn't mind seeing him have a nonfatal episode of choking on a schnitzel. But for the most part, she didn't much care.

"Evelyn," Josie said. "Make it so."

Chapter 34

Josie looked at the big clock on the wall behind the sales counter. Helen had been gone a while. Longer than it should have taken her to go across the street, retrieve a thimble, and come back. Unless she was having trouble finding one.

"I'm going to give Helen a call," she said. "She might need help hunting through Bea's supplies." She pressed in the number. It rang in her ear.

And rang somewhere else within Miss Marple Knits. Helen's purse was on the floor next to the wingback chair Helen had been sitting in before she left. Josie disconnected.

"She must have only taken her keys," Evelyn said.

"I just finished a row," Margo said. "Would you like me to go?"

"No!" Evelyn said, a little too sharply. Margo and Gwen turned to look at her, then looked at each other and shrugged.

"Uh, I'll go," Josie said. "Evelyn, you can mind the shop? I should only be a few minutes. Can you lend me your keys?" It wasn't that she didn't trust Margo and Gwen to know that

Josie had her own key to the Lair across the street, not that she'd used it anytime recently, but it wasn't her secret to tell.

Evelyn apparently understood, because she reached into her purse, pulled out a ring containing only two keys, and tossed it to Josie. Helen and Evelyn were best friends. It wouldn't be too hard to explain, if Gwen or Margo asked, why Evelyn had the key. But they didn't ask.

"See you in a few minutes," Josie said, and left.

After the earlier excitement, Main Street had returned to its mostly ghost-town appearance. At the end of the block she could just see a few cars parked at the general store. Unfortunately, none of this morning's onlookers had made his or her way from the store to Miss Marple Knits. But no matter. Once word got out that there were Sunday hours, the yarn people would probably eventually come.

Helen's car was not parked out front. Had she gone home? But then Josie remembered that Helen and Evelyn had come together in Evelyn's Buick. She crossed the street and opened the door to the side of the main shop. The stairway ahead of her was dim, so she flipped on the light. Fortunately, there seemed to be a minimum of cobwebs. She made her way up one, then a second flight to the third, top floor.

There were four doors up here. She chose the door to the Lair and went in.

The lights were on here in Evelyn and Helen's secret clubhouse. Josie hadn't been here in a few weeks. The floral couches covered in clear vinyl were still here, as were the small table, fridge, and coffeemaker in the kitchenette. They'd added some wicker bins lined with cloth to hold balls of yarn, some of which Josie recognized as coming from Cora's personal stash. Josie had brought that yarn here herself.

"Helen?" Josie called. "Are you here?" There was no answer, but there was a light layer of dust on the coffee table. Evelyn was an immaculate housekeeper, which supported the idea that they had shut down the probably illegal operations they'd been running here. A glance into the control room, which had once been the only bedroom in this apartment, confirmed it. Cords hung loose from some of their electronics, which were also a bit dusty.

Now that she thought about it, Josie realized this probably wasn't where Helen would be storing Bea's things anyway. The apartment was small, and there was a whole empty building full of choices. The only thing to do was to search it all.

She started with the other three apartments on this floor. They were all barren, except for an occasional odd piece of furniture here and there. A dining room chair whose faded blue upholstery had seen far better days. A wire birdcage, covered in peeling white paint. An empty cardboard box with dog-eared flaps.

As she opened the door to the last apartment on this floor, she thought of Bea Ryder again. Josie thought she remembered Helen or Evelyn saying that Bea had rented the street-level shop. Had she ever come upstairs for some reason and walked on these same floors? Opened these same doors? *Where are you, Bea?* Josie couldn't seem to get the question out of her head. It should be enough that the murderer had finally been identified.

Somehow, it wasn't.

"Helen?" she called again. Josie's voice bounced around the walls of the empty apartment. She headed downstairs.

The second floor contained what appeared to have once been small shops. Each had a glass door, with a transom over the top on which a number and a name were stenciled:

N. ROGERS, TOBACCONIST

S. TRELAWNEY, ELECTRICAL SUPPLIES

Back in the day, it appeared that each store had catered to its own particular niche. Josie supposed it was no different from shopping at today's outlet villages, where the stores stood alone or were separated by a common wall.

Josie started at the far end of the hall and entered three shops in turn. Helen wasn't in any of them. The fourth shop, the one marked ELECTRICAL SUPPLIES, was closest to the stairwell. Josie stuck her head in. "Helen? Are you here?" A figure appeared in her peripheral vision. She turned.

It was a dressmaker's dummy. An older model, probably from the middle of the twentieth century. Josie had seen and used enough of them during her career in fashion design to know that this one was heavy, pretty much indestructible. To its left, a sewing machine, covered in black enamel and dressed with gold scrolls, sat with its bed flush to a solid oak table. A few bolts of dusty, faded fabric stood upright in one corner.

"Helen? Helen, it's Josie," she called again. But there was no answer.

Here were Bea's things, presumably where Helen had come to find the thimble for Josie.

But where was Helen?

She felt her shoulders tense, then relax. Josie must have missed her. While Josie had been looking for Helen on the third floor, Helen had been here and gone. She pulled out her cell and dialed Evelyn, who answered on the first ring.

"Ev, I'm over here, and Helen isn't. Did she make it back to the yarn shop?"

There was a short silence. "No. She's not there? Did you try the second floor?"

"Yes, and the third floor too."

Josie could almost hear Evelyn thinking. "Look on the first floor, in the main part of the shop. There might be a few of Bea's supplies there too. And Josie?"

"Yes?"

"Call me again, one way or the other. Something doesn't feel right." Evelyn rang off.

Josie had to agree. But before she could know for sure if something was wrong, she would have to check out the first floor. Perhaps Helen had fallen, or had had some kind of medical event. Josie hustled down the stairs and into the empty storefront.

A quick search of both the public side and the storeroom revealed that Helen was not there. Josie dialed Evelyn again. "No sign of her," she said. "Can you call her house? Is it possible she walked home to get her car for some reason?"

Evelyn gave a little chuckle. "Of course. That must be it. She mentioned earlier that she had to pick up a few things at the general store before they closed today. And it's almost closing time too. I'll bet she's either home or at Dougie's. Let me just give her a ring at home, then I'll call you back. Wait there."

Josie's phone rang not more than a minute later. "She didn't answer," Evelyn said. "Margo volunteered to go to the general store and see if she's there. Gwen is going to drive past her house and see if she's walking. I hope she didn't fall. She'd never admit this to anyone but me, but her knees have been giving her trouble."

"Well, there's no point in my staying here. I guess I'll come back and wait for the other girls to get back."

"Good idea." Evelyn rang off.

Josie looked at the clock on her phone. Just how long had Helen been gone, anyway? She calculated back. It must have been close to an hour. Even if Helen *had* made a detour, her house was only two blocks away. Josie left through the front door, not the way she'd come in, and headed back to Miss Marple Knits.

When Josie got inside, she asked Evelyn for an update.

Evelyn shook her head. "No one can find her."

"Should we be worried?" Josie said. "Because I am. I know she's a big girl and all, but—"

"But this isn't like her," Evelyn finished. "What's that noise? It's outside."

Josie listened. She heard it too. It sounded like . . . a power tool. She and Evelyn went to the window and looked out. The view wasn't good enough, so they opened the front door and stepped out onto the sidewalk.

Josie's jaw dropped in surprise. "What the heck are you doing? You stop that right now," she said.

Chapter 35

A man Josie had never seen before, wearing a ball cap and a utilitarian coat and pants with a lot of pockets, was pressing an electric drill to the metal lock plate on the door of Nutmeg Antiques & Curiosities. The bit made a buzz that made Josie's fillings ache. Kai Norton and Taylor Philbin stood to one side. Kai, of course, had a camera in his hand.

Josie marched over and tapped the guy on the shoulder, realizing too late that that probably wasn't a good idea since he was holding a spinning drill in his hand. But he took his finger off the trigger and turned to her. "Just doing my job, ma'am."

Taylor had that insufferably smug look, the one Josie had seen more than once, on her perfect little face. Kai seemed keyed up, excited. He trained the camera on Josie. She was so angry, she didn't even care.

"You're damaging my property with the intent to break in." Josie pulled out her cell phone. "I'm calling the cops."

Taylor tilted her head and gave a little laugh. "Great," she said. "They can help enforce this court order I have." She held out a sheet of paper. Josie reached out for it, but Taylor snatched it away. She laughed again, then handed the paper to Josie. "Everything's in order. The judge granted me access to the property."

Josie scanned the sheet. It looked official enough, even had an original signature written in blue ink. It was dated that same day. Evelyn, who had followed Josie out, snatched the paper from her hands and examined it.

Josie narrowed her eyes. "You expect me to believe you got a Connecticut judge to give you an order on a Sunday? Sorry. Not buying it." Could Taylor have managed it somehow?

"Believe what you want. I don't care. It's legal. Now move out of the way so Burt here can get to work. I'm paying him by the hour." She folded her arms over her chest, daring Josie to protest.

Which she did. "Burt." He turned to Josie. "I own this property. I never received any notice of this order. And I am disputing it. Tomorrow, Monday morning, I will call the court that supposedly issued the order and verify it. If it's legitimate, you can come back. And Taylor can pay you again. But for right now, please put your drill away."

Evelyn glared at Taylor. "Young lady, you are making a serious mistake. Send this man home."

Taylor's face hardened. Kai turned the camera on her. "How about if I call your friends at the Dorset Falls police station and have an officer come down and enforce this?" Taylor said.

"Not if I call them first and have them stop it."

Burt looked from Josie to Taylor. "Look, Ms. Philbin. I don't want to get in trouble. This business is my only source of income. I can't lose my locksmith license."

"Why do you want in there so badly?" Josie asked Taylor. "You must have heard there was a new arrest in the murder of your uncle. Harry Oglethorpe will be out of jail soon. Maybe as early as tomorrow, depending on how fast he gets processed out. Why not just wait until then, and you and Harry can work out the details? You'll have to do that anyway. What's one more day?"

"I'll tell you why I want in there. Because it's half mine, and we still haven't found that partnership agreement. I want to know what I'm entitled to."

Entitled. That about summed it up. Josie opened her mouth to reply, when Kai butted in. "Tell you what, Burt. I've got a couple extra Ben Franklins in my wallet, and they say they think you should open that door. And you'll be on television, too. I can do a close-up of your jacket showing your company name."

Burt hesitated. But not for long. He pressed the trigger, and the drill buzzed to life. He started working on the lock again.

"You're paying for that lock repair," Josie said to Kai. She took her cell phone from her jacket pocket and dialed Sharla, but the call went right to voice mail. "Hey, it's Josie. You still on duty? I've got a situation here at the antique store, and I could use your help. Thanks."

Evelyn spoke into her own phone. "Sharla, you get down here right now." She turned to Kai and Taylor. "This order's not worth the paper it's printed on." She handed it back to Josie.

"Prove it," Taylor said. She put her hands on her hips and watched the drilling.

Josie didn't notice Margo Simmons until she came up and stood beside her. Margo glanced around at all the players, taking in the scene. "The police are on their way," Josie said. "Did you find Helen?"

Margo shook her head. "No one's seen her. She didn't go to the general store."

Evelyn put a hand to her mouth. "In all this excitement, I forgot about Helen for a moment. Josie, if you don't need me here, I'll go back to the yarn shop. We left the door open. And someone should be there in case Helen calls the business phone."

"Thanks, Ev," Josie said. "Hopefully I'll be back to join you shortly." Evelyn went next door.

"Gwen's not back yet?" Margo asked. "I can't stand the sound of that drill. It reminds me of the dentist."

"No, and neither can I. Where's Sharla, anyway?"

No sooner had Josie asked the question than a squad car pulled up out front. At the same moment, the drill shut off. Burt put his hand to the doorknob, and the door swung open. Heedless of the police, Taylor rushed inside, giving a shove past Burt. Kai followed her with the camera to his eye.

It wasn't Sharla who emerged from the car. It was Officer Fleming, the young cop who'd taken Josie's statement after she'd discovered Lyndon's body. Great. "Come on inside," she said. "And I'll explain."

"You," Fleming said to Burt. "You come in too. I'll want to talk to you."

Burt packed up his drill and went in, not protesting. Of course, he still hadn't received his couple of Benjamins, so he was probably in no hurry to leave.

Margo said, "I'll track down Gwen, see if she's found anything. We can rendezvous back at Miss Marple's when you're done here."

Josie nodded and followed Officer Fleming inside the antique store.

Taylor stood there with her hands on her hips, surveying the room. Apparently she hadn't considered how big a job this search of hers would be. Where would she start? Josie had a feeling the agreement wasn't even here. Taylor shook out her hair, letting it settle around her shoulders, as Officer Fleming approached her.

"There's really no need for you to be here, Officer." She had turned on the charm. "Though I'm glad you are. My uncle was the one who was killed here." She managed a fetching little catch in her voice. "And the landlord wouldn't let me in. This is my business now, and I've got to be responsible." Taylor turned those big green eyes on him.

Kai didn't seem to mind. In fact, he gave a little smile.

Officer Fleming, to his credit, seemed unaffected. Josie gave him a mental fist pump. She scolded herself. Just because he was young didn't mean he wasn't a good cop. He turned to Josie. "I know you own the building. Why don't you tell me what's going on here?"

Josie explained. She held out the order. "I'm fairly sure this is a fake, but I won't be able to verify that until tomorrow. And even if it isn't, there's no reason for all the drama."

Fleming glanced from Josie to Taylor. "What are you looking for?"

Taylor rolled her eyes. "As I've told Ms. Blair here, I don't know how many times, I'm the executrix of my uncle's estate. I need his computer, or his paper files at least, and I can't find them. Legal business, you understand."

"I can't think of too much legal business you need to conduct on Sunday afternoon," he said. "Ms. Blair? You own the building. What do you want to do?"

Good question. Josie was worried about Helen. But she had an obligation to Lyndon and Harry, too. "All right," she said. "Nothing leaves the property. You've got fifteen minutes to search. You don't need more than that since you've already been here and apparently didn't find what you were looking for."

"I don't know what you're talking about," Taylor said. "I've never set foot in this building." But she must have decided not to argue with Josie's fifteen-minute time limit because she started at the street-view side of the room and began to search.

"I'll be back here," Josie said to Officer Fleming. "I want to check on the broken lock on the back door." She made her way behind the counter. The door appeared to be in the same shape as when she'd left it, secured with a hasp and padlock she'd had Darrell Gray install for her. Based on Taylor's latest stunt with the probably fake court order, Josie didn't think she'd try the back door again anyway.

Taylor continued searching. Kai continued filming. Officer Fleming continued standing there, impassive, watching the show.

Josie sat on the stool behind the counter, then leaned her elbows on the scarred wood, so similar to the counter next door at Miss Marple Knits. She rested her chin in her hands. It had been a long day. She dropped one hand to the counter and began to trace the old grooves in the wood. Something rolled under her finger. Something light and fine, but she could feel it. Josie looked down, picked the thing up, and held it up to the light.

The strand of hair was more than a foot long. Wavy.

And an unmistakable shade of red.

"Officer Fleming? Do you have a plastic bag?"

He came over. "A small one. Why?"

Taylor and Kai both looked in their direction.

"Didn't Taylor just say she'd never been in this shop?"

"That's right," Taylor said, defiant. But she looked a little nervous, just the same.

"Because I've got a long red hair here that says you're lying."

Officer Fleming held out the bag, and Josie deposited the strand inside it. He zipped it closed, then pulled a pen out of somewhere and made some notations on the bag.

"You want to press charges?" Fleming said. "That B&E case is still open."

"Yeah, I probably do." More than probably. Josie couldn't take another minute of Taylor Philbin or Kai Norton. And she was getting more worried about Helen by the minute.

Taylor glared. "Even if I did do it—and you know I've got an alibi—it's not breaking and entering if it's your own property."

"I'm sure you can convince a judge of that, the same way you convinced a judge to give you this worthless court order. Fifteen minutes is up. You're done here."

"Burt, you can go," Fleming said. He turned to Josie. "I'll take these two down to the station and charge them with B&E."

"You might want to confiscate that camera, too," Josie said.

Chapter 36

Josie stood on the street and watched the squad car pull away. She wasn't counting on Kai and Taylor being tied up too long. One or both of them had broken in, but there was no evidence anything had been taken. But they were out of her hair for now.

She made her way through the familiar doorway of Miss Marple Knits.

Evelyn and Margo sat on the couch, knitting and crocheting away, respectively. Evelyn's hands flew faster than usual, a sure sign she was agitated. They looked up when Josie came in.

"Any word on Helen?" Josie asked.

"No," Margo said. "Gwen went to her house. Her car was in the driveway. The front door was locked, and when Helen didn't answer, Gwen found a partly open window and crawled inside. Helen wasn't there."

Evelyn yanked up some more yarn and continued her furious knitting. "There are only so many places she could be. And we've checked them all."

"Time to call the police," Josie said. "Although I have to think we've searched everywhere they would."

Josie's cell phone buzzed in her pocket. She pulled it out and looked at the display. The number was not one she recognized. She picked up. "Hello? If you're trying to sell me solar panels, you picked the wrong day—"

"Josie?" The voice was thin. Weak.

"Helen?" Evelyn and Margo sat up straight and turned toward Josie. "Helen, we've been so worried! Where are you?" Josie's heart pounded. Thank goodness.

"I . . . fell. Hit my head, and I think I've been unconscious for a while. Can you come and help me? I don't want an ambulance," she added quickly.

"Of course I'll come. But I can't promise I won't call an ambulance. Where are you?"

"I'm across the street. In my building."

Josie frowned. "Helen, are you sure you're thinking clearly? I was over there less than an hour ago, and I looked in every room. And where did you find a phone? Yours is here at the yarn shop."

There was a pause, as if Helen were thinking. Poor thing. She was probably disoriented. "I'm in . . . the basement. There's an old phone—a landline—I've been paying the bills on for years. For emergencies."

Which this was. "I'm on my way. Be right there, Helen. Stay put. I'll find you." Josie rang off. If she needed to call back, the number was captured in her phone.

"Where is she?" Evelyn demanded. "Is she all right? I'm coming with you."

"She says she's across the street and she fell. I'd rather have you stay here, Evelyn. No matter what she says, we're taking her to the emergency room. Can you make sure you've got a blanket, and maybe a bottle of water, in your car? You've got more room in your Buick."

"Then I'll come," Margo said. "Although I think I should call Darrell. He's on the Fire Department EMS unit."

"Honestly, she seemed a little embarrassed," Josie said. "I do think you should call Darrell, before we take her to the ER. I'll help her back over here, and we can say Darrell just happened to be here. To pick you up or something."

Evelyn nodded in approval. "Then he can check her out discreetly and see if she really does need an ambulance. It's not easy getting older, you know. If we can leave her her dignity, we should. I'll warm up the car and have it ready."

"Then it's settled," Josie said, and left.

She let herself in the front door of Bea Ryder's old dress shop using Evelyn's keys, which she hadn't yet returned. The stairs to the right of the door, which led to the apartments upstairs, didn't go down. Which meant there had to be a stairway to the basement somewhere in the storefront part of the building.

It didn't take long to locate it in the back. This store had a wall along the back with an opening that led into a hallway. A light was on overhead. A stairway was visible through an open door. Several other doors lined the other end of the hall.

Why would Helen keep any of Bea's things down there? She had a whole building. And really, if Josie had known Helen would go to all this trouble, go into that dank basement that Josie could smell even from here, let alone hurt herself, Josie would have told her not to bother. It was just a thimble, and Josie hadn't needed it that badly. "Helen?" Josie called into the stairwell. "I'm coming."

As she put her hand on the railing, a faint noise sounded from her right. She started, then turned. Just a short hallway, dimly lit by the leftover light from the single bulb over her head. Probably a mouse, though there was no sign of one. Maybe Josie would bring Coco over tomorrow. If there was a rodent, her cat would find it, kill it, and drop it at Josie's feet as a disgusting love offering.

She put out her foot to take the first step.

And jumped back, almost losing her balance, when she caught movement in her peripheral vision.

A hand reached out and grabbed her arm, steadying her. Josie's heart pounded from her near-death experience. She looked up, then blew out a breath.

"Dougie," she said. "You surprised me. What are you doing here?"

The mayor grabbed her by the shoulders and gave a shove, pushing her back against the wall. "What the hell are you up to?" he said, voice menacing. "Ever since you came to town you've been sticking your nose into other people's business. It ends here." His face was dark with rage.

Josie's gut tightened, but she got her New York on. "I don't know what your problem is, but you touch me again, and I'll knee your nuts up into your sinuses." She eyed him. He had fifty or sixty pounds on her, but he was out of shape. She wasn't exactly in fighting form after a few months of shepherd's pie and no gym, but she was a lot younger and was pretty sure she could outrun him.

Dougie snorted. "Did you belong to a gang back in New York City? They won't get here in time."

Keep calm and keep him talking. Evelyn and Margo knew she was here. If she didn't come back soon, with Helen, they'd call for help. "Dougie, settle down. Let's go back to Miss Marple Knits, or to the general store, and you can tell me whatever it is you want to talk about."

"I'll tell you now. Drop this Bea Ryder nonsense. The woman's been dead for years. It's nothing to you." He took a step closer, still holding onto her arm.

"Isn't it already solved? You confessed what you knew today, and now everybody knows it was Richard Steuben who killed her. And Rick Steuben who killed Lyndon to keep Lyndon quiet. So what if I'm interested in where Bea's body is? Lots of people are interested in mysteries and true crime."

Dougie's words repeated in her head. *It's nothing to you.* "It's nothing to you either. Is it?" she asked.

He yanked on her arm. She backpedaled and hit the wall, harder this time. Dougie's breath was ragged and smelled like some kind of spicy sausage. Lorna's lentil soup from today's lunch. Josie turned her face to the side so she wouldn't have to breathe it in.

Why was he doing this? She had to get to Helen.

Josie dodged to the side, breaking his grip, but she'd gone the wrong direction and was trapped in the hallway. Dougie was faster than she would have given him credit for. His fingers closed hard around her wrist, and he pulled. "Shut up!" He dragged her toward the door to the basement. She leaned back in resistance, but his greater weight gave him the advantage, and she felt herself being pulled along.

Dougie shoved her in front of him, twisting her arm across her back and holding on. "Downstairs," he ordered.

Not knowing what else to do, pain shooting up her arm and across her shoulder, she began to descend.

Because they were locked together by Dougie's iron grip, the descent was slow. Awkward. Could she use that awkwardness to her advantage? She had one free hand. But from her position below and in front of him, there didn't seem to be any way to trip him up or land any kind of blow without falling down the stairs herself. There was no guarantee she'd end up on top, with the advantage. No, her best bet would be to wait until they were back on level ground.

As they got closer to the basement floor, the air got danker. Heavier. It was thick with the moldy smell of damp bricks, and she found it hard to draw a breath. Or maybe that was the pain. Or the fear. Or all three.

Finally, they reached the bottom.

He gave her arm another twist, sending fresh pain searing

through her body. "Take it easy, Dougie," she forced out, sounding more like a breathy Marilyn Monroe than a tough girl.

"Keep that mouth shut," he ordered. "And keep moving."

Where was he taking her? This basement couldn't be that big. She glanced around, looking for something she could grab and use as a weapon, but the dismal room was empty. He seemed to be steering her straight toward the brick wall of the foundation, but as they approached, she could see the outlines of a door. She did a quick mental calculation. Based on the size of the empty shop above, this door must lead into the basement of the adjacent building.

He slid one arm around and in front of her and turned the knob. His sausage-breath was coming faster, shallower now, and she could feel moist heat radiating off his face. The door swung open. She ran through a self-defense scenario in her mind.

And took her chance. Josie jammed the sole of her boot behind her in a donkey kick that connected solidly with some part of Dougie's leg. He gave a sharp cry and stumbled backward, releasing his grip on her enough for her to twist away.

But she lost her balance and fell through the door anyway, into the blackness.

Chapter 37

Josie shook her head and rose on all fours on the dirt floor, attempting to catch her breath. She must have stirred up something because she could taste grit. She stood, spat, then blinked as the light came on overhead. Dougie limped through the door, his face contorted with anger.

"That was my bad knee," he said. "I might sue you."

If she hadn't been dirty, in pain, and, oh yeah, ripping mad, she might have laughed. "Dougie, you don't have any reason to sue—or kill—me. I assume that's what you're planning to do. You heard Sharla when they arrested Rick. He was never legally obligated to report his father for murdering Bea, unless he helped kill her or helped conceal the body. And neither were you. So why—"

A muffled noise came from behind Josie. Dougie's eyes darted to the far corner of the cellar. Josie turned, and her heart leapt into her throat. "Helen?" Her friend was bound to a wooden chair, a gag tied around her mouth. Helen's eyes were wide. She tried to speak, but only a muffled squeal came out.

Arms grabbed Josie from behind. Dougie lifted her a few inches off the ground and carried her toward Helen, grunting. She bicycled her legs, but without having one foot anchored, she couldn't repeat the donkey kick with any force behind it. "Let me go, you jerk!" She struggled against him. He couldn't keep this up for long. Probably, neither could she. Suddenly, she didn't regret the amount of Yankee food she'd been eating since she'd arrived in Dorset Falls, as those few extra pounds only helped in this situation. She twisted and shoved her elbow backward.

It accomplished nothing.

He tossed her to the ground next to Helen's chair and pulled out a knife.

"I didn't want to have to use this. Now sit down, and shut up."

Josie twisted her body and sat up. The damp from the earthen floor was soaking through her jeans, but she barely felt it. "You don't need to do this. Don't you understand? You're not liable. None of you were. You were just kids."

In the dim light, Dougie's face looked like the devil himself had taken up residence inside. He'd gone beyond anger. He was now clearly unhinged.

"You're the one who doesn't understand!" he screamed, waving the knife, which Josie could now identify as a chef's knife, in a wide circle. "It's not about me!"

Helen made another muffled sound. Josie didn't dare look up at her, just had to hope she was okay because there was nothing Josie could do at this moment.

Josie kept her voice level. As controlled as she could make it, considering that her heart was now running a four-minute mile. "Dougie." She drew a deep breath. "Whatever it is, we can figure it out. Just put the knife down, and let us go."

The knife made another swing. "It's not about me!" he repeated, breath ragged.

She watched him, calculating. She wasn't about to go down without a fight. Helen might be helpless right now, but Josie wasn't.

"If it's not about you, then who—"

Suddenly, she knew who it *was* about.

It *was* something to him.

Dougie was beyond prosecution, even though he'd been keeping a secret for years about Bea Ryder's death. She'd bet he'd always known that.

But it wasn't Dougie's own secret he'd been protecting.

It wasn't Rick Steuben's, or Rick Steuben's father's, either.

Dougie had been protecting his own father. Alden Brewster.

She had to be right. No one else had this kind of hold on Dougie, emotional, financial, or otherwise. And that meant that Rick had killed Lyndon to cover up a secret that wasn't even true.

"*Your* father killed Bea Ryder, didn't he? It wasn't Richard Steuben who'd beaten his wife, leaving bruises that only Bea saw when she fitted a dress. It was your father." Josie's mind raced with possibilities, but she could think of only one right now that made sense. "Mrs. Steuben and your father were having an affair, and it went sour, got physical?"

Dougie stood stock-still. Only his jaw quivered.

She'd hit her mark. "And when your father found out that Bea blamed Richard Steuben and was planning to go to the police, he killed her. Because even if Bea wasn't right about who had hurt Mrs. Steuben, an investigation could very well reveal the truth. And your father couldn't have that. Somehow you found out, and he made you keep his secret all those years."

"Shut. Up," Dougie said through clenched teeth. He held up the knife in front of him.

But Josie couldn't stop until she'd said it all. "Once Bea was dead, Mrs. Steuben was afraid to tell the truth. Afraid of what her husband might do. Afraid of what she knew your father was capable of. And she took the secret to her own grave."

Josie didn't know if she had it all worked out correctly, but it was close enough. Dougie stared at her. She stared back, waiting, her hand in her pants pocket.

A split second after Dougie lunged, Josie threw Bea's knitted doily and hit him square in the face. He jumped, and the knife dropped from his hand. The doily was too light, too small to do any damage, but it distracted him long enough for Josie to roll up hard against his legs and knock him off balance. He fell to the floor, breath pouring out of him in a loud whoosh.

Josie reached for the knife and quickly stood over Dougie. She gave him a solid kick in his bad knee, and he sucked in a sharp breath, then began to whimper. Could she stab him if she had to? The thought sickened her—she could almost hear that knife cutting into flesh, like a scene from *Psycho*—but she'd do it to save Helen or herself.

It turned out she didn't have to make that choice.

"Hands up!" a woman's voice barked. "Drop the weapon."

Josie complied and turned around slowly. Gratitude and relief washed over her.

Officers Coogan and Denton stood just inside the doorway, guns drawn.

Sharla gave a nod to Denton, who headed toward Dougie. Brewster was still groaning in pain but, wuss that he was, just lay there, defeated. Denton pulled a pair of cuffs from his belt and snapped them on Dougie's wrists, then manhandled him to his feet. "Come along, Mr. Mayor." Denton propelled him toward the doorway. "You're going to have a hard time explaining this to your constituents."

"Stay here," Sharla ordered. "I'll be back once we get Dougie loaded and secured in the squad car. Is that Helen? Check on her if you're all right yourself." Sharla followed behind Denton.

Josie didn't need to be told to check on Helen. She brushed the dirt from her hands onto her jeans—they were probably so filthy now, a little more wouldn't matter. "Helen? It's over."

She pulled the gag from Helen's mouth and threw it to the floor. "Oh, Helen! Did he hurt you?" Josie began to work at the knot securing Helen's left wrist to the chair.

"I—I'm okay," Helen rasped. "I need a drink."

Josie pulled one end of the rope free, then began to unwind it. "I'd say you deserve a whole bottle of Chardonnay, after what you've been through." When the rope had enough slack, Helen pulled her hand free, then began to flex it.

Josie freed Helen's other wrist, then unbound her legs. "Can you stand? Have you been here this whole time?"

"Just let me lean on you, Josie." Helen took Josie's hand, then rose. Josie put her arm around her friend's waist. "I'm not sure how long it's been. A few hours, I think." She swallowed. "I was up in the Lair, and he grabbed me, then dragged me down three flights of stairs."

"But why?" Helen's knees buckled slightly, and Josie held on tighter to keep her upright. "Do you want to sit down until Sharla comes back?" Josie wondered what it would take to put out a hit on Dougie in his future home in prison for having hurt her friend, but reconsidered. She didn't have that kind of money. Hopefully the sentence for kidnapping was a long one. And maybe the police could come up with some other charges against him. Attempted murder would be nice. He *had* pulled a knife on her.

"I'll stand," Helen said, determined. "And to answer your question, when Dougie found out about the doily, he assumed that Bea had told me everything before she was killed. He'd been following me, and when he saw me go into this building, he grabbed me. He asked a bunch of questions about Bea, and about Francine Steuben, then left for a while and came back. He forced me to call you, knowing you'd come when I asked."

Josie frowned. It looked good in the movies when the villain put both his victims in the same room and confessed, but she had a feeling that didn't happen in real life. Why wouldn't he have killed Helen as soon as he took her? Why go to all the trouble of tying her up? Helen was surprisingly calm right now, but she might have been in shock. The question was hardly something she could ask her friend.

"I think," Helen said, standing up a little straighter, and unwittingly answering Josie's unspoken question, "he never planned to kill me—or you—violently, even though he had that knife. He was always spineless."

"I sort of got that impression. Let me see your wrist."

Helen held one out. The delicate skin was raw from the ropes. Josie felt a fresh flare of anger. "We need to get you to a doctor. What do you think he planned to do with us, then?"

Helen paused. "I think . . . I think he planned to lock the door and leave us here." She cleared her throat. "To die."

Before Josie could respond, Sharla returned. "All set. He's on his way to the lockup." She strode over to them, hesitated, then threw her arms around both women. Josie felt her heart swell. In the few months she'd been back in Dorset Falls, she'd made friends. Real friends.

Sharla stepped back and put on her cop face once again. "Are either of you hurt? It's procedure to call an ambulance in a situation like this—not that Dorset Falls has *had* a situation like this, probably ever. We've certainly never made this many arrests in one day, as far as I know."

Helen shook her head. "I'll be fine once I have a cup of tea and can get my hands on my knitting." Before she came to Dorset Falls, Josie would not have understood what Helen meant about the knitting. But she'd seen the calming effect the rhythmic stitching produced. Tea and some yarn probably *were* all Helen needed.

"And all I need is a shower," Josie said. "There's no statute of limitations on murder, right? You're going to need to pick up Alden Brewster too. Dougie practically admitted to me that his father killed Bea Ryder all those years ago."

Sharla shook her head. "I can't wait to hear the rest of this story. There's hardly been a dull moment since you came to town, you know."

Josie wasn't entirely sure that was a good thing. "How did you know where to find us?"

Sharla eyed Josie, then her lips turned up into a smile. "Diantha Humphries called me and said that she was checking the Charity Knitters table at the general store, and saw Dougie acting strange. She watched him put a chef's knife into his briefcase, then followed him over here until he went inside. It took us a few minutes to find you," she said, apologetic. "This is a good-sized building."

Josie felt her jaw drop open. "But I thought Diantha and Dougie were tight?"

"I think," Helen said thoughtfully, "they're not tight so much as she wants Douglas Brewster's job. He'll have to resign as mayor over this, and there'll be a special election. This time, Alden Brewster won't be pulling the strings. I'll bet you a couple of skeins of that new opossum-blend yarn you have in the shop that her name will be on the ballot."

"Come and get the yarn anytime, Helen. Why wait for the election? That's a bet I know I'll lose." Josie turned to Sharla. "Alden Brewster will have to tell you where Bea's body is buried, won't he?"

Sharla nodded. "I'm sure that will come out. But you should know there's a chance he'll never see prison time. He's well into his eighties. The judge might sentence him to house arrest with an ankle monitor or something."

Josie could understand that Alden might be too old to go into the general prison population, but it would hardly be fair if he got to live out the rest of his days in his million-dollar lake house. She shook it off. Nothing she could do about that.

Sharla eyed her. "Do *you* have any ideas about where Bea's body is buried? You're awfully good at figuring things out. You must have gotten the same puzzle-solving gene your uncle has."

Bea's body. It was the last piece of this particular puzzle. "Well, I had thought she might be somewhere on her own property. And I still think that's a possibility. But now, knowing that Alden Brewster killed her, I'm wondering if she might be out on his Lake Warren property somewhere. That place is huge, and there's a special driveway that goes through the woods. She could even be *in* the lake."

Sharla frowned. "If that's the case, we'll probably never find remains."

Helen's face, which was always pale, went even whiter. She let out a small cry.

Josie reached for her. "Do you need to sit back down for a minute? I've been so insensitive, talking away while you should be resting."

"No, I'm fine. I can rest later." Josie and Sharla exchanged looks over Helen's head. "I think . . . I think I know where Bea might be."

"Where's that?" Josie's skin tingled. Had Helen had the answer all along?

Helen looked around the damp stone walls of the basement. "I couldn't have known. Not until the truth came out. So I shouldn't feel guilty, right? But I do, a little."

"Helen," Sharla said firmly. "You have nothing—*nothing*—to feel guilty about. Now where do you think Bea could be?"

Helen drew a deep breath. "I think she could be right here. Under this dirt floor. Or maybe in the other basement room we came through. Dougie probably thought it was fitting to bring you and me here to die, Josie. Sick, poetic justice."

"What?" Josie said. "Why?"

Helen looked Josie in the eye. "Do you know who I bought this building from, twenty years ago?"

Helen's question took only a moment to register. There was only one possible answer.

"Alden Brewster," Josie and Sharla said together.

"Let's get you out of here," Josie said. "And let Evelyn and everyone else know you're all right."

Epilogue

"The sign looks great, Harry." Josie put a hand to her brow to shade her eyes from the bright early spring sun. NUTMEG ANTIQUES & CURIOSITIES was carved into the sign over the shop door, each letter painted in gilt so it gleamed. A removable banner underneath it announced GRAND OPENING.

Harry smiled, but his eyes were misty. "I just wish Lyndon were here. This was his dream, to move back to his hometown."

Evelyn reached out and patted his sleeve. "Now, now. It's time to look to the future. I'm sure he would have wanted that. And you've put a lovely picture of him in the front window."

"This business is just what Dorset Falls needs to bring in the tourists," Mitch said.

"You're right, of course," Harry said. "Opening the shop on schedule is the best way to honor Lyndon's memory. Thank God there'll be no television show. I never wanted that in the first place."

Last Josie had heard, Kai Norton had gone back to California, and Taylor had gone back to her job in Mystic. Taylor would eventually inherit her uncle's personal belongings and accounts, but there was still a lot to sort through. Lyndon's copy of the partnership agreement, which Taylor had wanted and which Harry had also been looking for at the Gray Lady when Josie found him upstairs just after the murder, hadn't turned up yet. But Harry was able to retrieve his own copy from his apartment in Wethersfield. It proved that the antique business was all Harry's.

"And thanks for the tip about hiring Helen, here, to run things when I'm on buying trips," Harry added. "I have a feeling she'll be good for business. She's certainly prettier than I am." Helen looked pleased.

Harry pushed open the door. "And I won't forget to buy as many doilies as I can find for your business. Would you like to come in before I officially open up? Lorna Fowler sent a tray of the most heavenly-looking cookies."

"She'll be making a lot of cookies—and a lot of changes—at the general store," Josie said.

Diantha Humphries had gone to visit Alden Brewster, who was in fact at his lake house, out on bail and wearing electronic jewelry while he awaited trial. Dougie had not been so lucky. His bail had been denied, and he was currently residing at a Connecticut branch of the Graybar Hotel.

No one knew exactly what Diantha had said to Alden, but she'd come back with Alden's approval to sell Lorna the general store on a contract, with very low payments forgivable on his death. The first thing Lorna had done was hire a couple of part-time employees. She was now the proud possessor of a day off, every week, which she was no doubt using to come up with new and delicious recipes. But at least she now had a choice.

Evelyn shook her head. "Thanks for the offer, but no. I need to open Miss Marple Knits to be ready for your overflow customers, Harry. Josie here is taking the morning off. Right?" She leveled a gaze at Josie that left no room for interpretation.

"Yes, boss. Morning off," Josie said. Evelyn had probably been a drill sergeant in a prior life. "But I'll be back in later to see how things are going."

Mitch took her arm. "You've been holding out on me long enough, Blair. Let's go."

Josie stomach fluttered, as though a carbonated drink factory had suddenly materialized inside it. She felt a rush of heat in her cheeks, and she stood there, immobile. What did they think she and Mitch had planned?

Evelyn gave her a little shove. "Go on. Have some fun."

Mitch steered Josie toward his car, grinning. "I'll have her home before noon, I promise."

"Don't hurry on our account," Evelyn called out as Mitch guided Josie into the front seat and shut the door.

"Drive," Josie ordered as soon as Mitch started the engine. She hugged her purse—an oversized Coach bag she'd found in Cora's closet back at the farm—close to her body. It wasn't much protection.

"Your place or mine?" Mitch said, clearly amused. She was glad somebody thought this was funny.

The choice was clear. Eb was at home, probably adding to his inventory of thingamajig sculptures. Or thinking of new and improved ways to torment Roy Woodruff. So the farmhouse was out. "Roy's at the ham radio show at the Eastern States Exposition up in Massachusetts? You're sure?"

From the corner of her eye, she could see Mitch nod. "He'll be gone all day. We'll have the place all to ourselves. Promise."

Why was she so nervous about this? She was a grown woman, for the love of Wang. She took a breath and steeled herself. "Let's do it, then." *You want this,* she told herself. *You need this.*

"I thought you'd never ask," Mitch said, and pulled out from the curb.

Twenty minutes later, they were seated, side by side, on the couch in Mitch's living room in front of the big picture window. The couch gave a creak as he shifted his weight, then moved an afghan off the arm and onto the footstool.

This was ridiculous. She was thirty years old. She could handle this.

"Want a drink? I could probably find some cheese and crackers, if you're hungry." Mitch leaned back into the brown plaid cushions, clearly not planning to go anywhere, the food tease.

"Let's just get this over with," Josie said, opening her bag and reaching inside. "I brought my own supplies." She pulled out several items and set them in her lap. "Choose whatever strikes your fancy."

Mitch's grin now stretched from ear to ear. "Really? I can have whatever I want? You'll enjoy it, I swear." He leaned closer so that she could feel his breath, then the soft brush of his lips on her cheek, which was now tingling. She was about to turn her head to face him, when he pulled away. Drat.

She took a moment to compose herself. She would have kissed him. And she would have liked it, too. But there'd be time for that . . . maybe. Sometime.

"That looks good," he said, pointing to her lap. "And that. I'm so glad Evelyn suggested me for this job."

She picked up the objects. "Be gentle with me, Woodruff. It's not easy for me to admit I can't figure out how this stuff works."

Mitch put his hands over hers, and the tingle was back. And radiating to other places. He looked into her eyes. "Don't worry. I've done this before."

"I'll bet you have," Josie said, wondering who he was talking about. Yup, that was a little stab of jealousy that had just poked her. *You're insane,* she thought. *Completely bonkers.*

Mitch's hands moved over hers. "Put this here," he said. "And put this here. Now hold your hand like this." He positioned her fingers just so. *His hands are so warm. I could get used to this.* Her thoughts wandered . . . off topic.

"Earth to Blair," Mitch said. "You need to concentrate."

Concentrate. Yes, she could do that. "Sorry. I'll pay attention."

"See that you do." His voice was full of amusement again. He clearly knew exactly where her thoughts had been. "Now take this and wrap it around here. Good. Perfect, really." He moved her fingers again. "Pull it out, and give this a light tug. Not too hard."

Josie looked down at their entwined hands, then back up at Mitch. She had no idea this simple act could be so satisfying.

A stitch was on a knitting needle. A single, perfect, cast-on stitch.

And she'd put it there. With a little help, of course. And she was about to do it again. Now it was her turn to grin. "How'd you learn to do this, anyway?"

"My grandmother taught me. What do you think of this?" He pointed to the afghan he'd moved from the couch. "I made that while I was in grad school."

"I do like it," Josie said. "And I might get the hang of this knitting thing after all."

Knitting Patterns

SECRET MESSAGE PILLOW

Like Bea's doily, this pillow has a secret message knitted right into it. I'll give you a hint: The pillow is knitted with *L-O-V-E* (in Morse Code).

Requirements

- Approximately 250 yards bulky weight, light-colored* yarn, your choice of fiber.
- Size 10.5 needles
- 2 stitch markers
- One 14-inch pillow form

Gauge: 3 stitches equals 1 inch

Back

Cast on 41 stitches.
Rows 1–90: Knit. Bind off.

Front

Cast on 41 stitches.
Rows 1–13: Knit.
Row 14: K12, P17, K12.
Row 15: Knit.
Row 16: Repeat Row 14.
Row 17 (pattern row): K12, place marker, P1, P2tog, YO, P3, P2tog, YO, P2tog, YO, P2tog, YO, P2, P2tog, YO, P1, place marker, K12.
Row 18: K12, P17, K12.
Row 19: Knit.

*Pattern will show best with light-colored yarn.

Row 20: K12, P17, K12.
Rows 21–77: Repeat Rows 17–20 14 more times.
Rows 78–90: Knit.
Bind off.

Finishing

Sew three sides of knitted work. If desired, tack a 14-inch square of cloth in desired color to pillow form. Place pillow form inside knitted work, with colored side facing knitted eyelet pattern. Sew remaining side.

EASY LACY FINGERLESS GLOVES

These pretty fingerless gloves are perfect for cool fall or spring weather, when full gloves are too warm, or for when you need your fingers free, but still need to keep away the chill. Evelyn makes lots of these for Miss Marple Knits. Customers love them because they make lovely gifts and one size fits most.

Requirements

- Approximately 150 yards DK weight alpaca-blend yarn (Evelyn used Deerfield, from Webs, www.yarn.com)
- 4 double-pointed needles, size 5
- 4 stitch markers

Gauge: 5 stitches equals 1 inch (gloves will stretch)

Pattern Stitch

Rows 1 and 3: Knit.
Row 2: K2, place marker, *K2tog, YO, K1* Repeat from * 3 times, place marker, K1.
Row 4: K2 *YO, K1, K2tog* Repeat from * 3 times, K1.

Right Glove

Cuff: Cast on 36 stitches using your preferred method. Place 12 stitches on each of three needles, being careful not to twist stitches. Work in K2, P2 ribbing for 3 inches.

Row 1:   Needle 1:   Knit.

	Needle 2:	(Thumb gusset) K6, place marker, KFB (knit in front and back of stitch, to increase 1), place marker, K5.
	Needle 3:	Knit.
Row 2:	Needle 1:	Work Row 2 of pattern stitch.
	Needle 2:	K6, KFB twice, K5.
	Needle 3:	Knit.
Row 3:	Knit.	
Row 4:	Needle 1:	Work Row 4 of pattern stitch.
	Needle 2:	K6 to marker, KFB, K2, KFB, K5.
	Needle 3:	Knit.
Row 5:	Knit.	
Row 6:	Needle 1:	Work Row 2 of pattern stitch.
	Needle 2:	K6 to marker, KFB, K4, KFB, K5.
	Needle 3:	Knit.
Row 7:	Knit.	
Row 8:	Needle 1:	Work Row 4 of pattern stitch.
	Needle 2:	K6 to marker, KFB, K6, KFB, K5.
	Needle 3:	Knit.
Row 9:	Knit.	
Row 10	Needle 1:	Work Row 2 of pattern stitch.
	Needle 2:	K6 to marker, KFB, K8, KFB, K5.
	Needle 3:	Knit.
Row 11:	Knit.	
Row 12:	Needle 1:	Work Row 4 of pattern stitch.
	Needle 2:	K6 to marker, KFB, K10, KFB, K5.
	Needle 3:	Knit.

Row 13:	Knit.	
Row 14:	Needle 1:	Work Row 2 of pattern stitch.
	Needle 2:	K6 to marker, KFB, K12, KFB, K5.
Needle 3:	Knit.	
Row 15:	Knit.	
Row 16:	Needle 1:	Work Row 4 of pattern stitch.
	Needle 2:	K6 to marker. Remove marker. Thumb bind off: Bind off next 14 stitches, remove marker, K5.
	Needle 3:	Knit.
Row 17:	Needle 1:	Knit.
	Needle 2:	K6, pull yarn tight to close thumb hole securely, K6.
	Needle 3:	Knit.
Row 18:	Knit.	
Row 19:	Needle 1:	Work Row 2 of pattern stitch.
	Needles 2&3:	Knit.
Row 20:	Knit.	
Row 21:	Needle 1:	Work Row 4 of pattern stitch.
	Needles 2&3:	Knit.
Row 22:	Knit.	
Rows 23-38:	Repeat Rows 19–22 4 more times.	
Rows 39-41:	Work in K1, P1 ribbing around.	

Bind off loosely in ribbing. Weave in ends.

Left Glove

Repeat as for Right Glove, reversing shaping: simply switch instructions for Right Glove Needle 1 and Needle 3, above. (In other words, Needle 1 will always be knit, Needle 2 will contain the thumb gusset, and the pattern stitch is worked on Needle 3.)

BIAS-KNIT COTTON PLACEMATS

This pattern never goes out of style, and it looks great in a cotton yarn for an everyday placemat. It's also a good way to practice yarnovers and decreases. As soon as Josie gets a little more confident in her knitting skills by finishing a couple of scarves, this is the pattern she's going to try. Now that Eb's dining room table is temporarily cleared off, she'll have a place to use them!

Requirements

- One skein (about 95 yards) 100% cotton yarn, such as Lily Sugar'n Cream, per placemat
- Size 7 knitting needles

Gauge: Not important for this project.

Cast on 4 stitches, using your preferred method.
Row 1:K4
Row 2: K2, YO, K to end of row.
Repeat Row 2 until there are 50 stitches on the needle.
Next Row: K2, YO, K2tog, K to end of row. Repeat for 4 rows.
Decrease Row: K1, K2tog, YO, K2tog, knit across.
Repeat Decrease Row until there are 5 stitches on the needle.
Bind off and weave in ends.

These patterns are copyrighted by Sadie Hartwell and are free for your personal use. You are welcome to make and sell items made from these patterns, but Sadie would appreciate a link back to her website. You can see photos of all the projects at www.sadiehartwell.com. Sadie would love to see your projects too!

Connect with Us

Visit us online at
KensingtonBooks.com
to read more from your favorite authors, see books
by series, view reading group guides, and more.

for sneak peeks, chances to win books and prize packs,
and to share your thoughts with other readers.

facebook.com/kensingtonpublishing
twitter.com/kensingtonbooks

Tell us what you think!

To share your thoughts, submit a review,
or sign up for our eNewsletters, please visit:
KensingtonBooks.com/TellUs.